DEATH
IN
DUBLIN

ALSO BY BARTHOLOMEW GILL

The Death of an Irish Sinner

The Death of an Irish Lover

The Death of an Irish Tinker

The Death of an Irish Sea Wolf

The Death of an Ardent Bibliophile

Death on a Cold, Wild River

The Death of Love

The Death of a Joyce Scholar

McGarr and the Legacy of a Woman Scorned

McGarr and the Method of Descartes

McGarr and the P. M. Belgrave Square

McGarr at the Dublin Horse Show

McGarr on the Cliffs of Moher
(recently published as *The Death of an Irish Lass*)

McGarr and the Sienese Conspiracy
(recently published as *The Death of an Irish Consul*)

McGarr and the Politician's Wife
(recently published as *The Death of an Irish Politician*)

BARTHOLOMEW
GILL

DEATH
IN
DUBLIN

A NOVEL OF SUSPENSE

wm

WILLIAM MORROW
An Imprint of HarperCollins*Publishers*

This is a work of fiction. The characters, incidents, and dia-
logues are products of the author's imagination and are not
to be construed as real. Any resemblance to actual persons,
living or dead, is entirely coincidental.

HarperCollins books may be purchased for educational,
business, or sales promotional use. For information please
write: Special Markets Department, HarperCollins Publishers Inc., 10 East 53rd Street, New York, NY 10022.

FIRST EDITION

Designed by Shubhani Sarkar

Printed on acid-free paper

Library of Congress Cataloging-in-Publication Data

Gill, Bartholomew
    Death in Dublin: a novel of suspense / Bartholomew
Gill.—1st ed.
    p. cm.
    ISBN 0-06-000849-0
    1. McGarr, Peter (Fictitious character)—Fiction.
2. Police—Ireland—Dublin—Fiction. 3. Dublin (Ireland)—Fiction. 4. Police chiefs—Fiction. 5. Book of
Kells—Fiction. 6. Book thefts—Fiction. I. Title.

PS3563.A296 D38 2003
813'.54—dc21
2002032582

03 04 05 06 07 BVG/BVG 10 9 8 7 6 5 4 3 2 1

For Maddie and the McGs entire.

And for the wood woman whose lover was changed into a blue-eyed hawk . . . because of something told under the famished horn of the hunter's moon that hung between night and day.

A Note About
the Book of Kells

Scholars believe that the Book of Kells was created both at Kells in County Meath, Ireland, and on the island of Iona near Scotland around A.D. 800.

In 1185, the historian Giraldus Cambrensis was allowed to peruse the Book of Kells. Of it, he wrote:

"It contains the concordance of the four gospels according to Saint Jerome, with almost as many drawings as pages, and all of them in marvelous colors.

"Here you can look upon the face of the divine majesty drawn in a miraculous way; here too upon the mystical representations of the Evangelists, now having six, now four, and now two, wings.

"Here you will see the eagle; there the calf. Here the face of a man; there that of a lion. And there are almost innumerable other drawings.

"If you look at them carelessly and casually and not too closely, you may judge them to be mere daubs rather than careful compositions. You will see nothing subtle where everything is subtle.

"But if you take the trouble to look very closely, and penetrate with your eyes to the secrets of the artistry, you will notice such intricacies so delicate and subtle, so close together and well-knitted, so involved and bound together, and so fresh still in their colorings that you will not hesitate to declare that all these things must have been the result of the work, not of men, but of angels."

More recently, Umberto Eco, the Italian novelist and medievalist, called the Book of Kells "the product of a cold-blooded hallucination," perhaps because the illustrations meld Christian images with zoomorphic and other iconography that harkens back through the Celtic period to the very beginnings of European civilization.

Many of the designs and details partake of such subtlety that any reference to their meaning has been lost.

Yet few would deny that the enigma that is the Book of Kells is one of the premier creations of Western civilization.

PROLOGUE

Everybody has an inner voice, which is
the voice of God, Ray Sloane had been told by his mother.

"It tells you right from wrong, good from bad, what you should
think and do. And what you shouldn't, especially when somebody's
trying to lead you down the garden path. Don't let anybody lead
you down the garden path, Raymond. Not ever."

Which was the problem of arguing from the general (everybody)
to the particular (Raymond Francis Sloane himself), who was standing in the darkness of the guardhouse at the Pearse Street entrance
to Trinity College.

It was 2:37 A.M. of a perfectly soft night in early October. Fog off
the Liffey had stolen up from the quays and now mostly obscured
the gray stone Garda substation directly across from the gates. Orange halos ringed the cadmium vapor streetlamps.

The security guard on duty, who worked for Sloane, was on the
floor by his feet, bleeding rather profusely from the back of his head
where Sloane had sapped him from behind. He hoped the man
wouldn't die; it wasn't in the cards for him to die.

True, Sloane continued to reason, everybody probably had an

inner voice, the one that said, "Well, maybe you shouldn't be doing this or that" or "Get your bloody arse out of this pickle pronto, mate." Sloane had that too; usually at the last moment his inner voice knew when to skedaddle.

But increasingly in recent years the problem for Sloane had been that his inner voice didn't distinguish between good and evil, right action and wrong, positive and negative thinking. No.

For at least three years—ever since he'd got out of rehab and discovered Ox, which wasn't tested for—Ray Sloane's perverse inner voice had been leading him down paths with no garden in sight on any horizon. It then had wild fun watching him attempt to pluck his sorry arse out of the broth. For a completely accurate reason, Sloane called his inner voice I.V.

"Here they are," I.V. now said as a big Merc with blackened windows pulled up to the gate, its headlamps flashing thrice as agreed. "No going back now, arsehole. No fecking way."

Sloane didn't know why, but even though he had come from a good family and was now chief of security at Trinity, his I.V. spoke like a navvy from the docks. Or like his connection.

With a gloved hand, he picked up the receiver, then dialed the four-digit extension of his own phone in security headquarters on the other side of the campus, which he had programmed to pick up on the second ring.

That way, it would look as if he'd been sitting at his desk when the call came through. Later, he'd return to his office and erase the tape on the answering machine, while the main security computer would contain a record of the time of the call and could be made to replay a tape of the conversation.

"Hello, Tom—what can I do for you?" he heard his prerecorded voice ask.

Holding a glove over his mouth, Sloane said, "Jesus, Ray—get here fast. I don't know who these yokes are, but—" He then dropped the receiver near the unconscious man at his feet before punching the button that opened the gate.

The car pulled through; Sloane closed the gate.

"And what's this now?" I.V. continued, as Sloane nipped out of the guardhouse and into the back of the dark car. "Pointed hoods over balaclavas, no less. Better find out who your bloody wonderful mates are, bucko. And why they need to hide their faces."

"Who am I with?"

Neither answered, as the driver wheeled the car down the narrow lane toward the library.

"I'd like to know who I'm with."

Raising an arm, the passenger swung round with something in his hand. It was a handgun made larger by a silencer fitted to the barrel. Worse still, the man was wearing what looked like darkened welder's glasses, and not even his mouth was visible. In its place was a round black disk with holes, like something in the drain of a sink.

"Oh, Jaysus," said I.V. "Better shut your bloody gob, Raymond, and go through with the drill as planned. The less you know, the better off you'll be."

Should Sloane be subjected to a lie detector test, which, of course, he would. It was a clause in the contract of employment when theft was involved.

At the library, the passenger got out. Gun still in hand, he waited only a moment for Sloane to swing his legs out of the car, snatching up a handful of hair and wrenching him to his feet.

"Jesus Haitch Christ!" Sloane bawled. "Feck off, you bastard! I know the choreography."

"What if you don't?" I.V. asked.

The latex-gloved hand came away.

"Scares you, don't it? Feckers look like surgeons. Or undertakers. And what's with the *X-Files* costume, the bloody drains in their bloody gobs, and whatever it is that's strapped to their foreheads?"

Under the hoods and protruding from the forehead area of their balaclavas were miner's or caver's headlamps that were glowing red.

"Professionals?" I.V. asked. "Could it be? Maybe they're not the people you've been dealing with, Raymond. Maybe they have a different agenda."

At the door to the gift shop, which was also an entrance to the Old Library where Kells and the other old manuscripts were displayed, Sloane stopped, removed an electronic key from his pocket, and turned to them. "Once we're in, I'm going to start speaking. For the record, as we agreed. Right?"

Only the shorter man reacted, again flicking the barrel of the gun.

Having to stoop to find the slot of the electronic key, Sloane fumbled with the card and also with the key that turned the secondary lock.

"Jitters, eh?" I.V. asked. "Me—I'd turn and split, were I you. First chance you get. They don't know this place like you do. And they dare not switch on the lights or spend much time looking for you."

Which was what the goggles and miner's lights were all about, it now occurred to Sloane. Infrared. Unlike him, they could see in the dark.

"Strikes me, you're in over your head, Raymond."

And perhaps very much without it. Soon. How'd he get into such a mess?

"You mean meth. What we wouldn't give for a touch of that right now. Eh, lad?"

Stepping into the gift shop, Sloane tried to hold the door for the other two but was shoved forward. And—once the door was shut—he was spun around, both keys were pulled from his grasp, and something like a foot was placed against the small of his back.

In one wrenching thrust, he was launched clean off his feet into the darkness, where he fell heavily and brutally, the skin of his face grating over the flagged floor.

I get it, Sloane said to himself. They're playing the script to the letter. It's here I should begin objecting.

"Script. Choreography? What does it matter?" I.V. put in. "Fact is, you've no control here. You're a fecking sheep being led to the slaughter. Get out now, man. Run, while you still can."

But where?

Hauled to his feet, Sloane was shoved forward toward the Treasury room, which was off the gift shop on the ground level of the Old Library. Even in the pitch dark he knew the way.

"Haven't you spent most of your adult life here?" I.V. asked. "You know the aisles, the display cases, where the doors are. Think of them as escape hatches."

But suddenly a great sadness fell over Raymond Sloane: that in the fifty-second year of his life when, in fact, he had been an exemplary citizen in every regard but one, here he was involved in perhaps—not perhaps—the most culturally heinous crime possible in Ireland. Far worse than any mere bombing that killed only people.

He had to make sure that, if the worst were to happen, he'd be viewed as a hero. A martyr. And certainly not a coconspirator, in spite of the money he'd already taken from them.

"Agreed. If we're going to go out, boyo. Let's go out with glory. You should start now."

From his uniform jacket, Sloane now removed another electronic key, saying in a loud voice, "You don't know what you're doing. If you take away what's in this room, the police will hound you into your graves."

The card was ripped out of his hand, and he heard the door click open.

Again he was shoved forward until he was standing before the glass case that contained the Book of Kells.

"Use your hand. Kill the alarms and open it up," said a voice that sounded like Darth Vader's.

"Could he be speaking through a voice scrambler?" I.V. asked. "These yokes have thought of everything, which scares me."

"Do it!" the husky, disembodied voice roared.

Suddenly it felt like his stomach collapsed or that a fist had found his backbone through his solar plexus. Sloane doubled up and again fell roughly, his head and knees slamming into the stone floor.

Then somebody had him by the back of his belt and began dragging him toward the control panel, which was located under the display case.

"Now, your hand."

Grabbing his right wrist and tearing off his glove, they slapped his hand on the scanning screen. He heard the lock snap open.

"And the other two." Said a different, higher, but similarly disguised voice.

Whichever one of them had him by the belt was strong and brutal, whipping Sloane up against another display case.

"Get on your feet and run, lad. Run."

How could he run, when he could hardly breathe.

When his hand was placed on a second scanner, he realized what was happening. Not satisfied with two of the four volumes of the Book of Kells, they were also going to steal the even more ancient Book of Durrow and Book of Armagh, another ancient illuminated manuscript. All three, of course, were priceless irreplaceable treasures that would fetch a handsome ransom.

"I thought you said you were only going to take—"

With one heave, the man swung Sloane up against a third case. "Open your fist!" the deep voice roared. "Open your bloody fist or I'll stomp it to bits."

Sloane complied; his hand was placed on the scanner of the case with the Armagh book; the lock clicked; his belt was released.

Now, he would run, if he could. But as he tried to raise himself up to do as I.V. had suggested, something came down on his outstretched hand, and a blinding flash of pain seared his vision as he fell back onto the flags.

"You said you—" he began, tucking the damaged hand under his arm.

"I never said a thing," the higher voice said.

"And me—I lied," said the other, and they both rasped a horrible laughter, as Sloane, fighting through the pain, again tried to gain his feet.

But the moment he did, the tall one—silhouetted against the dim light from the open door to the library shop—took two quick strides and kicked him in the groin.

Sloane had never felt such total pain. Again he couldn't breathe or see or think. The hand no longer mattered, compared with the galling ache that now spread through his body.

And the fear; he knew what was about to happen.

"Why did you ever think they'd let you live? Somehow you've just got to get yourself gone from here, me boy."

In his need, Sloane had never once allowed himself to consider the possibility. And here it was.

"Give me a hand with him," said the deep voice.

Sloane felt himself being seized under the arms; the other one had him by the ankles. "Right enough—up he goes."

Opening his eyes, he could see enough to know what they were doing—stuffing him into the large Kells display case, which could be hermetically sealed by switching on a motor that sucked out the oxygen.

"No!" Sloane roared, pushing himself up.

But a fist slammed into his nose, again and again and again. "Blood enough for you?" he thought he heard, as the top of the case was closing.

"Enough to be taken seriously," said the higher voice. "Pity is—there's not enough. A man like that deserves all this and more."

And then the top was forced down, squeezing his shoulder, arm, hip, and head into the small space. It clumped shut, and the lock snapped.

"Serious," said I.V. "That's just the word. This is very serious."

Panicked, terrified, Sloane tried to force his legs, shoulder, and hip up against the glass top and sides of the display case. And then, twisting around, his back and buttocks.

"Which are the strongest muscles in the body," said I.V.

But not strong enough.

His feet—maybe if he banged them against the glass he could shatter it. But his sponge-rubber security-guard soles only thudded against the thick surface, which was slick now with his blood.

Only then did he remember the sap, the sock of coins that he had thumped the gate guard with.

"Too-da-loo," said one of the voices, rapping on the glass.

"Ta," said the other.

Sloane then heard the motor switch on, the one that sucked out the air, and suddenly he became hysterical.

"That won't help," I.V. remarked. "Not one bit."

 Peter McGarr stepped out of the laneway into Dame Street, at the end of which stood the granite eminence of Trinity College about a quarter mile distant.

It was early morning—half 8:00—and the street was thronged with automobile commuters creeping to work. Cars rolled on a few paces, stopped, and their drivers looked away blankly, used to delay. Faces of passengers in double-deck buses, through windows streaked with urban grime, were careworn and bored.

A solitary articulated lorry appeared lost amid the clamor, its wide headlamps searching for a street that might lead to a highway and freedom.

Like Trinity itself, where McGarr was headed, the early traffic on Dame Street was a given of his day, something he seldom noticed.

But since the murder of his wife, Noreen, more than two years earlier, McGarr had gone from being an acute observer of the city to being necessarily blind to its changes and nuances. Save those, of course, that concerned his family, who had been reduced to his daughter, Maddie, and his mother-in-law, Nuala. She now cared for the child while he worked.

Trinity, which he was now approaching, was a case in point, he realized. Back when he'd been a student, the bastion of Protestantism and privilege had been declared off limits to Catholics by the bishop of Dublin. Of course, as the seventh of nine children of a Guinness brewery worker, it was no place he could have had hopes of attending, anyhow.

And yet in his own way, McGarr had coveted Trinity's complex of mainly Georgian and Victorian buildings that walled off traffic and noise and provided a quiet haven of wide lawns, cobbled footpaths, and civility in the heart of the city. It was a gem of a place, a kind of urban diadem. But for the nearly twenty years of his marriage, he had associated the college with Noreen, who had studied there.

The arched entranceway was crowded with returning students, and across a wide courtyard, he could see uniformed police cordoning off the Old Library. In front of the barrier stood press and television crews—details that he'd sooner forget, if he could.

But Peter McGarr was chief superintendent of the Serious Crimes Unit of the Garda Siochana, the Irish police, and since the tragedy, his work had become the sole sustaining element in his life, the one constant activity that helped him forget.

Also, there was the chance—however slight—that he might discover who exactly had murdered his people. And why.

At the corner of the Old Library, McGarr paused for a few tugs on a cigarette before running the gauntlet in front of the police line, even though he'd promised his daughter he'd quit.

More guilt. How could he have failed to recognize the danger that his occupation posed to his family? How could he have allowed the tragedy to occur?

Feeling as he did most waking hours—that his life was effectively over in his fifty-fifth year—McGarr dropped the butt into a storm drain and stepped toward the reporters.

A somewhat short man with gray eyes and an aquiline nose bent slightly to one side, he still presented a rather formidable appearance with wide, well-muscled shoulders and little paunch.

Courtesy of Nuala, who had taken charge of his appearance, he was well turned out in a heather-colored tweed overcoat, razor creases in his tan trousers and cordovan half-cut boots polished to a high gloss.

"You've got to get a grip on yourself and get on with life, Peter," she had told him going out the door. "If only for Maddie. And forget the bastards what done it. They're a sly and craven lot, not at all like your common run of criminal, and more than a few, I'm thinking. And if they thought you were onto them . . ."

Unless, of course, they didn't know he was before he struck. The niceties of the law being dispensed with. Revenge was what McGarr sought, not justice.

As he waded through the clutch of reporters, whose questions McGarr fended off with his eyes, all that hinted at his inner turmoil was a certain drawn look and his deep red hair that tufted out under the brim of his fedora. He'd been too distracted for barbers.

While waiting for the door to the gift shop to be unlocked, McGarr glanced up at a sky freighted with clouds moving in from the east. Although it was only early October, the wind carried an edge. The fair weather would not hold much longer, he could tell.

Bernie McKeon—McGarr's chief of staff—had already arrived, along with a pathologist and several members of the Tech Squad.

A man and a woman, who McGarr supposed were library officials, were standing off from the others.

McKeon handed McGarr the notes he'd taken since arriving.

"You've heard of squab under glass. It's served at the finest restaurants, I'm told. And duck too. But blue-d uniform security cop is a new one on me," McKeon said in an undertone.

McGarr glanced at his colleague, whose dark eyes were bright with the grisly irony that passed for humor in the Murder Squad.

The victim was encased, literally, under thick glass or high-quality Plexiglas. Not only was his security uniform a deep, midnight blue, but his face was some lighter shade of the color, rather like cornflower blue, except for where it was covered in blood, which had also smeared the glass.

"To control the deterioration of the manuscripts, the cases are hermetically sealed and the atmosphere's withdrawn. Or so says your man," McKeon continued. "He's the head librarian and she's the keeper of old manuscripts."

"Trevor Pape?" asked McGarr, glancing over at the two. Pape was a well-known figure in academic and arts circles and had attended openings at the picture gallery that Noreen had owned.

"Aye. She gave her name as Kara Kennedy. She found the victim, after getting a call from Pape about another guard at the Pearse Street gate. He's in the hospital with a fractured skull."

McGarr pointed to the victim, who, although a rather large man, had been stuffed down into a quasi-fetal position in the narrow space. Alive. He had struggled for any air he could find; his mouth was open and his eyes—blue, as well—were swollen and protrusive.

"Raymond Sloane, head guard here for decades."

"What's that in his hand?"

"Hard to tell through the blood. There's more over here." With a penlight, McKeon flashed the beam over the flooring stones that were splashed with drying blood. "Looks like he put up a fight, he did. One hell of a way to cap off a career."

"Know him?"

"Not well. Started out with me in the army. I'd see him now and then. Around town." Before joining the Garda decades ago, McKeon had been a drill instructor in the Irish army.

It was Dublin again. In spite of the population explosion and recent influx of immigration, in many ways it remained a small town.

"What's missing?"

"The books, of course—two of four Kells books, also Durrow and Armagh," McKeon said.

There lay Raymond Sloane, devoid of life and spirit and now merely a subject for a pathologist's scalpel.

"Let's see what's in his hand."

McKeon waved the librarians over and explained what was needed. Reaching under the case, Pape threw a switch and the case hissed as air entered the chamber.

Suddenly the lid sprang open, with Sloane's arm and shoulder rising up. The woman gasped and jumped back, sobbing.

A forensic photographer aimed his camera, and cold achromatic lightning raked the room. Closing his eyes, McGarr watched the light burst red through his eyelids as the camera continued to flash.

With surgical gloves, a tech sergeant removed the object from Sloane's right hand—a thick black sock that was filled with a stack of maybe thirty 50P coins.

"Because he didn't carry a weapon?" McKeon asked.

McGarr shrugged. Nevertheless, it had proved useless against the glass.

"Couldn't swing it."

Shattered capillaries in the man's protrusive eyes swirled down, like tiny red worms, into his sclerae. McGarr thought of the small red wet hole in the back of Noreen's ear. It was all the damage she had suffered, but enough to kill her.

"You, I know," he said to Pape, who with hands clasped behind his back only nodded. "And you are?"

Her hand came forward. "Kara Kennedy. I'm in charge of the stolen books. I mean, the books that were stolen. Or, at least, I was. In charge, that is." Her eyes strayed to Pape, who only maintained his stony consideration of McGarr.

A woman in her early to mid-forties, she had brown hair, pleasant features, good shoulders. "Tell me everything you can about this. Who the victim is. How the theft could have happened. Impressions." McGarr swirled a hand.

"Well, I think—"

"When I am present, I speak to the public about library matters," said Pape.

"We're the police," McKeon objected, "not the public. And that man over there"—he jabbed a finger at the display case—"is dead. Murdered."

McGarr touched McKeon's arm. "Perhaps I might speak to you alone, Doctor—it is Doctor, isn't it?"

The man nodded.

"Dr. Pape. And, really, we should make some room."

Tall lights on stanchions were being set up around the display case. With halogen torches, others were searching for evidence on the floor, while another team lifted prints from the cases.

The pathologist, Dr. Henry—a blowsy woman McGarr's own age—was leaning over the case with a kind of loupe held to one eye.

Pointing the way, McGarr led Pape in one direction, while McKeon took the Kennedy woman in another.

"What were the security precautions?"

"I've already explained that as well. To the police."

McGarr cocked his head; if so, McKeon would have filled him in.

"To Jack Sheard, your superior."

Younger than McGarr by an easy dozen years, Sheard held the same rank, chief superintendent, but had far less seniority. Money laundering, major thefts, and frauds were his area of responsibility.

"When?"

"Earlier."

"Here?"

"No—over the phone. Jack's a graduate, you know."

And proud of it, McGarr remembered, Sheard one night having

arrived at a Garda banquet wearing a tie emblazoned with the Trinity College crest. Few high-ranking Garda officers had attended university, much less a college with such cachet.

"Well, Jack is otherwise occupied, and you may have left something out."

After a sigh, Pape explained that at night the college posted a guard at each of four gates, with a fifth guard patrolling the grounds and buildings. Sloane himself maintained a command post at security headquarters, monitoring a bank of surveillance cameras. "Here in the Treasury and gift shop, surveillance also included voice and movement sensors.

"Unfortunately, we've been one guard shy since the recent death of a member of the security detail, and Sloane was performing both functions."

"Death, how?"

"Motorcar. He was knocked down in the street."

"How recent a death?"

"A fortnight ago."

If the gates could be locked and monitored, why had Sloane not taken a guard off a gate for foot patrol, McGarr reasoned. "In other words, when Sloane was on patrol, there was nobody back at security headquarters."

"There you have it." Pape's smile was slight and superior.

At least sixty-five, he was nearly gaunt with a long face and light brown hair that was thin on top but swept back in a gray-streaked mane that hung to his shoulders. His nose was thin, hawkish, and lined with crimson veins; his eyes were blue but ruddy.

Without question donnish-looking, Pape was wearing a muted green-checked jacket over a beige shirt and dun tie.

"While on patrol, would Mr. Sloane have entered the building?"

Pape shook his head. "Not unless the sensors or cameras detected something."

"What about an alarm system or a silent alarm connected to the Garda barracks in Pearse Street?" It was just across from an entrance to the college.

"It was disabled."

McGarr waited.

Pape raised his head and looked down his nose at McGarr. "I'm afraid we're the library that cried wolf, Inspector. Every time a student or visitor rattled the door after hours, wanting in, the alarms went off. With students now returning to campus, I imagine Sloane decided to take a hiatus from alarms."

"Were there students resident in college last night?"

Pape shook his head. "During the day, yes. But only this morning were they allowed to move back in."

Planning, McGarr thought. The theft had been engineered to a fare-thee-well. Then why murder Sloane in such a dramatic way? Why not simply disable him, even with some violence, as they had the other guard?

"What about here, the library—how do you get in?"

Pape ran through the procedure: electronic and deadbolt keys to the gift shop, then electronic hand recognition to open the cases.

"Whose hands?"

"Mine, Miss Kennedy's, and Raymond's alone."

Could Sloane have refused, McGarr wondered, so they beat and murdered him? Why, then, was the sap still in his hand? Why hadn't he used it to defend himself? There was blood on the flags around the display cases.

And surely, knowing about the hand-recognition device with only three hands keyed suggested—no, declared—involvement by some insider.

"Who knows—knew—about the hands?"

"We three, of course. And, I'd hazard, staff who'd observed us performing the . . . maneuver."

"What about the security firm that deployed it?"

"They were not present in the building when we initialized the system. By policy."

"Could somebody on your staff or some other Trinity employee be responsible for this crime?"

Pape shrugged.

McGarr waited, noting that Pape had averted his eyes. "You seem unsure."

"Do I?" The eyes returned with anger. "Truth is—I don't know, and frankly I don't much care. Possessing that damn book"—he waved a hand at the display cases—"has been a double-edged sword for this institution.

"Yes, it brought the college notoriety, and it was a mighty cash cow. But"—Pape's voice had risen—"hordes, veritable legions of patent fools and ignoramuses pile off tour buses and troop through the college in their Aran caps and jumpers to ogle the bloody thing. Which was, mind you, in its own time designed to be ostentatious. No, garish! The 'Oh-wow!' of the ninth century.

"It's . . . it's"—he wagged his head, his mane tossing from shoulder to shoulder—"the bloody Blarney Stone of academia and banal. Très ban-al!"

Even the Tech Squad had now stopped to watch him.

"And I'll confess something else. This theft and Raymond Sloane's murder would not have occurred had Trinity remained the college first intended by its founders. Now that it's been turned into a bloody diploma factory, I call it immanent justice that its talisman has been stolen."

A curious opinion for a man charged with preserving and protecting books, thought McGarr.

"That said"—Pape paused, flaring his nostrils and pulling in a chestful of air, as though to get hold of himself—"a true loss is Durrow and Armagh, which in their time had more than simply liturgical value. But I have every confidence that Chief Superintendent Sheard will get them back.

"You're done with me, I assume."

McGarr only regarded the man, who turned and walked out of the room as though conscious of his heels ringing on the stone.

Turning to McKeon and the woman, McGarr raised a hand and flicked his fingers into his palm, a gesture redolent of both veteran police practice and his gloom, he realized as she moved toward him.

Here he was involved in perhaps the most important murder/theft of his career, and he felt as though he were just going through the motions. Maybe he should retire and try something different like . . . well, there was the rub. He couldn't think of anything he really wanted to do, and police work was really all he knew.

Yet he managed a smile for the women. "This must be difficult for you," he said, noticing her unusual jade-colored eyes. Contacts, perhaps? "Obviously, it's been trying for Dr. Pape."

"Please excuse him," said Kara Kennedy. "Trinity—the college and the library are his life. He's been here . . . well, I'd say the better part of forty years, counting his student days, and I'm certain this is a greater blow to him than—"

Glancing at the corpse, which was now being littered from the room, she lowered her head and tears splatted on the stones by her feet. Her shoulders shook, and her body moved into McGarr.

He raised a hand to her back. Close, like that, he breathed in the warmth of her body and the complex scent of whatever shampoos or perfumes or emollients she used. And he was disturbed by what he felt, not having been so close to a woman such as she, in more than two years.

She moved her head, and her hair brushed against his face. "Why don't we sit down for a moment? Out there would be better."

Taking her elbow, he drew her into the exhibition room where at least the lighting was less funereal. They sat on a bench against the wall.

"Did you hear what Dr. Pape just said? The bit about Trinity being a diploma factory and better off with the Book of Kells being gone?"

She shook her head and blotted her eyes. "That's just anger and frustration. Trevor's an antiquarian who loathes change, and his world—like the rest of the world—is marked by change these days. It's the one constant, isn't it?"

Sobbing now and then, she explained that there remained a few on the Trinity faculty who had never accepted the "democratization" of the college in the early seventies, when the Catholic Church lifted its ban on attendance and enrollment surged from twenty-five hundred to close to fourteen thousand students, mostly of Catholic background.

"No longer was it a sleepy, insular place, its faculty riddled with dilettantes and academic eccentrics protected by tenure. Trinity stepped into the twentieth century, acquiring true scholars and exploiting the resources at its command." Her hand moved toward the door of the Treasury.

"It became what it should have been all along—the oldest and best university in the country. But there were—and, I'm afraid, still are—those who are averse to change."

With cupped shoulders, Kara Kennedy leaned forward, elbows on her thighs, and McGarr noticed for the first time that her hair had begun to gray. He also glanced at the smooth slope of a breast that could be seen between the plackets of her pearl-colored silk blouse.

And a pang of longing seized him—for warmth and the perfumey aroma that he could still detect and for other comforts as well. Up until that moment, he had kept himself from remembering what being with a woman could be like, knowing how disconcerting the remembrance would be. And was.

"Unfortunately, Trevor is one of those who fought and still fights the change, not—please don't misunderstand me"—her fingers touched his knee—"not because he is in any way incompetent. It's just that not everything was awry in the old Trinity College, which was collegial in many of the best ways. I think he still harbors fond thoughts of those years."

Her hands were long, gracefully formed, and well tanned, as though she'd spent the summer outdoors. Also, McGarr was hearing the hint of a Scottish burr in her voice.

"I'm certain he'll think better of what he said. The Book of Kells is truly a treasure of"—she had to pause again—"a treasure of inestimable value both intrinsically and to the Irish people, and I'll never forgive myself that this . . . this debacle occurred on my watch."

McGarr frowned. "Are you in charge of security?"

"What?" Her head swung up to him, and it was as though he plunged into the jade pools of her eyes.

"Were you Raymond Sloane's superior?"

"No, of course not. I'm . . . an academic." She looked back toward the Treasury.

A handsome, if not a pretty, woman with a long, thinly bridged nose, a strong chin, and high cheekbones. Her dark hair, which was a chestnut color, formed a deep widow's peak, and the skin on her neck had begun to take on the wrinkles of age.

McGarr glanced at the backs of her hands, which she had clasped in front of her—forty-five, he guessed, from the sheen and wrinkle of her skin. He was seldom wrong.

"But I should have made it my business."

Guilt—it ruled the culture. It ruled McGarr.

"Apart from you, Dr. Pape, and Raymond Sloane, who else knew of the hand-recognition device beneath the cases?"

She swung her head to him, and he noted how her hair grew deep on the sides of her forehead and rather complemented her widow's peak. And as had been Noreen's, her upper lip was noticeably protrusive.

McGarr looked away; he was feeling uncomfortable.

"Cleaning people, I should imagine, if they knew what they were seeing."

Kara Kennedy flicked a hand to clear the hair from her face, and McGarr again smelled—what was it?—chamomile, vanilla, and verbena?

She had crossed her legs toward him, and he followed the gentle line of her calf to a narrow ankle, before looking off into the gift shop.

"Also, there's the security firm who set the device up, perhaps some other library staff. No, surely some other library staff who have been present when we've turned the pages.

"To answer your question, Chief Superintendent"—she waited until their eyes met—"I suppose our security measures were rather common knowledge to those of us who work here. But I hope you don't suspect—"

McGarr shook his head. "I don't suspect anything yet. I'm just gathering information. What can you tell me about Raymond Sloane? Personally."

"Apart from here in Trinity . . ." She shook her head before pulling her eyes from his.

Or did he imagine that? He stood. He was so emotionally at sea it rather frightened him. "Do you have any idea who might have done this?"

There were no rings on her fingers.

"No. Some madman. Mad*men* to get Raymond into . . ." Again she could not continue.

"What about the possibility that whoever did this was in league with somebody here in Trinity, somebody who knew the security precautions, somebody who—out of disaffection with the college or the book itself—"

"I hope you don't mean Trevor Pape." Leaning back against the wall, she placed her palms on the bench in a way that spread the plackets of her suit coat. "Trevor has spent his life—literally, spent it—working here for little or nothing, preserving and protecting books. Why would he throw all that away?"

She was wearing a pearl-colored silk blouse.

She smiled slightly, exposing a single dimple. "It's refreshing that you didn't mention greed. Disaffection was a nice touch."

Pulling a card from his pocket, he extended it toward her. "Scots, are you?"

"Kennedy can be a Scottish name as well, I'll have you know."

"And how do I reach you?" It was said without thinking, which was doubly distressing to McGarr, since he knew that with every waking moment he had not yet got over—and he sometimes thought he would never get over—the presence of Noreen in his thoughts. And her absence in his life.

"Oh—I've got a card." She fumbled in her purse and came up with a card and a smile, which quickly faded. "Who's going to inform Raymond's wife? I mean, how is it handled?"

"We'll take care of it."

Her brow furrowed. "Oh, yes—I suppose you have to do this regularly."

And it was never easy. "Many thanks." McGarr turned toward a kind of clamor outside of the gift shop.

"Will you catch who did this?"

"I suspect we'll be hearing from them rather soon."

The noise was coming from what looked like an impromptu news conference that was being held on the gift shop steps.

There stood Trinity grad, Chief Superintendent Jack Sheard,

answering questions from the press. About what, McGarr could not guess, since they knew only that the books were missing and Sloane was dead. But not even his name could be given out until the family was notified.

But there Sheard stood, resplendent in a navy blue pinstriped suit that had been tailored to his at least six-foot-four frame. His tie was pearl colored, like the handkerchief sprouting from his breast pocket.

In his early forties, Sheard was a handsome man with sandy hair and a rugger's angular body. With shoulders squared and hands clasped at his waist, he looked like a Janus figure—a bigger, better guard at the portals—but too late.

Over his—how many?—fifteen or so years with the Garda, Sheard was periodically the darling of Sunday news features both on television and in print. Early on, he was billed as "the new face of the police" and pictured with his blond young wife and three towheaded children on the lawn in front of their rambling suburban home on the flanks of the Dublin Mountains.

Later, after he'd been admitted to the bar, the press called him "Commissioner Inevitable," which so browned off the actual commissioner that he delayed Sheard's inevitability by rusticating him to the desk that kept tabs on "unlawful organizations," which was a euphemism for the IRA. It was a police dead end.

Because Garda commissioners were political appointees, all that changed with a new government, and for his patience Sheard was rewarded with the Fraud Squad, which also investigated major thefts. Most recently the press had dubbed him "The Cop for the Twenty-first Century," noting his Trinity background—he had studied finance and organization—his legal degree, and his work against terrorist organizations.

McGarr had only skimmed or lent half an ear to the pieces, since publicity for a cop—twenty-first century or otherwise—was something to be avoided. Unless, of course, the cop had another agenda entirely, which McGarr and some other senior Garda officers suspected Sheard had.

Fitting on his hat, McGarr opened the door and stepped out behind Sheard's broad back. And with a hand raised to the brim, he set off down the stairs on a flank of the crowd.

Sheard was saying, " . . . of inestimable value. It is the chief bibliographic treasure of the people of Ireland and all those others of Celtic heritage. The Garda will spare nothing in pursuing those who assaulted one guard, murdered another, and made off with the volumes."

Saying, "Police, please. Police, please," which in his pancake Dublin tones sounded like an apologetic yet intentional plaint, McGarr weaved his way through the crowd.

He wondered if Raymond Sloane's family had begun to worry about him, and how they would react to Sheard's comments. And how they would react to McGarr himself, when he arrived on their doorstep to announce Sloane's death. After Sheard's public remarks.

Had Sheard himself ever been in the position of having to announce a death to a family? McGarr doubted it, the man's specialty being more white-collar crime.

2

after McGarr, but he stretched out his stride and was soon alone.

It had become a pleasant autumn day filled with the golden light, peculiar to October, from a sun that was surrendering the heights of summer. Angling in from the east, its rays were warm not hot, and glancing at the smooth chartreuse carpet of lawn that filled the quadrangle, McGarr thought of his garden, which he had ignored for weeks.

Some time soon, he should pull up the stalks of the summer plants, fertilize the soil, and sow more "winter wheat"—a crop rich in nitrogen that he would turn into the ground come spring. But for the last two years his heart had not been in gardening either, which had once given him real pleasure.

He had reached the guardhouse from which the tall wooden gates that gave onto Pearse Street could be monitored. A uniformed guard, standing before the entrance, touched his cap, as McGarr ducked under the yellow police tape and stepped into the building.

Pale blue chalk marked off where the injured Trinity security guard had been found; green chalk surrounded the pool of his spilled blood; and yellow chalk detailed where somebody had stood and shifted his feet before taking a stride toward the door.

The two stationary prints were enlarged and blurred, as though the person had stood there for some time, shifting his feet now and then. The striding print lay beyond the pool and was fainter but more well defined.

The victim had been seated in the chair, which lay on its side, when he had been sapped from behind. Bright orange chalk indicated the position in which he had been found.

"What d'yiz think, Chief? Inside job?" a voice asked, startling him.

McGarr swung round on a young woman. Late thirties, pixieish; her black curly hair was pulled back and woven into a long braid. She was wearing a navy blue fleece jacket and jeans. McGarr had seen her before, but he couldn't place where.

"Orla Bannon, *Ath Cliath*." She held out her hand. He only stared down at it.

Ath Cliath was a weekly tabloid that through the cunning use of innuendo, unnamed sources, and front-page hyperbole had grown from a mere weekend listings rag to one of the most influential and certainly the most profitable newspapers in the country.

Only two days before the murder of its founder, Dery Parmalee, nearly two years earlier, ownership of the tabloid had fallen to one Charles "Chazz" Sweeney, who had ordered the hit, McGarr had believed but could not prove.

He also believed Sweeney had played some part in the deaths of Noreen and her father, Fitz. But he couldn't prove that either.

Orla Bannon was a columnist, McGarr now remembered; a head shot, which made her look rather like an American Indian princess, ran with her articles. In it, she was gazing out at her readers sidelong and assessing, with that same slight smile on her face, her eyes so black they were jet.

"You shouldn't be here. This is a police zone."

"Didn't I see the tape?" she replied coyly, cocking her head. "But not to worry—I'm here to help you." The voice was Northern, working-class, and the pluck he recognized—the one that came from a lifetime of having nothing to lose.

"Inside job, right?" she continued. "There's the hand-recognition device, and the other security guard who got bumped off a fortnight ago by a hit-and-run driver, so's Sloane would have to walk the beat himself. And their knowing that if they clapped him into the case and withdrew the air, his corpse would look frightful. Did you get a look at it yourself?"

"Why would they want him to look frightful?"

Now knowing he wouldn't make her leave, she pulled back her jacket and placed her hands on her hips. The press passes hanging from her neck made her breasts, which were contained in a white jumper, all the more obvious. "For the effect. The drama. So you'll take their demand for ransom serious, when it comes."

"How do you know where Sloane was found?"

"And would you look at this chair—where the other guard was sitting, right? He must have known whoever sapped him." Hands still on hips, she stepped over the area stained by blood and lowered her head. "Footprints, eh? The craven inside yoke stood here in the poor bastard's blood, while waiting to open the gate for whoever murdered Sloane and stole the feckin' books."

McGarr wondered as much at her hardened tone as her seasoned observations. The voice in her column was urbane, even elegant. "Crime reporter once?"

She only moved her head to the side, as though to say, of course. As she bent to peer around the side of the desk, a shaft of sunlight struck the top of her head, and McGarr noted rows of stitched scarring where the dark wavy hair would no longer grow. "How do you know about the crime scene in the Old Library?"

"Like I said, we can help each other." Turning her head, she caught his eye. "But it'll have to be a two-way street. Not all give and no get."

She raised herself up. "Lost a lot of blood, Tom Healey. Little wonder he's fighting for his life."

McGarr glanced at the notes McKeon had given him. It was the name of the Trinity security guard who had been attacked there at the desk. "How do you know all this?"

"Didn't I tell you I'm a shape-shifter straight out of Celtic myth. I can travel about in a lordly mist, I can. Whenever I please."

Which was something McGarr had heard years before in school.

There was a sparkle in her jet eyes. "I can tell you don't believe me."

"How will you help me?"

Turning to leave, she presented herself in profile, and his eyes devolved on the radical angle of her breasts. "I already have. Look into the death of Greene—you'll see what I mean. But I think we're both going to be needing some help. Down the road. D'yeh have me card?"

"Who's Greene?"

"The Trinity security guard who bought the bumper of a BMW a fortnight ago."

From the back pocket of her jeans, Bannon drew out a contact card. "It's a bit wrinkled and hot, but you can reach me, if you've a need." Again, her eyes fixed his. "And I'm thinking you'll need."

McGarr did not offer his hand to take the card.

"Take it."

Still McGarr did not reach for the card.

She stepped in on him, so close her breasts grazed his chest and her breath was hot on his neck. She slid the card into the breast pocket of his jacket.

"I've been following you for years. I know your story. You don't know me yet. But you will. I have contacts that you would not believe. And, incidentally, what I know about you, I like."

McGarr stepped back, having known more than a few journalists who for insider access would say or do just about anything.

He pulled the card from his pocket. "Thanking you all the same, Orla."

She cocked her head again and looked up at him assessingly. "Know what I'd hazard? I'd hazard Sloane was on Ox, and that's why he sold out Kells, Trinity, and Ireland."

It sounded rather like a headline, and McGarr tried to remember what Ox was, exactly. Some drug he'd read about in a Garda report that concluded its addictive power was greater than that of any known drug, including heroin and cocaine.

"Of course, you'll discover all that in the postmortem. Look at me."

He raised his eyes from the card and gazed into her dark eyes.

"You and I are similar people. Apart from geography, we come from the same place. You were born and brought up in Inchicore; your father worked for Guinness and had nine kids. You went into police work, which is a more immediate form of journalism.

"I, well, chose less risk, even though I'm from the Short Strand and the tenth of eleven kids, I kid you not." It was a small, often besieged Catholic enclave in a Protestant section of Belfast.

"Sure, me da worked at what he could, given the inset. And he did as right for us as any man there. Ring me up, if you think I might help. Otherwise, I won't bother you—unless I have something . . . critical."

Slipping her hands in the front pockets of her jeans, she turned and walked out of the security office.

At the desk, McGarr scanned the logbook of cars admitted to the college. The final entry was at 11:07 P.M., when the automobile of a Professor Hurley left. McGarr flipped the pages, noting that it was either policy not to admit cars after nine at night or none seemed to arrive after that hour.

An arm of the chair had broken, where the man had fallen heavily. He had not bothered even to get up when his assailant had entered. Or had sat back down, trusting him.

Outside, a crowd of students had gathered at the police tape, where the uniformed Guard was keeping them back.

"How did that woman get by you?" McGarr asked.

"You mean the one who was just inside with you, Superintendent? She flashed a Garda ID and said she was with you."

"Did you check the ID?"

"Yes, I did, sir."

"Her name?"

"Bresnahan, Ruth. Serious Crimes Unit."

It was the name of a former detective.

"And the photo?" Ruth Bresnahan was a tall redhead.

"It matched. I took particular notice because I thought I'd seen the woman's face before."

Moving through the crowd, McGarr pulled his cell phone from his pocket.

The number answered on the second ring. "Bresnahan and Ward," said a deep yet womanly voice. "Aren't you busy? Or are you in need of expert help?"

Along with her common-law husband, Hugh Ward, another former Murder Squad staffer, Ruth Bresnahan now ran a successful security firm.

"Orla Bannon—know her?"

"Who doesn't? She's the diva of *Ath Cliath*. Column, front page whenever she wants it, features with miles of space."

"She just got herself into the crime scene here. The ID had her head shot with your name."

"Go 'way."

"How would she have got hold of your ID?"

There was a pause.

With cell phone to ear, McGarr was weaving through a stream of students.

"Let's see—I still have my last ID in the glove box of the car. But maybe four or five years ago, I lost another when my purse was nicked at a pub in Enniskillen where we were staking out Eva Morrisey. Remember?"

He did. Bresnahan had been undercover, trying to get a lead on an IRA squad leader who had murdered her lover in Donegal.

"Orla Bannon had covered the story from Morrisey's arrest and trial to her sentencing. It was all hearts-and-sorrows. She portrayed her as an unloved child, the victim of an abusive upbringing and a social and court system that failed to address her obvious psychological needs.

"And now that you've mentioned her name, I also remember her ringing me up around that time, wanting to know how the 'Mata Hari of the Murder Squad' had fared, north of the border, up Enniskillen way. She even sang it. At the time, I wondered how she knew.

"But it's classic Orla Bannon, all right. It's not how you get the story, but that you get it. Which doesn't bother her boss one bit, I bet."

Sweeney, who used *Ath Cliath* as his own literally bloody pulpit.

"Although I hear there's bad blood between them, with Sweeney wanting to sack her but the editors telling him she's too well known and too knowledgeable of him and the paper to let her go."

"Would some other paper have her?"

"In a heartbeat. Nobody comes through with new takes and evidence on old dead stories like O.B."

"She's called that?"

"With the allusion to the all-knowing *Star Wars* character not disavowed by her."

"She's well scarred."

"On the head from truncheons. She was a kid during the civil rights marches, and it's said by those who would know that she's got other scars that are not merely physical.

"Fetching, wouldn't you say? Small, dark, fine-boned but full-figured. Yet she's never married, never been in a serious relationship that I've heard about. And any word of one would be all over town in a jiff, given who she is.

"If we can we help you with the Kells thing, Chief, you only have to say the word." McGarr detected more than a little interest in her voice.

Since leaving the Murder Squad, Bresnahan and Ward—with their knowledge of computers and databases—had provided McGarr with information he could not have obtained otherwise.

And none of what they came up with would have to be entered into Garda files and shared with the likes of Sheard.

"Call round at six"—when McGarr held his evening squad meeting. "And, thanks, Rut'ie." He rang off.

McKeon was waiting for him in what had been Sloane's office in the Trinity security headquarters, a small room with a gas fire in the grate and a tall, paned window that looked out on a playing field.

"Listen to this." McKeon hit a button on what looked like a recording machine. "Hello, Tom," a man's voice said. "What can I do for you?"

Another somewhat muffled voice replied, "Jesus, Ray—get here fast. I don't know who these yokes are, but—"

"One, I guess, is Sloane, the other the guard at the gate, the one who got thumped. Problem is"—McKeon again worked the answering machine, spooling back—"this is the prerecorded message for incoming calls."

McGarr again heard Sloane say, "Hello, Tom—what can I do for you?" Thereby establishing an alibi about where he was when the vehicle was let through the gate.

"Later, he'd come back, erase it, and put in a regular 'You've reached security headquarters at Trinity College. Please leave a message' . . . and so forth.

"As well, there's this." Moving toward another machine, McKeon punched two other buttons. "It's the voice recorder in the Old Library. It's switched on whenever sensors detect movement in the gift shop and book Treasury rooms after hours. When I walked in, it was the first thing I noticed. This light?" His finger swung to a red light the size of a 50P coin. "It was blinking."

"You don't know what you're doing," said the same voice. Sloane's voice. "If you take away what's in this room, the police will hound you into your graves."

"Use your hand," said a deep, gravelly, and obviously scrambled voice. "Kill the alarms and open it up."

There was a pause and then "Do it!"

McKeon stopped the tape. "Scramblers like that are used on the teley for interviews with informants on news shows. You know, for anonymity."

McGarr nodded as McKeon began to fast-forward the tape.

"I thought you said you were only going to take—"

Again, McKeon stopped the tape. "There he's so frightened he's forgot they're being taped."

"Open your fist!" the curious voice continued. "Open your bloody fist or I'll stomp it to bits."

"You said you—"

"I never said a thing."

"And me," another scrambled but much higher voice put in, "I lied."

There followed noises of something or somebody falling, a groan, grunts, scraping.

Then, a scrambled: "Give me a hand with him. Right enough—up he goes."

"No!" Sloane wailed.

They heard a clump, then another and another, then: "Blood enough for you?" Even through the scrambling, a kind of evil joy could be heard. "Enough to be taken seriously. Pity is—there's not enough. A man like that deserves all this and more."

"Too-da-loo."

"Ta."

What they then heard, McGarr assumed, was a rushing of air, as the atmosphere within the case was evacuated. And footsteps as the two left with their booty—the books of Kells, Armagh, and Durrow.

"Any word on the guard, Tom Healey?"

"Still unconscious."

"We'd best speak to Sloane's family directly."

3

RAYMOND SLOANE HAD LIVED IN A SECTION OF the Liberties that had been gentrified, the former commercial buildings rehabbed into lofts.

Others had been torn down with "Georgian-inspired condominiums," McGarr had read, erected in their stead. Randomly, it seemed, unpaned arched windows studded the facades, and every doorway carried an exaggerated fanlight.

The Sloane residence was far different and the genuine article altogether, McGarr could see as the car rounded a narrow corner in the warren of ancient laneways that marked the area.

It was a low two-storied affair with a sharply gabled slate roof and narrow windows. The front door opened directly on the footpath, where a uniformed Guard was standing, keeping the Fourth Estate at bay.

"Would you look at this cock-up."

A clutch of television vans had gathered before a dusty attached row house.

"All because of Sheard, who is a piece of work. He had to know how quickly the press would suss out who got whacked, once he said it was murder. There were only four guards' families to ring up.

"But him—he didn't give a shit, not being the one having to deal with it."

McGarr raised a finger to the windscreen. "Go down the block to the second alley. We'll go in the back." As a child, he had roamed the area with his mates; the buildings may have changed, but the ancient streets and laneways had not.

But a large BMW with tinted windows blocked the laneway, and they had to walk.

"How ya keeping on?" It was a question McKeon had been asking McGarr now and then since Noreen's death.

But he only nodded and reached for the handle to the back gate of the Sloane residence. McGarr was not used to divulging his feelings, nor did he do that easily.

The small back garden had been paved with concrete and filled with sheds from which they could hear pigeons cooing. Planters, some still in bloom, lined a sunny wall.

McKeon knocked on the back door with a frosted glass window. From the inside, they heard a deep man's voice say, "Jesus fookin' Christ, Ma—didn't I tell yeh to lock the back gate?"

Then, louder. "Yeah?"

"Police."

"What police?"

"Murder Squad."

"And bloody fookin' late, yiz are."

They heard a lock turn, and the door was jerked open. In it stood a large young man with a kind of silver ring through the septum of his nose.

His head was shaved, and over his broad shoulders he was wearing something like a woolen half-tunic. His trousers were light green and looked more like pajama bottoms. On his feet were sandals.

Apart from the ring, most noticeable were his bulging biceps that were mottled with patterns of tattoos. Yet from his long face and beaklike nose, McGarr could see he was Raymond Sloane's son. Early twenties, maybe twenty-five.

"Yiz fookin' cunts—nice of yeh to stop round. We thought you'd taken to informing families of murder victims on the teley. What's next, E-mail?"

"Would your mother be at home?" McGarr asked, noting that the nose ring was shaped rather like a Claddagh with azure studs on either end. He wondered how it must feel to have something like that there. Always.

"And now sneaking in through the back." His eyes, which were dark, played over the two smaller older men assessingly. "Two poncey codger cunts. What's wrong—gone suddenly camera shy? Or did yiz leave your balls back at Trinity?"

McGarr glanced at McKeon before pulling out his Garda ID, which he held toward Sloane with his thumb covering his name. "And you are?"

"Does it fookin' matter?"

When Sloane's eyes fell to the card, McKeon's hands shot out, one thumb digging into the young man's neck, the second finding another pressure point on the triceps of his right arm.

Sloane actually yelped, as McKeon jerked him out of the doorway and over an outstretched knee—depositing him rather gently on the concrete. Stepping back, he advised, "You. Stay. There."

McGarr moved into a low hall that led to what had been a scullery in days gone by but was now used as a kind of closet.

A small kitchen with a bedroom off it came next, then more narrow hall.

He found an older woman seated between two others, who were younger, in a small sitting room that was packed with overstuffed furniture, tables, floor lamps, more potted plants, framed photographs, curios, and even a spinet piano.

Eyes on McGarr, none said a word.

"Chief Superintendent McGarr." He took a step into the room. "I have some questions for you."

"Took you long enough," said one of the younger women.

From the back, he could hear McKeon. "And don't even think about getting up."

"But it's me own fookin' house."

"Shut your bloody gob. You think your mother needs you giving out like this?"

McGarr took a seat opposite the three women.

With eyes red and swollen, the wife had a fistful of photographs in her hand. Her cheeks, which had fallen into loose folds of skin, were streaked with tears. With prominent teeth and a weak chin, she had never been a pretty woman. But somehow she looked older than Sloane himself had in death.

Her eyes flickered up at him. "I know you know what it's like. But . . ."

McGarr only nodded, his personal tragedy having been played up by the press. Even now, his name was seldom mentioned without reference to the still-unsolved case.

One of the younger women twitched and opened her mouth to speak. But her mother's free hand came down on her thigh. "It's unfortunate how you came to learn of this tragedy. But my job is different. I'm here to gather information." He turned to the young woman on the mother's left. "And you are?"

"Siobhan Sloane."

"And you?"

"Sally."

McGarr addressed the wife. "Was there anything unusual in your husband's life of late?"

Siobhan rolled her eyes.

"What wasn't?"

"Derek Greene—" Sally began saying.

But her mother cut her off. "Please, let me. There're things you don't know." She drew in a breath and looked at a point over McGarr's shoulder. "You could say it began with the death of Derek Greene about a fortnight ago. But"—her eyes fell to McGarr's—"it began much before that. Two years ago, at least."

"Ah, Ma—he don't need to know that, now that Da's dead. That's family business. Private like," said Sally.

"You see, Raymond had a drug problem."

"But he was over it. Why bring it up?"

"First, it was marijuana when he played in a band, back when we was young. Then it ran on to pills, cocaine, and finally heroin, which he kicked three years ago, when Trinity announced it would begin taking urine samples from its security staff.

"So nobody would know, he went away to Holland, he did, on what should have been his holidays. Came back clean." Her eyes veered off. "For a while.

"All along, you see, he'd been a maintenance user, and clever like that—holding down the job, pleasant even home here, not like the other men hereabouts, always down the pub pissing away any extra money. Seldom jonesing in any way noticeable.

"He had the dose down, and it was like other people on Prozac or antianxiety tablets. He'd be alive today if he could have stayed on it.

"But once off, well, he became another man altogether. Nervous was not the word for it. Frazzled he was, all the time. He seldom slept for the first year.

"So, he tried drink, which made him sick and was no good for the work. Methadone, which he said was like weak heroin and just made him want to go back to the real stuff. And they might test for it without telling.

"All of which made him miserable until . . . until he found something new he wouldn't tell me about, apart from saying his troubles were over.

"And they were, sure. For maybe six or seven months, when I discovered he'd been into our savings for old age. He'd even taken a loan on the house.

" 'Not to worry, me love—I've got it all worked out. We'll be in the chips big-time by year's end. And I'll be saying *hasta la vista* to effing Trinity and all the bluenose pricks who teach there.'

"It was the way he'd been talking since he'd found whatever he'd found to calm him—wild like."

"And stupid," put in Sally.

"Then Derek died, who was Raymond's assistant, and it was like all hell broke loose for Raymond. Suddenly, he was hardly home. 'Work, work,' he said. 'Who's to say it's not a good in itself.' "

"Even stupider," said Siobhan.

"And when he was here at home, he was either on the phone or nipping down to the pub for a chat with some barfly or other. But the money improved. Last Friday didn't he show me a deposit slip for all the money he'd taken from the savings and a receipt for what he'd screwed out of the house."

"Then there was the car," said Sally.

Mrs. Sloane shook her head. "Whatever will we do with it now?"

"Ray-Boy will want it," replied Sally.

"Out in the alley. A big shhh-tu-pid car," put in Siobhan.

"Ray-Boy will take it," said her sister.

"The hell he will. We'll turn it back in."

"He'd just signed the hire-purchase agreement," said the wife.

Asked McGarr, "Do you know the source of the money?"

The wife shook her head.

"What about people? The new people around him recently. On the phone, in the pub. I'm only asking because whoever stole from the library had to have studied Raymond's rounds, the layout of the college, and the security protocol for the display cases. One way to do that would be to befriend the security chief."

"Are you saying our father was a thief?"

The wife shook her head. "Friends—it was one thing Raymond didn't have."

"Or had only one of," said Sally. "It's a curse."

"Do you know who was ringing up your husband?"

She shook her head.

"What about down in the pub—who was he going out to see?"

"Myself, I don't go in there."

"The name?"

"Foyle's. It's down the corner and to the right."

"What about Derek Greene, your husband's workmate—how did he meet his death?"

Suddenly, McGarr heard a commotion in the hallway, and the son burst past the archway to the sitting room. "Let's put some air into this thing," he roared. "We'll burst this fookin' bubble."

"Ray-Boy!" his mother shouted.

Before McGarr could get up, McKeon also appeared in the archway, blood streaming down his face. "Bastard has a sap . . ." He collapsed.

"Come in," the son could be heard saying obviously to the press gathered outside. "Come in all of yiz. The Guards—two poncey codger cunts—they snuck in the back. Forced entry. They attacked me, Ma."

On his feet now, McGarr only reached the archway when a television camera swung round the corner, topped by a brace of blinding lights.

McGarr knelt by McKeon, who raised a hand. "Get him, Peter. I'll be fine."

Arms out and elbows high like a rugger out of a scrum, McGarr vaulted forward into the journalists, pushing them toward the door. "Out! Get out!"

"But we're in," one said.

"We were invited."

"You're abrogating the freedom of the press, McGarr," said a female voice he thought he recognized.

At the door, he raised a foot, kicked out at the cameraman with the bright lights, then scanned the street. Sloane the younger was nowhere in sight.

Nor was the BMW in the laneway, when, at length, they got there.

4

After tending to McKeon's injuries, which required medical attention, McGarr drove out to his daughter's school, where almost daily he picked her up. Nuala—his mother-in-law, who now cared for Maddie and was elderly—only drove in emergencies.

It was a ritual that at first he thought would be an impediment to his work. Instead, it had become a welcome relief from his duties, a two-hour hiatus and the only time, if truth were told, that he got to be with her alone, given her schedule and his.

Located in Sandeford, a village south of Dublin, the school was private and nonsectarian.

Among the Mercs, Audis, Volvos, and Jags of the other parents, McGarr's unmarked Ford squad car stood out like a rolling eyesore. But, truth was, one day his own daughter would be wealthy if not rich.

Fitz—Noreen's dad, who had died with her—had been a key member of the Dublin in-crowd that had thrived in good times and bad, no matter the vicissitudes of politics. Nuala had been Fitz's heir, and Maddie was hers.

Which was a felicity that McGarr rather feared for his daughter, knowing little of its demands. How should he prepare her for the responsibilities and burdens? Or direct her toward happiness, which was, really, all he had ever wanted for her? And what, he suspicioned, had been lost because of who he was? If he'd been a banker or a barrister, like the fathers of some of the other students who were filing out of the handsome, half-timbered building in front of him, Noreen and Fitz would be alive.

Watching Maddie now, as she larked down the stairs with her classmates, she appeared happy enough, smiling and laughing with her friends, all of whom were wearing charcoal blazers with the school crest on the pockets.

But at home, where so much of Noreen lingered, she was often different. Somber. Given to sudden tears. And her need for his time, his attention, and the constant reassurance of his love was nothing short of pitiable. Which only jacked his guilt sky-high.

Pulling open the door, Maddie tossed her book bag on the floor and slid in. "H'lo."

"H'lo."

She leaned over and brushed her lips against his face.

"How was school?" McGarr eased the car down the drive.

Her brow furrowed. "You know—you always ask that, Peter."

In the last year, Maddie had gone from calling him Daddy to Father and now by his first name. "Can't you think of something original to ask?"

"Well, I'm interested in how your day went. In school."

"And you always say that."

"Because you always say what you say."

"And the next line is—how were your classes? Did you learn something interesting, something I don't know, something that will keep me from being the obvious dolt that I am?"

McGarr glanced at her, noting how much she had begun to resemble her mother. Like Noreen, she was fine-boned with a thinly bridged nose and dimpled cheeks. While fair, her coloring was darker than that of either of her parents, and her skin still carried a golden hue from the summer she had spent on Nuala's estate in Kildare.

Noreen's eyes had been green. McGarr's own were a very light gray. Maddie's were starburst blue, like McGarr's own mother's had been.

"Well, here's something that might interest you. Picture this: There we were in the buttery, taking lunch, and Eithne says, 'Maddie, isn't that your father thumping those cameramen?' And everybody—I mean the entire blessed school—looks up, and there you are, my special da, on the teley.

"Your face in the camera, elbows out, and your eyes—well, your eyes are only your eyes, when you're mad. And there you were shoving the entire bloody lot out into the street.

"The truly great thing, of course, was when you raised your foot and vaulted that last man from the house. Before slamming the door.

"What you couldn't have seen, since you were on the other side of the door, is how he landed. On his face with the camera smashing to bits.

"Of course, we kept watching. I mean, how often do we see somebody's father on television when, you know, they're not running for a political office or announcing a corporate merger.

"And, sure, they did show why you did what you did—Bernie all bloody and down on the floor in the hallway of the house. But they kept running the shots of the cameraman flopping down on the footpath and his camera crashing into the street.

"It was then—" Maddie turned to him, and he watched her slight smile crumble. "It was then Brianna Cauley said—" She looked down at her hands, which she had placed palms up in her lap. "She said, 'No wonder somebody murdered her mum. That man must have lots of enemies.' "

Tears burst from her eyes, and McGarr looked for a place to pull over, so he could comfort her.

Clinging to him as she now often did, Maddie sobbed into his chest, and he stroked her brow. When she had quieted, he asked, "Did you say anything back to Brianna?"—who was one of Maddie's earliest friends and had probably overheard the assessment from her parents.

Maddie shook her head. "I didn't have to. Cassie said, 'Maddie's dad does what he does to protect society from the likes of you, arsehole.'

"And Brianna shot back, 'Really? Since when has he begun protecting us from television?' That's when somebody else told her to shut her bloody gob, and a teacher came over."

McGarr let some time pass before offering his handkerchief. Then: "Don't think I haven't thought of just what Brianna had to say."

Maddie straightened up and blew her nose. "You mean, if you weren't who you are, Mammy would still be alive?"

McGarr nodded. "And your grandfather."

"If you were instead—"

"A banker or a solicitor or a businessman, say."

"But you weren't. And you're not. You are who you are, and Mammy's dead."

Which was the painful—and, McGarr suspected, the ever-painful—reality of their lives.

"Got much homework?" He twisted the key and put the car in gear.

"Reams and reams of it."

When they arrived at their house on Belgrave Square in Rathmines, he reached for her before she could get out. "I want you to forgive Brianna, and be gracious when she apologizes to you."

"Peter! You think I won't?"

"No, I knew you would. But I thought I'd mention it."

Probably because he himself wished he could forgive whoever had worked the two deaths, but he knew he never would. It just wasn't in him.

And because he did not want the poison that had spilled into his life with the murder to spread to his child.

THE BAR UP THE STREET FROM RAYMOND Sloane's house was a relic from the Liberties of old—a low, dim kip clouded with smoke from the clutch of old men at the bar and a sooty fire that was smoldering in the hearth.

McGarr pulled back a stool, the red leatherette seat of which was split and curled like the skin of an apple. He sat, noting that all conversation had ceased.

The others were staring at him, one man even having rose from his seat to get a better look.

Climbing down from her own stool positioned at the farther end of the bar, a slatternly old woman with a pronounced limp and a cigarette at the corner of her mouth approached, muttering something he couldn't quite make out.

He thought he heard, "Fookin' cop shite . . . never see them . . . grass on the locals."

She stopped in front of him and raised her head to look through a pair of grimy glasses on the end of a long nose. Her wrinkled face was the shade of putty; her brown eyes were milky with age.

"Yeh drink on duty, it's said."

"By whom?"

"It's why you did what you did on the teley." She flapped a hand at a screen that was showing a rugby match. "Drunken snit. It's on all the channels. With young Sloane—who's known as J.C. hereabouts—saying yous two broke in the back of his house, roughed him up, then grilled his mammy and sisters. Before he busted out.

"Then there's yourself, beatin' the piss out of the press. Finally. At last. Feckin' bunch of fakes, frauds, and fairies. What are ye havin' besides the time of day?"

"Malt."

She shuffled around to reach for a bottle. "If you want ice, you can go to feckin' Iceland and hell in that order. We serve no feckin' ice here."

Some of the others began laughing.

She poured the drink and placed it before McGarr.

He slid some Euros toward her, but she slid them back. "You gave me a laugh, which is hard to come by these days."

McGarr nodded thanks. "Why J.C.?"

"Jesus Christ. It's how he once looked, with a dust mop beard and feckin' sandals in winter. And because 'J.C.' browned him off. But all that's gone. Now he's Kojak with a ring in his nose."

"Like a feckin' bossy cow," said one of the men at the bar.

The old woman pulled the stub of cigarette from her mouth and flicked it at the man. "Another word from you, and you're out of here. The man's speaking to me."

"The father, Sloane, he came in here." It was not a question.

"Not to drink. No toper, Raymond Sloane."

"Why drink? How high is up?"

"That's it. You're gone."

The man turned his head and smiled to the others. He did not move.

"Feckin' ee-jit."

"Drugs?"

"Raymond?" She nodded. "Years ago. Him with a steady job but the family and no money, the missus told me. Any other place but Trinity—bein' a college and all—would have booted his arse into

Liffey, where it belonged. But he did the rehab, and then he was back acting . . . different.

"At first we put it down to the 'pink cloud' thing—you know, clean. Off the shit. I get 'em in here all the time. Turning over a new leaf, clean—yous is all drunken mots and bowsies, they say. Then, sooner or later, they show up, worse than before. Locked—morning, noon, and night."

Turning her back to her customers, she lowered her voice. "But Raymond was different. He was better at first, then better than better, if you catch me drift. More . . . alive, smiling, happy"—her sad old eyes scanned McGarr's face—"too feckin' happy.

"Chattin' everybody up a mile a minute. Then he was, like, gone. Not there with you. You could say, 'Raymond, you just won the Sweeps.' He'd give you his contented cow look and say, 'That's gas, Lizzie. Gas.'

"Pink feckin' substantial cloud, says I to meself. Without a penny in it for me, more's the pity." Again she paused, as though to assess McGarr's reaction.

"Tell me now—why would anybody want to kill Raymond Sloane? So you nick the Book of Kells and them other two yokes. So you're all dressed up in black and balaclavas, and you've disguised your feckin' voices and all. Why off a feckin' security guard like Raymond, who'd probably messed his britches the moment he sussed out what was happening.

"Because"—she glanced down at McGarr's drink, which was untouched—"because Raymond must have been in on it.

"Because the moment they got the goods in their hands, it was nightie-night, Raymond. No probable touts allowed, no druggie informers. They clapped him in the box and sucked out the air."

Although bemused by her detailed knowledge of the crime, McGarr waited. She had more to tell him.

A cigarette came out of the pocket of her cardigan jumper, then a lighter. Her wrinkled lips jetted smoke at the teley. Then, with the palm of her hand, she vigorously worked the crook of gray flesh that was her nose.

"Itchy. Bad air in here. The worst. But"—she drew on the cigarette—"I suppose it's a condition of life, as I've known it.

"Take them chancers behind me." She jerked a thumb over her shoulder. "Years ago, a good half of them were beggin' me to throw a leg over their lousy hides, don't you know. Eyein' me, buyin' me little thises and thats, reachin' for me hip when I passed.

"Says I to meself, says I, Whatever would I want with anybody who comes in here? All they see in me is this bar, sorry as it is. The till. And me, an only child with an aged father. I'd only get the best of a bad lot.

"No, I wanted a gent who would take me out of this motley shite. Somebody like the bloody tall man who came into the lounge over there with a lady maybe a fortnight ago to speak to Raymond." She jabbed the cigarette at a low battered door, which was closed.

"It's hardly used. There's a separate entrance. A buzzer goes off when the other door gets opened from the street, is how I knew they was in there."

"You get a look at them?" McGarr touched the drink to his lips.

"Only when the door opened and closed. Raymond had been in here at least an hour before, nervous like."

"Playin' with himself, as ever," put in one of the men at the bar. "Sloane was a feckin' wanker, if there ever was one."

"You too," she warned through the laughter. "You can go as well."

"Nervous, how?"

"Pacin', looking at his wristwatch. Must have smoked a packet of fags."

"Describe the gent." McGarr reached for his drink. "What did he look like?"

"I only got a look at him when the door opened and closed, don't you know. But I'd say he was a tall man. Early forties. Soap star looks. Cashmere top coat, silk scarf.

"When Raymond come out saying he needed a gin martini and a glass of white wine, says I, 'The feck would I be doing with vermouth.' Says he, 'Just fill it up with gin. Fecker's got the bag on, he won't notice.' Fortunately, I found the bottle of white wine I made the mistake of buying years ago. For the lady."

"What did she look like?"

"Had her back to the door, but upmarket altogether. Tasteful coat, good shoes. Legs crossed to make a show of them. It's all I saw of her."

"Hear any names?"

"Only Raymond's."

"He speak with you later?"

" 'Twas the last I seen of him. Ever, as it turns out."

"Big BMW up the street," said one of the men behind her. "Midnight blue. Gold wheel covers."

Like Raymond Sloane's new wheels, which, McGarr supposed, the son, Ray-Boy, had driven off in.

"How long did they stay?"

"The drink, is all. Fifteen minutes, twenty. They had business with Raymond, if you know what I mean. After it, he was out of here like a shot."

"Big shit-eater on his puss" came from one of the men.

"He could see his future before him," said another.

"Notoriety. Front-page headlines."

"Stardom and a big glass box." Laughter gurgled from the crew.

"Warped arseholes," the old woman opined. "Imagine swearing any one of them in a court of law."

More immediately, McGarr was interested in the possibility of one or another having got a good look at the man or woman who met Sloane in the lounge. "Would you mind if I sent an artist over here?"

"Depends on her act. If she gets the lads all riled up, then leaves, no telling what might happen." Behind the soiled lens of her eyeglasses, one rheumy eye winked.

McGarr tossed back his drink, put a ten on top of the singles, then slid the bank notes forward. "Buy the lads a drink and one for yourself." Warped or not, later he might need them.

"Where'd you learn about the balaclavas and all the . . . crime scene details?" He slid off the stool.

She swung her jaw at the teley. "Some big fella—one of your own—was on twice. Once at Trinity, a second time from Garda headquarters in Phoenix Park."

Sheard. What possibly could he hope to gain in releasing those details? McGarr wondered. "Your name?" He held out his hand.

"Does it matter?"

He nodded. "You've been helpful."

"Foyle. Annie Foyle, like the name of the place. But I don't think I'd do you much good in court, either."

McGarr now remembered—Foyle's had been the name of the pub at least since he'd been a child.

He had actually known her father, who had been a friend of his own father. "Small world."

"It's occurred to me."

Twenty minutes later, McGarr found himself climbing a battered staircase toward his headquarters on the third floor of a building in the complex of structures called Dublin Castle in the heart of the city.

The brick structure, Edwardian in style, was a former British army barracks and still reeked of coarse tobacco, dubbin, leather, sweat, gun oil, and fear. The British had been oppressors and in that role hated and sniped upon. Like the Garda itself, these days.

And paper, McGarr decided, bumping open the door into the office proper. The place now also stank of paper, reams and reams of it, as Maddie had said of her homework. Along with a more recent smell—the acrid plastic stench of simmering circuitry.

"Chief," said one staffer, as McGarr passed down the rows of desks.

"Chief," said another.

"Chief," some of the others then chorused.

It was the standard greeting.

"You got Rut'ie and her consort in your cubicle," said John Swords, who since Bresnahan's removal had acted as McGarr's amanuensis. "Bernie's in there too, nursing his stitched pate."

"Which you're calling a heads-up?" McGarr asked, if only to break his somber mood.

"Only the 'nursing.' You'll see what I mean."

With the next step, he did:

McKeon was ensconced in McGarr's chair, feet up on the desk. In front of him was the bottle of whiskey that was usually kept in the lower left-hand drawer of the desk and could get McGarr sacked, given long-standing regulations prohibiting drink in Garda facilities. McGarr's personal cup was in McKeon's right hand, doubtless filled with the potent fluid.

Bresnahan, on the other hand, was seated in McKeon's usual chair, with Hugh Ward occupying the edge of the planning table.

"Chief," the three said together.

McGarr made a point of staring at the bottle and then at the cup.

"I'd offer you a touch but, as you can see, there's only one drinking vessel," said McKeon, his dark eyes bright from the drink. "I asked for OxyContin, but they warned I couldn't snort and gargle at the same time. Please don't tell me I have to get up."

McKeon's thick white hair had been shaved around the wound, which was covered by a bandage plaster.

"Did anybody ever tell you you need a television in here?" McKeon continued.

"Acting lessons," said Ward.

"And a blue pinstriped, double-breasted suit with a hankie in the pocket," put in Bresnahan, who now crossed long shapely legs that were encased in buff-colored stockings.

The swish of one silky thigh gliding over the other caused McGarr to turn and look out the sooty window. He removed his hat and placed it on the filing cabinet.

She—Bresnahan—was a tall woman with an angular—no, a spectacularly angular—build. In her midthirties now, she reminded McGarr of a larger, better-looking Rita Hayworth, if that were possible.

In his youth, McGarr had been entranced by Rita Hayworth. She had been his first love, he had more than once thought. Even Noreen, his wife, had looked like a diminutive, finer version of Rita Hayworth, and here was Bresnahan—Rita gone large and in the shape of her face prettier.

Rita Hayworth, McGarr had decided when watching *Pal Joey* for the umpteenth time, was only pretty in the pose of command—head tilted back and slightly to the side, staring down her rather ordinary nose at some hapless sap as though to say, "Grovel, swine."

Bresnahan, on the other hand, always looked markedly handsome from every angle, with a long, straight nose, high cheekbones, and a dimpled chin. Her eyes were the color of dark smoke; her hair was auburn.

But not only was she decades younger than McGarr, she had also worked for him too long for anything other than friendship. Add to that, she was the common-law wife of Hugh Ward, McGarr's erstwhile second in command and good friend.

Nevertheless, he wondered—not for the first time—how it would be to have Bresnahan in bed. The touch of her, the heft of her body.

Reaching for the bottle on the desk, he squeaked the cork into the top and slid it into the drawer. He turned to Ward. "Got something?"

Ward hunched his shoulders. "Maybe. But first you should see this."

Dark, with matinee-idol good looks and an athletic build, Hugh Ward tapped a few keys and turned the screen of the large laptop so the others could see. Ward had been touted as McGarr's successor before the debacle that led to Noreen's and Fitz's deaths and resulted, later, in Bresnahan and Ward being drummed out of the Garda.

The screen brightened, and a voice said, "Mr. Brendan Kehoe, taoiseach, will now make a statement about recent events at Trinity College."

Kehoe was to McGarr's mind the consummate down-country politician. A small, wiry man with an unruly tangle of blondish hair, he maintained a perpetual slight smile, as though to say, no matter the situation—some reversal of progress toward a settlement in the North; the malfeasance of a minister in his government; or here the theft of perhaps the chief treasure of the country—all was right with the world. Or could be made right, if we just keep our aplomb. Or cool.

At first Kehoe's smile had been the subject of derision in the press, with columnists lampooning it as "daffy," "imbecilic," and "ga-ga." Cartoonists had a field day, picturing him as a pukka or Lilliputian among a forest of Brobdingnagians. But as his leadership matured, all learned that the bemused smile was balanced by a political deftness and savvy that had been missing from Irish politics in recent years.

A barrister and legal scholar, Kehoe still spoke in the broad tones of his native West Cork, and along with the smile, he maintained an avuncular manner, like some poor country farmer you might meet in a pub or hear phoning in one of the chat shows that were a feature of rural Irish radio—at once garrulously good-humored, folksy but sly.

Surrounded by taller men at the microphone, Kehoe studied his notes and shook his head before speaking. Then:

" 'Tis a sad, sorrowful day for the Irish people and the world. Our greatest national treasure has been stolen, one brave man murdered egregiously and seemingly to no purpose, and another is seriously ill in the hospital.

"The Book of Kells, along with the books of Durrow and Armagh, are collectively a trinity which represents the highest form of Celtic-Christian art that the world possesses, and are a testament to the cultural preeminence of Celtic peoples during a period in Europe that was otherwise turbulent, benighted, and militaristic.

"The manuscripts are also holy objects, divine talismans of the Christian faith.

"That said, we who are gathered here represent all political parties but one. And we are united in our resolve to get the books back undamaged in any way. We will also see those cultural terrorists who perpetuated these several crimes apprehended and punished to the fullest extent of the law.

"Every resource of the government and Garda will be brought to bear on this effort, which will be led by Chief Superintendent Jack Sheard."

The camera swung to Sheard, the largest and certainly the most striking-looking man there. His expression was bathetically grave, McGarr judged—hands clasped at waist, eyes down, brow glowering. A knob of flesh on his wide jaw had blanched from compressed concern.

"The government has also established a reward of thirty thousand Euros for information leading to the arrest of the perpetrators and the return of the treasures. Needless to say, the identities of all patriots willing to come forward to help the police in this matter will be kept strictly confidential. You need not fear reprisals."

A graphic with a telephone number now appeared on the screen. It was the public information number of Sheard's office.

"Which political party is absent?" McGarr asked.

"Celtic United," said Bresnahan.

"The who?" Swords asked. He was standing in the opening of the cubicle, pad and Biro in hand to take McGarr's orders.

"What rock have you been skulking under, boyo?" McKeon asked.

"It's the political party of the New Druids," Ward explained. "The gang from the North Side."

Who were responsible for much of the organized crime and drug dealing in the working-class sections of the city, McGarr well knew.

The New Druids were a group of former IRA thugs and anti–organized religion zealots who were suspected of torching churches, Catholic and Protestant alike, on both sides of the border—and of other crimes, such as bank holdups, protection schemes, car thefts, and drug dealing.

Particularly they preyed upon Ireland's growing immigrant population and thus appealed to the young native Irish who were either unemployed or unemployable, along with the marginally or downright poor who had watched their neighborhoods become Moroccan, Nigerian, or Slavic.

Taoiseach Kehoe did not take questions. Instead, for the third time that day, Jack Sheard stepped before the cameras to field questions from the media.

He reprised what was known: the theft, security guard Raymond Sloane's murder, the probability that more than one thief/murderer was involved, and the injured security guard.

McGarr could only admire the panache with which Sheard rephrased his answers to make what was essentially only a few details seem like further information. In all, with wide shoulders, the big knobby chin, and youthful blond hair, he looked stalwart and competent.

"Then there's Orla Bannon," said Bresnahan. "The *Ath Cliath* reporter with my ID. Turns out she was snooping into the hit-and-run death of Derek Greene a fortnight ago, mind you, before what happened last night in the Old Library. My source at *Ath Cliath* tells me she's doing a big story on the New Druids."

"Who's Derek bloody Greene?" McKeon asked.

As one, the others turned their heads his way to assess his level of sobriety.

"How'rya getting home?" Bresnahan asked.

"On me pins."

"Which will needle you, if you drink any more of that." She pointed to the cup.

"Oh, really now—I'll tell you who Derek Greene is. He's"— McKeon looked off, his dark eyes glassy, features knitted before breaking into a sly smile—"the bloody security guard. The one what et the bumper of a BMW, the one who wasn't there, which forced poor Sloane to walk the beat.

"By choice, of course, Sloane having been bought. Witness the big car and the payback of the money he'd filched from his family's savings to feed his drug habit." McKeon looked down into the cup. "My prediction?"

"Delivered by himself, the new druid of Dublin Castle," Bresnahan quipped.

"The postmortem will confirm that."

"Confirm what?"

"Oxy-effing-Contin."

"This Orla Bannon knew what was about to go down," said Ward, if only to keep them on course. "Just like she knew the details of what had happened in the Treasury—case and point of how Sloane was murdered. How could she have known that and not been in on it?"

Pape, the head librarian, McGarr thought. If Orla Bannon wasn't in on it, then she could only have got the information from Pape, who had viewed the crime scene and had left the Old Library while McGarr was still interviewing Kara Kennedy. A skilled and fetching younger woman reporter with an angry old man—she probably now knew the brand of his jockey shorts.

"Ach, forget about her," said Bresnahan, flapping a hand dismissively. "She's only looking for a scoop. It's her MO."

"Yah—scooping up your credentials and representing herself as a Garda senior officer," put in McKeon. "Both are crimes."

But crimes that were best ignored, given how foolish Bresnahan and the Garda would look. And how resourceful Orla Bannon would appear. McGarr reached into his jacket pocket and felt for the cards that the two women—Orla Bannon and Kara Kennedy—had given him.

"All right—what do we know?" Ward asked, as he had for years when he'd been McGarr's second in command.

McGarr and McKeon supplied most of the synopsis:

That Derek Greene, a security guard, was knocked down in the street and killed a fortnight ago by a hit-and-run driver, freeing up the chief guard, Raymond Sloane, to walk Greene's beat. It might be a coincidence, but why had Orla Bannon been investigating the death?

That Sloane, who had a drug problem, made some kind of deal with either the two people who met him in Foyle's or some others that resulted in a windfall right before the event at Trinity College.

Sloane also probably assaulted his colleague, the guard at the Pearse Street gate, rendering him unconscious before opening the gate for the thieves who would also become his murderers. The sap that was found in Sloane's hand would produce evidence of that, McGarr was certain.

That there were at least two thieves was apparent from the voice transcription of their garbled voices. Near the end of the heist Sloane dropped any pretense of objecting to the theft and began objecting to their treatment of him.

As well, Sloane had not known that they had planned to steal the books of Durrow and Armagh in addition to Kells.

They murdered Sloane to send the message that they were "serious." About what? The ransom demand that was coming; there could be nothing else.

That Trevor Pape, the head librarian, and Kara Kennedy, the keeper of old manuscripts, were the only other two people who knew definitively how the cases could be opened and by whom— Sloane and each other alone. No others.

"Which leaves us?" Ward asked.

"Waiting for the demand," Bresnahan concluded.

"Anything else?" Ward asked.

Swords cleared his throat, stepped fully into the cubicle, and reached a printout toward McGarr.

The E-mail message was from the commissioner, repeating what they had heard the taoiseach announce on the television: the 30,000-Euro reward and that Jack Sheard would head up the investigation. With a final remark that cut McGarr to the quick.

"Jack's expertise is theft. He's studied these things, Peter. He knows how thieves think."

As if McGarr, with more than thirty years of police work both in Ireland and on the Continent, did not.

Turning to Swords but actually speaking to Bresnahan and Ward, McGarr said, "I want to martial the staff. They're to drop everything else and concentrate on Trevor Pape, Kara Kennedy, the victim Sloane, this Derek Greene, and Orla Bannon. I want to know every little thing about them, from their last phone calls to bank balances, mortgages, liaisons, what programming they watch, how many fillings in their molars, the works."

Still smarting from the commissioner's message, McGarr tugged on his hat. "Finally, send an artist over to Foyle's in the Liberties. I want a mock-up of an upmarket man and woman who met with Sloane two weeks or so ago."

"Look at that big pumped-up pussy," McKeon was muttering, as he stared at Sheard on the computer screen. "He can yap more nothing about nothing much than any man alive."

Among his handful of admirers within the Garda, Sheard was known as "The Communicator," McGarr now remembered it said.

They would now see how potent an investigator he was.

"By when, Chief?" Swords asked to McGarr's back.

"Ten. Tomorrow."

5

Going home, being home, enjoying the home he once loved was a trial for McGarr, filled as it was with so many memories of Noreen.

A detached Georgian house made of brick and stone, it occupied a corner on Belgrave Square in Rathmines, a suburb of the city that was now also filled out with recent immigrants, students, pensioners, and the working poor. It had not always been so.

McGarr parked his Mini-Cooper down a narrow cul-de-sac that bordered one side of his property and got out.

The night, like the day had been, was fair, and even with the ambient light of the city and a quarter moon, the stars were myriad and deep.

Instead of walking round to the front door as he usually did, McGarr moved toward the laneway and the low door that opened into his back garden.

There in the dim chalky light, striped with brighter luminescence from the kitchen windows, he surveyed his garden, which he had all but abandoned for three entire summers.

But in hopes of carrying on in the coming spring, he had planted a bit of winter wheat that would add nutrients to the now-well-rested soil, when he turned it under before planting.

There had been a time when gardening had been a passion for McGarr, a way of truly recreating himself while producing a satisfying variety of vegetables, fruits, and flowers. When engaged in gardening, he had no thoughts other than those related to the pastime, which were few since he'd been gardening for decades. It was like second nature to him.

McGarr knew other people who had suffered losses as great as he is but whose hobbies had given them succor and solace.

Well—he glanced up at the house where he could see Nuala's head moving to and from the stove—maybe in the coming year. A light was on in Maddie's room, where she would be doing her sums.

He should go in and find out how she was and how her work was progressing, make small talk with Nuala, who would be interested in the trouble at Trinity, maybe pour himself an aperitif and make a few phone calls about other cases that would now go ignored.

And yet McGarr removed his jacket and began pulling up dead plants and tossing them on the compost heap. He worked steadily but without passion for perhaps a half hour, before he heard the back door open.

"Peter—is that you out there?" Nuala asked, squinting into the darkness. "I thought I saw you. Put that down now. And come in. Your tea is ready."

Climbing the back stairs, he caught the aroma of baking plaice with black olives and mild peppers, some fresh tarragon, and butter. Less apparent were the odors of parsleyed potatoes and hot bread.

Like her daughter had been, Nuala was an excellent cook. And yet he who had eaten next to nothing the day long had little appetite for the food. He reached for a glass of wine, which was white, cold, and calming, he hoped.

"Maddie tells me you were on the teley today."

McGarr nodded and glanced over at Maddie, who had brought a book to the table in spite of his having asked her not to do so some weeks earlier.

But he could hardly blame her, dinner conversation usually taking the form of "How was your day?" "Grand." "And yours?" A nod. "The same." This, in spite of Nuala's having once been accounted as one of the notable conversationalists in Dublin society.

"The Kells affair, now—will you catch the blighters who killed that poor watchman?"

Eating the dinner if only to respect the effort, McGarr glanced up at Nuala. In all but coloring she resembled Noreen—dark where Noreen had been fair. But now in her early seventies, she was gray; her skin had grown slack and her hips wide.

"Yes. Surely. We will. Eventually, I suppose." There would be money involved, which always left a trail in some way or other.

"But will you get the books back?"

"Yah. It's why they were stolen."

"For a ransom."

"Yah."

Maddie's head came up from the book. "How much?"

"We haven't heard from them yet." Unless, of course, Jack Sheard had, and McGarr and the Murder Squad were being kept out of the loop.

He thought of the taoiseach's press conference, the commissioner's note, and he placed his fork on the plate. He knew why Sheard brought out all his insecurities and fears.

Younger, taller, handsome, well-spoken, with the picture-perfect family and legal background, Sheard was the future of the Garda.

As for McGarr . . . well, he had no university degrees, no other training, and apart from Maddie and Nuala, his work was all he had in life. All he knew.

"But how much do you think?"

Pushing back his chair, he stood and moved toward the pantry where he kept the malt. "Millions, I'm certain. Why murder for less?"

"How many?" Nuala paused. "What's wrong—don't you fancy your dinner?"

"It's grand. I'll be right out." Pouring himself a stiff drink and then adding to it, McGarr knocked it back, set down the glass, considered another but instead corked the bottle and returned to the table.

"I've no idea how many millions," he continued when he could, as though he had not left. Through his watering eyes, Maddie's image was distorted. "But they're obviously professional thieves." And killers, he did not add. "So the sum could be high."

"Millions and millions?"

He nodded and again reached for the wineglass that he drank from, rather like a chaser.

Nuala's jet eyes, now a bit rheumy with age, moved from the glass to his face, and then back down at the glass. "Have you heard from them?"

"Not that I know."

Later, up in Maddie's room, he said good night to her rather early, as she continued to read the book in bed.

"The bit on the television—it bothered you?"

Eyes in the book, she only shook her head.

"Bernie was assaulted by the dead man's son, who let the press in. Seven stitches in his pate. I had to do something. I was going after the son. The others just got in the way, letting him escape."

"Peter—don't you think I know that?"

It might be necessary for her friends to know that as well, however. "Well"—he bent and kissed her forehead—"I was just doing my job, such as it is. And I love you."

"Yah." She raised her head and closed her eyes.

Their lips met briefly.

"I love you too, Peter."

And then, as McGarr descended the stairs, Maddie called out, "Love you."

"Love you," McGarr answered her call again and again, until he reached the kitchen and picked his hat from the rack.

Nuala was washing the dishes. "Going out?"

"Yah."

"Back to work?"

"Up the street. Above in Flood's."

Glancing up into the window, which at night became a mirror, she took him in. "One of these nights you should get some rest. And tomorrow a haircut. You're looking a bit tatty."

FLOOD'S WAS PACKED MAINLY WITH THE immigrants who were now as local to the neighborhood as McGarr himself had been for nearly thirty years—people of all shades and hues speaking languages from Asia, Africa, and Eastern Europe, not a word of which McGarr understood.

Most were young, their conversations loud and animated, their smiles bright. Smoke—from a turf fire and cigarettes—was everywhere, and the din was deafening.

Without having to ask, he was slid a drink, which he carried into the lounge, if only to escape the noise. There he found a low stool, the last by the hearth that was glowing with the cracked red eye of a mound of real peat.

Although the burning of anything but EU-approved solid fuel was now illegal in the city, the turf fire was a nice touch, McGarr decided—a bit of old Ireland amid what had become very much a motley international country peopled by a motley international crew.

Tugging on his drink, McGarr turned away from the fire to find somebody standing before him. Pleated black slacks, black stockings, black pumps.

He looked up. It was Kara Kennedy, the keeper of old manuscripts at Trinity.

"Twice in one day. Could it be coincidence?"

McGarr only cocked his head and regarded her—the chestnut hair, the jade-colored eyes.

"D'you live around here?" She had a glass of wine in one hand, her purse in the other.

"For ages. And you?"

"Not far. I just couldn't stick to my flat tonight—all the bother on television and my still feeling so much . . . really, so much the failure." The hand with the purse came out. "Despite what you said about my not being responsible and all. I appreciated your concern, I really did. But I'm afraid when it comes to guilt, I'm quite a mess." She looked around, as for a stool.

McGarr stood. "Sit here."

"No, really—where will you sit?"

"I'll stand until another frees up. In fact—" He caught the eye of a barman and pointed to a stool.

The barman nodded. Producing one from the storeroom in back of the bar, he passed it across to McGarr.

"You have clout here, I see."

"And elsewhere, as it turned out today."

"So I've been watching."

He regarded her—the protrusive upper lip, the umber eyebrows that nearly met, with the arch repeated in a deep widow's peak. Long neck, fair skin, square shoulders.

She had changed since he'd last seen her into something like a black tank top covered by a cashmere cardigan just the color of her eyes.

"I don't know why this has affected me so completely." As though embarrassed by what she was saying, she was looking down into her wineglass. Two bright patches had appeared in her cheeks. "But earlier tonight, back at my flat, I felt . . . well, nearly suicidal. It's such"—she shook her head, then brushed her longish brown hair off her shoulder; it was slightly tinged with gray—"such a huge loss, such a crime, such an enormity. And, of course, there's Raymond's death."

When she turned to McGarr, her eyes were brimming with tears.

She had said all that earlier in the day, McGarr thought, but suicidal was different.

Also, beyond her good looks, there was something he found attractive about the woman, perhaps how vulnerable she seemed. Or how much she had taken on responsibility for the event.

Noreen had been like that—always thinking there was something she could have done or said that would have prevented or ameliorated some unpleasantness.

"It should have occurred to me that the security structure was not what it should be."

"Who set it up?"

She raised her head, her nostrils flared, and she looked away, as though suddenly having realized something. "Dr. Pape. Actually, it's rather new. Under a year."

"Were you at all consulted?"

Pursing her lips, she shook her head. "Well, I should have thought about it a bit, I suppose—if it was truly secure, what was the potential for theft." Attempting to smile, she again glanced over at him, the glowing fire dancing in her eyes. "Something, anything. I feel so . . . foolish."

"What might happen to the books now? Apart from a ransom demand? Is there some other way they might be disposed of for a pile of money?"

She sipped from the glass of wine. "Well, I suppose, some rich eccentric bibliophile, who wished only to possess and admire the books, might pay some portion of their worth. You know, to turn a page a day, as we do . . . did in the library, and admire the intricate weave of iconography and design, which rather mirrors the plot and other complexities of the gospels and of life.

"At least that's why I would want to own it. But connecting with such a person would be difficult. Unless, of course, whoever did this was commissioned by somebody like that." Her smile was now more complete. "As you can tell, I've been thinking about this.

"Otherwise"—she drew in a deep breath—"there's simply no market for art objects of such notoriety and uniqueness. Unless they were stolen by cultural terrorists interested only in their destruction."

They both looked off, thinking of past events in the North and other parts of the world.

McGarr took another sip and glanced into the fire.

"Do you know that the Book of Kells has been stolen before?" Kara asked. "Back in the Middle Ages, when it was called the Great Gospel of Columcille. Thieves stole it from the sanctuary of the church in Kells where even then it had been kept for centuries."

"*The Annals of Ulster*?" responded McGarr.

Kara nodded; it was one of the only early histories of Ireland.

"Describing the book as 'the most precious object in the Western world,' it said that for 'two months and twenty days' the four Gospels went missing until found in Donegal, 'covered by a sod.' "

"Was it damaged?"

"That's not known. But over the years it's suffered some damage. Yet for all its antiquity, the manuscript is in rather splendid shape." Her brow glowered. "Or at least *was*."

She raised her glass and drank.

If only to keep her talking, McGarr asked, "I thought the Book of Kells was a Bible with gospels and the like."

"It is, surely. But the Latin text, as copied from St. Jerome's Vulgate translation, is rife with errors—misspellings, missing words, solecisms—as though the words are inessential.

"But not the illustrations, on which great care and artistic attention was lavished. That's because it was not meant to be read. Rather, it served an evangelical purpose."

McGarr took note of the way she gestured with her left hand, as though chopping off little wedges of information while speaking.

"Many of the early evangelists carried with them beautiful, supposedly holy objects to wow the pagans. Bede reports in the *Historia ecclesiastica* that when Augustine arrived in England to preach the gospel in 597, he came bearing 'a silver cross and an image of our Lord and Savior painted on a panel.' He raised it on high for King Aethelberht to see.

"Later, Pope Gregory advised the clergy that images were aids to understanding the sacred text, saying that pictorial representations provided a living reading of the Lord's story for those who cannot read."

Again catching the barman's eye, McGarr pointed to their glasses, requesting another round.

"And the more richly embellished with gold and other colorful and precious materials the better. Books like Kells were meant to impress and be viewed and admired by communicants in processions during holy days and as part of the Mass. You know, almost like another form of altar furniture."

"But what about the—is it?—iconography of the thing?" Mc-Garr asked. "The Christian images are plainly there, but many others look like particularly Irish designs. And the intricacy, the interweaving, the whole image-within-an-image-within-an-image bit is definitely Irish. That's there as well."

"Oh, definitely. The free association of ideas seems to have been not only acceptable among the monks who produced Kells but rather encouraged. Which resulted in the sheer sumptuousness of its multilayered images that were in play among other artists of the time, as seen in the stone and metalworking designs that have survived."

"What about the animal shapes—lions, sheep, snakes, and so forth?"

She took another touch of wine and set the glass down. "Most refer to Christ, even the snake, which is an image of renewal. You know, the circularity of the snake swallowing its own tail?"

McGarr suspected he had heard something like that from Noreen.

"Zoomorphic forms also harken back to antiquity and Celtic and Pictish carvings. But what makes Kells special and more than simply another, albeit outstanding, illustrated manuscript is the tension that obtains between the Christian purpose of the book and the underlying motifs drawn from so many other non-Christian sources.

"It's a curious mix, but one that was carried off with consummate panache. In spite of the eclecticism, there is not a moment of doubt or confusion. The entire work communicates surety and the power of belief. As Giraldus Cambrensis, the thirteenth-century chronicler, put it, 'the work, not of men, but of angels.' "

A cigarette, McGarr thought. What he needed most now was a cigarette. But he didn't know if she smoked, and he didn't want to ask if he could, although plenty of others around them were smoking. "Any idea of its value?"

"As I mentioned this morning, inestimable."

"But a money amount. I'm trying to get a handle on the size of the demand. What the thieves might possibly ask, when they do."

She took another sip and turned to him, her jade eyes now a bit glassy. "It could be any figure and every figure. Millions, surely."

"Ten, twenty?"

"Or more. It depends on what you're willing to spend."

Which was the question: Who would be willing to pay for the return of the books? The government, in the guise of Taoiseach Kehoe, could not be seen as selling out to thieves and murderers using public money of great magnitude without, of course, recovering the funds and catching them with the books intact.

Also, the government did not own the manuscripts. Trinity College did. And in spite of much governmental aid, the college was officially a private entity which certainly could not afford a ransom in the amount that McGarr feared would be asked.

At the same time, allowing the books to be lost would be tantamount to political suicide for Kehoe. He would be known forever as the taoiseach who botched the Book of Kells Affair.

The only possible outcome that would keep Kehoe out of political trouble in office would be the safe return of the books and the capture of the thieves along with the ransom.

Glancing up at the television screen at the end of the bar, where Jack Sheard was again pictured fielding questions during an earlier press conference, McGarr realized that in at least one way he'd been freed by not having been placed in charge of the investigation—he would not have to make himself available to the press. And he would not be held directly responsible if in some major way the investigation/recovery failed.

But it still galled that Sheard had been granted the preferment. Also, Sheard, being ambitious, would sequester for his own use entirely whatever unsolicited information came in, yet he would expect McGarr to funnel any and all information to him without foot-dragging, McGarr suspected.

"Does that bother you?" Kara Kennedy asked. "That he's been named lead investigator?"

McGarr drew in a breath and nodded slightly. "To be honest, it does. But obviously this theft takes precedence over the murder. And his brief is theft."

"But don't you outrank him?"

"No. But I am more senior."

"Could that be why you're out here tonight?"

Hunched over with his elbows on his knees, McGarr was still staring at the screen. Somehow, the whiskey he'd drunk had not done the trick, and he felt a bit bleak without knowing why. "Perhaps. But you could make a case for my being here most nights."

"Since when? Since your wife died?"

Slowly, McGarr swung his eyes to her.

"I don't mean to be cruel, but you're at least as well known as he." She pointed to the screen. "And it was in all the papers. I'm sorry. It only just occurred to me." Her hand came out and touched the back of his.

The new drinks were ready, and McGarr rose to retrieve them. Now he himself was on the television, booting—literally—the final cameraman out into the street.

"Gooo-ooooooh-aaaaaal!" crowed one of the barmen, like Andres Cantor, the Argentinean football announcer, and the men at the bar—many of whom knew McGarr personally—roared their approval.

"To put it in Latin, *Ars ejectica*," said one.

"*C'est bootiful*," said another.

"Forget that—it's a documented case of police bootality," put in a third before singing the Sinatra lyric "All the way—all the way!"

"The natives are restless," said McGarr, picking up his change.

"You have only yourself to blame. They need no encouragement."

Carrying the drinks back to the hearth with its fire, McGarr noted that voices hushed as he passed other tables.

From deeper within the room he heard, "Book of Kells . . . murdered a security guard . . . browned off entirely, did you see his eyes? . . . millions and millions . . . spineless government fooks . . . they'll feckin' get away with it, you'll see."

Handing Kara Kennedy the fresh glass of wine, McGarr attempted a smile.

"You're a celebrity."

"And doubtless the subject of a future lawsuit."

"What would happen in that case? Would you have to provide your own defense, or would you be covered?"

McGarr nodded. "In the line of duty." He had been sued more than a few times on frivolous grounds, only to see large sums awarded by a legal system that was notoriously arbitrary. "But enough about me. What about you? Are you married?"

Her eyes dropped to her glass. "Yes. I think I am. Or, at least, I was." She then explained in halting tones that she had been married four years earlier to an oil broker who, fifteen months ago, was sent to Yemen by his firm.

"Either he walked away from me, all his responsibilities, and his life, or something catastrophic happened to him over there. Nobody's heard from him—not his firm, his parents, nor I."

When she raised her eyes, they were again brimming with tears. "Sorry, I'm just not in good form tonight. Not good company."

"Nor am I, I'm afraid."

"Ah, that's nonsense. Haven't you been good company tonight? Haven't you cheered me up?" She clinked her glass against his. "It's the way to get out of a depression, I'm told—putting your own troubles aside and helping others."

"My thoughts exactly," said a deep male voice. "It's why I've come."

McGarr looked up. It was Chazz Sweeney himself—immense and in a powerful way formless—his nose beaked, his fleshy face pocked from some childhood malaise. He smiled slightly, and his bloodshot eyes surveyed them, looking sly and not a little bit predatory.

Charles Stewart Parnell Sweeney—his complete and sardonically apt name—was a man whom McGarr thought of as more dangerous than any violent criminal in the street.

Although only ever a Dail backbencher—and that time out of mind—Sweeney had once been said to virtually control the country through his contacts with the movers and shakers in commerce and industry.

Nominally the director of a private merchant bank, Sweeney had a small, drab office on the Dublin quays. But he was said to have been the bagman for an older group of politicians who had been exposed, publicly shamed, stripped of much of their known wealth, and even—a few of them—placed in jail several years earlier. But not Sweeney.

Not even when—two years ago, following the deaths of Noreen and Fitz—Sweeney was arraigned and tried on a variety of charges including the murder of Enda Flatly, a Drug Squad detective.

A brace of the country's best barristers, however, convinced a jury that McGarr and Ward were "contaminated with hatred for him [Sweeney] because of his stalwart religious beliefs." Sweeney was an adherent of Opus Dei, the ultraconservative Catholic religious sect.

McGarr himself had little history of church attendance, and Ward was shown to be "living in sin under one roof with not one but two common-law wives and children by both of those women."

Sweeney's weekly newspaper, *Ath Cliath*, became a daily during the three and a half weeks of the trial, with coverage of both the trial and continual exposés of Ward, Bresnahan, and Ward's other "common-in-law wife," Leah Sigal, whose Jewish background was referred to often.

During what came to be known as the Barbastro Affair, Sweeney was convicted only of possessing an illegal handgun. Sentenced to six months in prison commuted because of time served, he walked out of court the day of the decision.

The following Monday he sued the government for "a consistent pattern of police harassment" and was awarded 2.7 million pounds.

Yet for all his millions, Sweeney was wearing his signature wrinkled and soiled, if expensive, mac, a rumpled shirt, and a patterned red tie. His cordovan bluchers were in need of polish. There would be a navy blazer the size of a small sail beneath the mac.

"Yes?" McGarr asked.

"I've come for a wee chat. About the book." He was sweating, in need of a shave, and his skin as always looked sickly and gray.

Turning to the bar, Sweeney raised a finger and swirled it. There was a drink in his other hand.

"Which book?"

"Sure—is there any other at the moment?"

"How did you know I'd be here?" Certainly Nuala, who loathed the man, would not have told him.

"How did I not? What's the phrase—to be predictable is to be controllable. But you can risk that, not being controllable in any way that's been determined thus far. Which is your great strength, McGarr. And don't let anybody ever tell you otherwise."

A barman, whom Sweeney had obviously tipped handily, now appeared with a tray of drinks.

"Not to worry—I won't interrupt your cozy fireside chat for long. Fancy how convenient it is, given what went on last night—

yous two living so nearby. Curious how life throws people together, is it not?"

Sweeney raised the drink in the maw of his left hand, drank it off, and set down the empty glass. From under his mac he then brought out what looked like a videotape in a clear plastic sleeve. "My purpose in coming—to give you this." He held it out to McGarr, who only regarded the object.

"Right enough." Sweeney set the box on the table and picked up a full glass. "I'm no part of this. I don't know why they chose me to be the messenger. Did I look at it? Of course I did, curiosity as always getting the better of me. And then, amn't I a publisher these days?" His slight smile was rueful and exposed a clutch of yellowing teeth.

"But I'm passing it on to you and not that gobshite Sheard out of concern for the cultural heritage of the country. He's no real cop and will just make a balls of the situation.

"Look, McGarr." Because of his height, which had to be all of six-five, he had to bend to pick up the fresh drink. "To put it mildly, we've had our differences over the years, and I know you think I'm in some way responsible for your wife and Fitz, which I'm not."

Tilting back his head, he opened his mouth and tossed off the second drink in one swallow. As Sweeney set the glass back down, McGarr noticed that the rough contours of his face were now running with sweat.

"But after you watch what's in here, you'll see that these motherless pricks aren't bluffing. Sure, the urge is to bring all the force possible down on them, which will not change one thing—they've got the bloody books, and we don't."

"It's a ransom demand?" asked McGarr.

Sweeney nodded.

"How did it come to you?"

"Motorcycle messenger—dropped it on the desk in the news-room and said it should be brought to me immediately."

"Messenger?"

"Standard-issue leathers, boots, helmet, and goggles—I checked. No different from any other."

"When?"

"Maybe two hours ago. I gave it a gander and thought it should be passed along to you pronto."

"How did you view it?"

Sweeney's massive head moved to Kara and back to McGarr. "How else? In a feckin' videotape player." There was a pause, and then, "Ooops—fingerprints. I never thought of that. Did I chuck a spanner in the works?"

Sweeney touched his index finger to his lips, as though cogitating. Then, "No, not likely. You'll see—they're professionals. The entire shenanigan has been thought out to a sweet good-bye. I'm sure they considered everything. Why, even in the burn sequence, the bastards are wearing black gloves."

He pulled back a cuff to check a large gold watch nestled in the bramble of hair on his wrist. "Shite and double shite. I've got to run. If you need anything, don't hesitate to give me a shout. I'm still at the old stand, when not at the paper. You know where it is.

"Ms. Kennedy." Sweeney touched a hand to his brow.

Pivoting, as though to leave, he then careened back. "By the by, how be young Ward and his mot, Rut'ie? Thriving, I'm told. Don't tell them but I myself—Chazz, the Terrible—contracts with them through a brace of dummy corporations, of course. I only ever hire the best, and don't I know their quality firsthand. Ouch.

"Give them my regards on their next stop by your shop, the whole magilla between yiz all and me being just part of life. And profitable. But I'm happy for them they landed on their feet.

"Remember, I'm only the messenger. Just the messenger."

In arresting Sweeney two-plus years past, Ward—a former All-Ireland and European boxing champ—had give Sweeney a thorough beating, which had cost the country an additional 500,000 quid. And, in part, had cost Ward his job.

"Somehow, he seems larger and more ominous in person," Kara observed.

Watching as Sweeney stopped at the bar for another quick drink and to pay his tab—his broad but shapeless back and bent head looming like a kind of carrion bird—McGarr remembered that Flood, the publican, had an office in the cellar with a television and video player for taping World Cup matches.

He turned to Kara Kennedy. "Would you mind if I took a look at this?"

"How would you do that?"

"In the pub office. I'm sure it won't take long."

"You mean, you're not inviting me?"

"Think of this as my work. I'll be back shortly." Ransom demands almost always being brief. "If you have to leave, I understand. Perhaps we might do this again. Or dinner."

"I understand as well. You don't trust me. I'm just another suspect. And you couldn't have it said you allowed a suspect to view evidence."

Turning her head, she raised her glass. In profile, he decided, she was truly beautiful, given her long, slightly aquiline nose, the rake of her forehead, thick darkish eyebrows, and a definite widow's peak.

Moving down the stairs into the cellar of the pub, McGarr remembered how miraculously Sweeney had appeared at McGarr's father-in-law's door in Kildare two years earlier, just as McGarr was beginning his investigation into the murder of Mary-Jo Stanton.

At the time, she was perhaps the wealthiest woman in the country and, like Sweeney, an adherent of the secretive and reactionary Catholic sect Opus Dei.

Having enjoyed McGarr's parents-in-law's vaunted hospitality and knowing the doors were never locked, Sweeney had entered the house whole hours—it was later determined—before any of the family had returned and was found sitting in the very room where Fitz's and Noreen's guns were kept unlocked.

Others, including Delia Manahan, the woman who actually murdered Mary-Jo Stanton and her gardener, had also spent time in the house alone. But whoever had spiked Noreen's favorite shotgun—inserting a 21-gauge shell into the 12-gauge chamber so that it would block the barrel and explode when the larger shell was fired—knew guns.

And Sweeney did much more than Manahan, whose death—McGarr suspected—Sweeney later arranged.

In the darkness of the stairwell, McGarr stopped. He could not go on. His eyes had yet to accustom themselves to the dim light, and behind his eyelids the death scene was unfolding again.

McGarr had not been far away—down in the sleepy Kildare village near Fitz's estate—when Noreen rang up his cell phone, asking him to come home. The gun had exploded, Fitz was down, and it was an emergency.

Commandeering a car, McGarr caught sight of them in the distance by the shooting blinds: Noreen down on her knees with her father's head—looking like a bright red berry—in her lap. His arms were stretched out, his legs splayed.

She did not rise to meet him, and once out of the car, he could see it was serious. It seemed as though the older man no longer had half of his face. One eye was untouched. It was open and staring up at her. But his brow, his other eye, his cheek, and even most of his left ear looked like it had been wiped away with one pass of something sharp.

There was blood everywhere—on Fitz, on Noreen, in a puddle on the ground around her knees. She looked up at McGarr, her green eyes glassy. "Is he gone?" she asked in a strange, disembodied voice.

McGarr then noticed a black and cratered spot the size of a 10P coin just behind her right ear. It looked like a splotch of dried blood, although he knew it couldn't be.

He was hearing the steady, distant thump of rotors from the emergency helicopter that he'd called in while driving there. He rose to direct it in.

"Oh—where are you going, Peter? I'm not sure I can support his head much longer."

When McGarr glanced back at Noreen, he saw she was not speaking toward him, as though she could neither turn her head nor follow him with her eyes.

Fitz died first, Noreen several days later.

In a coma.

6

McGarr found Niall Flood in the pub office, going through a stack of delivery invoices.

"I'm glad you're here, Peter. The police is just what I need. Fookin' help'll steal you blind, if you let them. Look at this—charged for two dozen cases of Saxenbrau, twenty came over the threshold. Here, a dozen bottles of Black Bush with a bottle missing.

"But it's nothing compared with the two chancers I had in here Monday week." A tall, thin man with silver hair, a bright red bow tie, and blue straps over a white shirt, Flood had taken over from his father, who had taken over from his father, and so forth. "Since before the flood," the chuckle went.

"One says to me, says he, 'None of the theft, nor the rash of broken windows, nor the trashing of the jakes will continue,' if I 'bring them on board,' says he.

" 'In what capacity,' says I.

" 'Protectors,' says he. 'People do stuff, you tell us, we fix 'em.'

"Says I, 'More easily said than done.' No geniuses, they were at a loss. 'For you to fix yourselves.' I threw them out and rang up your cohorts over at the substation."

"Immigrants?"

"Nothing of the kind. Irish as you and me, apart from the bangles and rings in their ears and noses. The one had a bloody big stud—like a tie tack—through his tongue. Made him lisp."

"Tall fella? Blond with broad shoulders?"

"Nah. More like a midget, he was. Dark. The one with him was blond with broad shoulders, though he didn't open his mouth."

"Anything in his nose?"

"Snot, I should imagine. But I didn't check."

McGarr explained what he wanted, and that it was official. "Won't take but a sec."

"I'll go up, then, and see who's stealing from me aboveground."

McGarr thumbed on the machine and took Flood's chair, wishing he'd thought to carry a drink down with him.

The video began with a blank screen and pipe-and-fiddle music, some traditional tune McGarr had heard before but couldn't name.

As the screen brightened, Newgrange—the ancient passage grave on the banks of the Boyne near Slane—appeared, and the voice-over declared:

"This is what the Irish were capable of building without metal tools or the wheel five hundred years before the oldest pyramids were constructed in Egypt. The structure is so perfectly aligned with the sun that only on one day per year does sunlight strike the central altar—on winter solstice, the shortest day of the year. In more than fifty-three hundred years, never has the massive corbeled stone roof allowed a drop of water to penetrate the sanctum."

In travelogue fashion, the video went on to describe the high points of Celtic civilization: brehon law, Beaker people pottery, La Tène design, the "proto-Arthurian values of chivalry and gentilesse, as developed within the Fianna, which was the group of legendary heroes who were said to have ruled the Ireland of Celtic myth.

"Also democracy—rule by the consensus of the clan. The Celts had a way of dealing with each other on a daily basis that was based on warmth, clan solidarity, and trust. The most extreme punishment that could be meted out to an offender was not death. It was expulsion from the community—to be declared pariah."

The voice was what McGarr thought of as "mid-Atlantic," one that could not be identified as demonstrably Irish, British, or North American. It was, however, surely urbane, and McGarr wondered if the entire piece had been lifted from some television show run on the BBC.

"But Christianity, which arrived in the latter part of the fifth century, proved disastrous to Ireland," the voice continued, noting that early Christian converts were encouraged to renounce the world and retreat to abbeys, monasteries, and other sanctuaries. "This alien movement not only usurped and supplanted the ancient religion of Ireland's native Celts, it also led to the central religious division of the country that obtains to this day.

"The most immediate deleterious effect was the escapist teachings of early missionaries, their advocacy of converts becoming 'exiles for Christ.' "

Family, clan, and nonreligious community ties suffered—the video continued—such that 350 years later, when Vikings began raiding the Irish coast, there was no effective militia in place to defend the country.

"Abbeys, monasteries, and churches had waxed fat, amassing great wealth, while secular institutions, which might have countered the Viking threat, were all but absent.

"Even after seventy years of sustained Viking pillaging, Christianity with its otherworldly ethos could not bring forth a common defense. In A.D. 863, Christian Ireland allowed a Viking force to sack Newgrange and other nearby megalithic tombs in the Boyne Valley.

"For over thirty-five hundred years, those tombs and religious relics of former greatness—the very gateways to the Celtic Otherworld—had been revered by the Irish people and kept sacrosanct. Having withdrawn to its many stone keeps with its own booty, Christianity simply allowed those treasures of Ireland's ancient past to be plundered.

"The remains and artifacts interred there were not relics of the Christian past—the past of their prophet from the deserts of the Middle East. No. Oenghus, to whom the site was sacred, was an indigenous god of the older religion. Therefore, Newgrange was deemed expendable and valueless."

After showing photos of Newgrange before its restoration in the 1990s—when it was a near ruin in a wet pasture with boulders strewn about—the screen presented a collage of the tall medieval keeps that monastic communities had built as sanctuaries. During Viking raids, the monks had retreated there with whatever precious objects they could carry or had stored there, drawing up the ladder after them.

"Even more than four hundred years after the initial Viking attacks, Christian Ireland remained so weak that the country was easily overrun by their coreligionists, the Normans, beginning in A.D. 1169. It ushered over in eight hundred years of foreign domination that has not ceased to this day.

"Question—what is the most divisive and destructive issue in this country today?"

A pastiche of rioting crowds, bomb-related destruction, and corpses appeared, along with clips of grieving families at funeral processions and gravesides.

"What might Ireland have become, had she cleaved to her culture? Had Christianity not displaced the older Celtic verities of life and Druidism?"

Suddenly, the picture on the screen began rotating and diminishing in a spin-fade, as though being drawn down a drain.

The drain—replete with circular drain holes—reappeared, glowing and reddish as though made from some fiery chrome. "Which makes this book what?" a deep, gravelly, and disembodied voice asked.

As the camera panned back, it revealed that the drainlike covering was obscuring the mouth of a person dressed in black with a black balaclava over a hooded face and what looked like blue-tinted welder's goggles wrapped around his eyes. Strapped to his forehead was a bright red light that cast a film of red glare over the lens of the camera, further obscuring the image of the figure and book.

"A Judas book." The figure was holding up a book with the pages turned to the camera. The voice was one of the voices from the Trinity security tape, one of Raymond Sloane's killers. "And expendable."

The picture on the screen then broke to a shot of the same black-gloved hands in some other setting, holding the blue flame of a gas torch to what appeared to be a page of the Kells book. After only a few seconds of smoldering, it burst into flame, curling up into a roll as it was consumed.

"Like your fookin' Christ, you have three days to come up with fifty million Euros. On the fourth, we'll contact you with the drop. If you balk, on the fifth we burn a page and another every day until you do. Publicly." The screen went black.

McGarr's first thought: Was it genuine? Or a ruse by Sweeney to . . . what? To enrich himself by 50 million. Why had the thieves chosen to go through him? Because they knew Sweeney was certain to copy it and make the entire matter public if the government were to balk?

And how could its authenticity be established? McGarr thought of Kara Kennedy upstairs in the lounge—perhaps she could tell from the look of it on the screen. Or the way it burned. While the tape was rewinding, he climbed the stairs two at a time, but she seemed to be gone. "She still here?" he asked the barman who had served him. "The woman I was with." He pointed toward the hearth.

"Told me to tell you she was tired of waiting. And just tired. She gave me this to give you."

On the back of her card was written, "Knackered. Going home. Thanks for the drinks. If you need me, please call." She had included a second phone number.

Back down in Flood's office, McGarr rang up McKeon, Swords, and Ward and Bresnahan, asking them to assemble at his house.

Out on the street, he met Orla Bannon, the *Ath Cliath* reporter, who was sitting on the bonnet of a car with her legs folded under her.

"Ran out on you, did she? Never trusted academics much meself. It's the whole tenure thing. What the fook is tenure but a way of saying you can breeze through the rest of your life and still be in the chips? With all the time in the world.

"Drink?" From under a brightly colored cape that looked like a serape, she pulled a pint bottle and held it out. "It's me pukka pose. Like it?

"What did Sweeney hand you? Looked like a video. Buds now, are you? Into swapping naughty films?" She tsked. "Men are so inscrutable. How quickly things change for you. Or is there something I should know?"

McGarr had stopped in front of her, again wondering at her appearance there just as Sweeney was handing him the tape? Could it have been felicitous, merely her having tailed either Sweeney or McGarr himself there to witness the exchange? Or did Sweeney and she have some other purpose that was, at least for the moment, inscrutable? And finally, what was her work arrangement at *Ath Cliath* if, as Bresnahan had said, she and Sweeney were at odds? "Chazz didn't tell you? You, his diva. His ace reporter."

Becoming more complete, her smile crinkled the corners of her eyes, making her seem rather feline, given her pose. "Done some legwork, I see. Which is good. But not complete enough by half, I'd hazard. Your man Sweeney? He'd sooner give me the sack than the time of day. What's in the video?"

"Why do you work for him?"

"Beyond money? Space. Where else could I get pages and pages and no—I repeat, no—editorial interference. He touches me copy, I'm gone."

"Gone with what?"

She only smiled and raised the bottle.

"What about Opus Dei? Ever write about them?"

She nodded. "But I wasn't working for him then, and we all have our sacred cows. Could it be, McGarr—you and Sweeney share that particular bovine but from different ends?"

Fair play, thought McGarr, all three of the potential murderers of Noreen and Fitz having been associated with the reactionary Catholic sect.

"What about the New Druids? Ever write about them?"

"There's little I haven't. They send you that via Sweeney?" She waved the bottle at the video that McGarr now slipped inside his jacket.

"A ransom demand on tape? It's a nice touch. Eliminates the whole handwriting analysis thing." The legs came out from under her, and she swung them off the fender. They were shapely legs encased in black stockings.

As though pondering, she raised them and stared at her shoes, which were suede with heels that gave her some height. "But why Sweeney of all people, considering who they are—anti-Christian and all their other rot."

When she glanced back up at McGarr, her eyes narrowed.

"Officially—as written on the papers they had to file when register-ing as a political party—Celtic United is unattached to any other organization and is run by a woman who calls herself Morrigan." She pronounced the name "Mor-ee-GAN." She cocked her head slightly.

McGarr nodded, the name being known to every schoolchild. Morrigan was the unconquerable goddess of war who battled Cuchulainn in the Celtic legends that made up the books of the Ul-ster Cycle.

"But, really, she's just another big, blowsy, middle-aged woman full of herself along with mounds of shite and drivel that she un-loads at the slightest provocation. But who controls things is a man who calls himself Mide." Again she gave McGarr a look.

It was another name from old legend, but beyond that . . . He shook his head.

Orla Bannon raised her head to pipe a short laugh at the dark sky. "Wouldn't you know it—us from the North always being more up on things Irish than you who've secured your own country in part because of those myths."

"Mide," he prompted, now remembering. "The chief Druid of the Nemedians." Only a few years ago he wouldn't have had to reflect.

"Yes, and—"

"And what?"

"Go on. About Mide."

"Well, none of this is fair. Obviously you've researched this recently—for one of your articles."

"Not so recently."

"And me—I've not been to school recently." McGarr glanced at his watch.

"And not too attentively when you did, I'm thinking."

She paused for his reaction, and he wondered if—beyond her obvious attempt to pump him for information—she was actually trying to flirt with him. Or was it just the drink?

Her smile was full; she was enjoying herself. "Thought as much. After the Nemedians conquered Ireland, your man Mide came up with this scheme. To demonstrate his power, he built a big ritual fire that he kept burning for seven years, some say, without adding fuel. As a prize or reward, he was allowed to exact a tribute of one pig and a sack of grain from every Irish household.

"Two questions: In what way can the dealing in OxyContin, heroin, speed, and the two cocaines be considered the building of a fire, consubstantial or otherwise? And could seven years possibly have elapsed before Mide and his gang began their protection schemes?"

McGarr smiled; it was the "back story" humor that cops and journalists shared, if only to keep sane.

"Morrigan's real name is Sheila Law. Don't know much about her apart from gossip saying she's into young men in numbers, which she has, of course—the recruits, addicted, down-and-out whom they take in. It's the other side that's not reported much—the hostels, soup kitchens, methadone clinics they've set up. Day to day, they're run on the up-and-up but are really recruitment centers for culling prospects. The ones who'll do their bidding competently with few fuckups."

"What about him? Mide."

"Fergus Mann. 'The Fergie Man,' he's called. A codger now, but still a nasty piece of work. Former IRA stalwart in the old never-grass-on-nobody-no-matter-the-pain mold. Convicted for two murders, he did the Maze thing with Bobby Sands and the other hunger strikers, then nearly two dozen other years until he became by his own say-so a visionary."

"And his vision?"

"Thick, it is. The whole anti-Christian, IRA thing wrapped in different language—that Ireland was better off with the bunch of bloodthirsty bastards who were our ancestors, the Celts. It appeals to anybody who's ever had their ears boxed by a priest or a nun, which is everybody. But poor kids from worse backgrounds are targeted. He's a fookin' viper, and the New Druids with its CU facade a viper's nest. Literally." With her thumb and her first two fingers, she imitated the action of pushing a hypodermic needle into her other arm.

"You've written that."

"I have. You'll have to start reading me. How much ransom do they want?"

"Where does 'The Fergie Man' hang his hat when he's at home?"

She hunched her shoulders. "Elusive, he is. As you would suspect, given his present involvements and the years he spent in the drum. It's said he tells people he's 'allergic' to prison, but I bet he keeps in touch with Morrigan at all times. Being a power monger and control freak."

McGarr turned and began heading off.

"Ah, just when I thought were getting to know each other. Ten million? Twenty? If you tell me, I'll tell you something I'm only after learning, something you can't possibly know."

Stopping, he turned his head and shoulders to her. So far she'd been forthcoming, and without question she had good sources. Maybe she had more for him.

"Thirty?"

He shook his head.

"Forty?"

Again.

"Jaysus, Mary, and Joseph—fifty fookin' million, which is, mind you, a nice round figure. But Kehoe will never pay it. He can't."

Pushing down with her hands, she virtually hopped off the bonnet of the car. "McGarr—you're a gas. Haven't we got a wee neat story brewing here?" She hugged her elbows and spun a circle, her long dark braid whipping behind her.

"Well?"

"The something you can't possibly know?"

He swirled a hand. "Think of it as a lane in the two-way street you mentioned when we first spoke."

"Okay. Remember, you asked for it." On heel, then toe, she sauntered up to him, as though to whisper in his ear. She slipped her hand in his jacket pocket and pulled him closer. "Derek Greene?"

McGarr nodded. It was the name of the Trinity security guard who was knocked down and killed two weeks earlier.

"A witness told me the killing car was a BMW." Their bodies were touching, and her breath was hot in his ear. "The big one."

"Midnight blue. Gold wheel covers," McGarr guessed. "Now, for something I don't know." The point being to pump her as hard as she was pumping him.

"Two things, darlin' man—the car, or a car like it, is often parked round back of CU party headquarters."

"And where would that be?"

"Off the Glasnevin Road near Ballymun. Big place, can't miss it. Office is open twenty-four hours a day, methadone center upstairs, a 'dormitory/hostel' out back down a laneway for in-patient rehab, the brochure says. Most are New Druid recruits or CU operatives, with the whole health-care operation financed by the government. Mide, 'The Fergie Man,' being quick on his feet.

"Need more?" she again breathed into his ear. "Your man, Derek Greene? He was interred in the Fairview Cemetery six days ago. But the family phoned me this after'. They've been told the grave has been disturbed."

"Disturbed how?"

"Somebody took off his bloody head."

McGarr waited.

"Grisly, no? Dug up the casket and chopped his block right off the body. And very much the New Druid thing. Rumor has it, they do it to rival gangs, other thugs horning in on their territory. Sends a message, one told me. Fook with the New Druids, you end up not only dead but headless. Your mammy pines."

Sending a message—it was the purpose of Raymond Sloane's murder, according to the voices on the security tape.

McGarr turned his shoulder to move away from her, but she pulled him back. "What are you doing later?"

McGarr suspected there would be no later for him, only morning. "I imagine I'll be busy."

Kissing his ear in a way that made him flinch and sent a shiver up his spine, she then shoved him away. "Imagine, then—it's all you'll get tonight. But remember—you have my card."

Walking quickly toward his house, McGarr couldn't help speculate on what any involvement with somebody so—what was it about Orla Bannon?—seemingly self-possessed, so sure of herself and her talents, might be like.

But then, of course, how to separate the Orla Bannon of the by-line from Orla Bannon herself, if there were in fact another person beyond the journalist.

And why, with commerce being brisk along their two-way street. Now, if only all of it proved genuine . . .

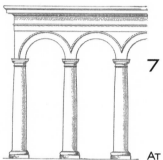

7

AT HOME McGARR WENT UP TO MADDIE'S room, where the light was still on. "How go the sums, Madz—done yet?"

"Nearly."

"Do something for me?"

Her tousled red head came up from the book. "What?" She was dressed in her pajamas, and the covers of her bed were pulled back.

"Copy this for me while I'm on the phone. Use the original for the first, then copy its copy on however many blank tapes that we have."

"Or tapes that I'll make blank."

"There you have it, if they're expendable. Five will do." He placed the videotape on the desk, then moved back toward the door and the phone in his study.

"Does it have to do with the Book of Kells?"

"It does, indeed. And after you're done, I'd like you to see a portion of it." So you understand what else I do apart from brutalizing the press, was his intention.

In his study, he called his office and asked for the exact address of Celtic United and if the whereabouts of one Fergus Mann, convicted felon, were known.

"The Fergie Man? Mide himself?" Swords asked. "Finding him won't be easy, Chief."

"Any way we can." Which meant touts, illegal searches, wiretaps. "Pull out all the stops."

"He behind the book theft and murder?"

"Possibility. I'll also need the accident and police reports on the hit-and-run killing of Derek Greene."

"They're sitting on your desk."

"Any witness statements?"

"Two, both describing the car as big, dark blue, with gold wheel covers. One said she thought it was a BMW."

McGarr hoped Orla Bannon's other tips were as accurate.

Next, he phoned McKeon and Bresnahan and Ward, asking them to meet him on the Glasnevin Road near Celtic United headquarters.

Downstairs in the den, where the television was located, Maddie was finishing up the final tape. "We only had two blank tapes and one more that was 'expendable.' "

"That's grand. Sit back there, now." He pointed at a chair. "And I'll give you some idea what we're up against. It's between you, me, and the lamppost, of course. No friends, nobody in school. But I don't have to remind you of that at this late date."

"No, Peter, you don't. I know what to say." Which was, "My father never mentions his work at home. Not a word."

In the past, the parents of Maddie's friends—to say nothing of the children themselves—had tried to extract any little bit of information they could about some ongoing investigation.

"I came by this only a little while ago. It could be the ransom demand, if the page is genuine. You'll see." McGarr slipped the tape in the VCR. Stepping back, he found Nuala standing in the doorway, her arms folded across her chest.

McGarr spooled through the first part of the video until the black, hooded figure came on with the demand per se. In silence, the three watched.

"Is it a real page from the Book of Kells he's burning?" Maddie asked.

"We don't know yet." McGarr switched off the tape and hit rewind.

"How can anybody, the government even, pay that much money? And how will it get paid? I mean, that much must be a heap of money."

"Maddie—you should be in bed," said Nuala. "I want you upstairs. Now." She stepped away from the door.

"But Peter let me . . ."

"No ifs, ands, or buts—you're past time as we speak."

"But Peter—"

"Now!"

Her eyes wide and filling with tears, Maddie glared at McGarr, as though to ask why he had not come to her defense. She rushed toward the door. "Granny, sometimes you're such a witch."

"And, Peter—I'd like a word with you before you leave."

Not happy with Nuala, he caught Maddie by the arm and swept her into his arms. "I'd carry you upstairs but you're getting too big. Night, now." He kissed and released her.

"Night, Daddy. Love you." And the "love you" chorus echoed in the hall until she reached her room at the top of the stairs.

Nuala was back in the doorway, as though blocking it. "Think you it wise to let your thirteen-year-old daughter see something like that?"

It was the first time in two years that she had ever questioned McGarr's raising of Maddie, and he had to check his first impulse, which was to push by her and attend to his pressing business.

"Kehoe will have that tape on every screen in the country by tea tomorrow, so he will."

Her old dark eyes, which had followed countless politicians over the years, widened, then blinked, as she realized the sense in that. The video of the thieves actually destroying the book would allow Kehoe to take extraordinary measures—deploying the army squads or actually paying the ransom as a last resort.

The public would have witnessed the demand and the destruction of the book. The press would play it up big, running daily features about the history and value of the relic from a time when Ireland enjoyed cultural preeminence in Europe.

In that way and handled with savvy, which was the man's hallmark, the theft and the drama of its salvation from the forces of evil—again, as witnessed in the hooded, masked figure on the tape—might initiate a revival of interest in Ireland's medieval Christian past that no 50 million Euros' worth of advertising could equal. Or at least spark a revival of interest in Kehoe's remaining taoiseach for another several years.

"I think you know what I mean. I'm not blaming you. You are what you are, and we knew that. But are you doing it for her? Or for yourself?"

"Why would I be doing it for myself?"

"I think you have to ask yourself that."

Now McGarr pushed by her and started down the stairs. "D'you think I haven't?"

"Not completely enough."

At the bottom, he turned and looked up at her. "But you have?"

She nodded. "To absolve yourself of the guilt you feel, when there should be no guilt to be felt. I've asked you before, and I'm asking you again—see somebody. Priest, counselor, anybody. But do it. For us."

"WHAT GALLS ME IS HOW DUPLICITOUS AND in-your-face it all is," McGarr could hear Bresnahan telling McKeon through the receiver/transmitter that was looped over his right ear. "Look at that building, bold as brass with a methadone center and even a rehab out back when bottom line is they're in the effin' trade. They have to be stopped."

The three private cars—Bresnahan's battered Opel surveillance sedan, Ward's new Audi, and McGarr's old Rover sedan—were parked at the curb on the busy Glasnevin Road several hundred yards from Celtic United headquarters.

It was an old brick commercial building of four floors with a brightly lit shop front over which hung a large green flag with CU in white Celtic script across its face. Interweaved through the letters were designs in bright orange that seemed to mimic the images and symbols seen in the Book of Kells, it occurred to McGarr. There was the tongue and tail of a snake, one paw and the head of a lion, and within one tangle appeared the eyes of a sheep, but deep and soulful, looking out.

Milling in front of the building was a clutch of mainly young men but a few women as well. Most of the men had long hair or beards, and in spite of the weather, which had turned chilly, many were wearing only half-vests that exposed swirls of tattoos and other body designs.

"And would you look at those effin' wankers—probably not a job among them in spite of their muscles, tattoos, and perms," said Bresnahan, the rose pin on the lapel of her jacket actually being a speaker connected to the other two cars via radio.

Although once radically chic herself, Bresnahan hailed from rural Kerry where conservative values, such as the work ethic, were revered.

But few in the throng could be blamed, McGarr imagined. Ireland's educational system was disparate, to say the least, and more than thirty years of police work had shown him that poor districts tended to have poor schools, poor community values, and much poverty of the spirit at home. And not all of Ireland's young had ridden the Celtic Tiger, as the recent economic boom had been called.

"The dole, the drug trade, and whatever they can nick from the public being their stock-in-trade."

"Ruthie, go ahead now," McGarr advised through his own headset, as he removed the Walther from under his belt and checked the clip. "And remember to leave the tape with her."

They watched as Bresnahan stepped out of the other car and waited for traffic to pass before crossing the street. Tall, angular, her red hair flowing behind her, she immediately attracted the attention of the young men in front of the CU building.

She was wearing a black leather jacket and short skirt that made the most of her shapely legs. When one of the men kept stepping in front of her, she said, "Ah, look—you've a bit of shit on your shirt."

When he looked down, she raised an elbow, shoved past him, and stepped into the open door of the shop. "My mistake, 'twas only you."

Patches of color had appeared in her cheeks, Bresnahan could see as she caught sight of her image in the glass of the open door. Why? Because she was in high dudgeon, she now realized.

Nothing browned her off more than hypocrisy of the sort that preyed upon people—the innocent, the trusting, or here, she suspected, the ignorant: young, poorly educated, inner-city kids with little hope of even duplicating the straitened lives of their parents. Somebody had to be to blame. Why not the church, Christianity, and by extension the society that had accepted and continued to endorse that religion.

She herself and Ward—her colleague, paramour, now business partner, and common-law husband—had run afoul of Christian strictures. But they had well understood the risks they'd been taking and the possible fallout.

Stepping up to a counter covered with stacks of brochures and flyers touting Celtic United, its aims and accomplishments, she palmed a bell several times, until a woman appeared in the door of what looked like an office. "Help you?"

"If you're Morrigan, I've got something for you to see." She held up a videotape.

"I hope it's licentious. Or at least naughty. I'll consider nothing less." A full-length, wheat-colored tunic made the woman look like a classical goddess out of Greek or Roman, not Celtic, myth.

There was even a garland of tiny flowers in her long and flowing gray hair. Unlike her body, which was formidable, her face was long, well structured, and thin in the way some middle-aged women lose rather than gain facial flesh as they grow older, Bresnahan noted. Late forties, early fifties.

"And to whom do I owe thanks for this present?"

"I'm Ruth Bresnahan."

"The detective?"

"Former detective."

"Ah, that's right—she who lives in harem sin, according to *Ath Cliath*. Albeit, a small harem and thoroughly liberating sin, I should imagine. How's life? The three of you still together? Or is it five?"

"Six, counting all of the children." Bresnahan could feel the blush that now suffused the light skin of her face. Even now, more than two years later, she rankled at being branded wherever she went because of Chazz Sweeney's "exposé" of her relationship with Ward and Leah Sigal and the thoroughly happy life they had made for themselves there in Dublin. Which *Ath Cliath* now billed as a "world capital."

There were communes, groups that functioned as families, openly shared wives and husbands all over Europe. But no such grouping was to be tolerated in Sweeney's Ireland, where every other class of license and crime was allowed. Which was, of course, yet more hypocrisy. "Yes, we're still very much together, which is something I would have thought you here would applaud, given your . . . Celtic perspective."

"And do, do. You're one of my heroes. Welcome. It's not often the police arrive bearing gifts. What do you have? Give us a look."

She held out a hand.

"Former police."

"Ah, yes—former police, which we both know is a patent oxymoron, don't we, dear. Come." She took the tape. "If it's really exciting, I'll insist you sit on my knee. Did I tell you I like that skirt and those legs. My, my."

Out in the Audi, Ward commented, "And the report said she liked boys."

"No, no—it said she liked sex with young recruits," replied McKeon, who was sitting with McGarr in the Rover. "Gender was not named."

"Can you give me some hint as to what I'm about to see?"

"You'll know soon enough why I brought it to you. For comment."

As the introductory music began playing, McGarr thought of time and how, really, the Celtic era, while over a millennium past, was only a blink in the history of mankind. Who were a blink themselves in the history of the earth.

And how Celtic lore and legend still resonated in the country, perhaps because the images of the Celtic revival in the early nineteenth century had lingered in the old money that was in the process of being retired, in the government and other publications, in "traditional" music, clothes, jewelry, literature, the theater, and now as a cover for a drug gang who were probably also involved in murder and grand theft. The grandest.

More minutes went by as the two women in the office watched and the three men in the two cars listened, until Morrigan said, "So, at last—the other shoe drops."

The deep scrambled voice was making its demand.

"I hope you're not pointing the finger at us. All you people make the assumption that, just because Celtic United and the New Druids tap into the same rich fodder of Ireland's Celtic past, we're one and the same organization. We're not. We're independent of each other and discrete."

Bresnahan had to struggle to keep her eyes from rolling.

Behind the wheel, McKeon shifted in the seat and reached forward to wipe the windscreen.

"Nor is Celtic United responsible for the citizens, mind you, who hang outside this office. By law, they have the right to assemble."

"Speaking of which, take a look at the tall one there," McKeon said, "the one with the Kojak and—could that be?—a ring in his nose?"

McGarr moved forward to peer above the condensation that had gathered on the glass.

"We're only allied in our core values. And these people—whoever made this tape—are not wrong in blaming Christianity for having usurped and supplanted the ancient culture of Ireland's native people, which has led to the central religious division that obtains to this very day."

Either the woman, Morrigan, had a good memory, or she had viewed the tape before, McGarr thought, since her phrasing was nearly identical to the videotape.

The man McKeon had spied was tall, bald, broad-shouldered, and was wearing the same woven jumperlike top that they had seen young Sloane in earlier. Opening the glove box, McGarr reached for the binoculars that Noreen, an avid birder as well as a shooter, had kept there. The Rover had been her car.

"And that book—I hope it was in fact a real page that he burnt, because the entire literally bloody thing should be torched to a cinder if only to demonstrate that we've unshackled ourselves from our wretched Christian-Brit past and embraced the New Celtic order."

Raising the binoculars to his eyes, McGarr thought of the many times they'd stopped so she could follow the transit of waterfowl or scan a hedgerow for some rare and errant songbird that had been blown to Ireland during a storm.

"And do you think for a moment that we'd be so stupid as to identify ourselves so baldly and risk sacrificing all of this?" Morrigan swept her hand to mean the building. "Two seats in the Dail and a burgeoning electoral base? Somebody is setting us up. Whoever stole the bloody book has a double agenda, and I know who it is."

"It's him," said McGarr. "Ray-Boy."

"You're shittin'—what luck."

"Nose ring and all."

Bresnahan waited.

"He's twirling a set of keys."

"The car," said Ward. "If we just could get that, it might provide evidence of how Derek Greene died."

"Chase him, he might run to it," McKeon mused.

Finally Bresnahan asked, "And who might that be?"

"The man who is threatened most by Celtic United, whose party lost those very two seats to us in the last election and will lose more in the next, all the polls say."

"Brendan Kehoe, the taoiseach?"

"None other."

"Bernie—pull up to the far corner, in case he goes that way," said McGarr.

"I was thinking you'd let me be the one to approach him."

"Patch on your head and all—he'd never see you coming," Ward put in.

"Haven't I got me fookin' hat? Let me at the fookin' bastard."

Said Bresnahan, "I think if you think Brendan Kehoe would stoop to stealing the Book of Kells and murdering a security guard—"

"Not Kehoe himself, but one of the cowboys around him. Think of Charlie Haughey and all the bagmen he surrounded himself with while taoiseach. And there was Watergate. Kehoe's indirect involvement is not so far-fetched."

Thought McGarr: Another flap would not do. And with all the other young men milling about CU headquarters, any provocation might spark an unwanted incident. Tact or, rather, tactics were called for.

"Top of the street, Bernie. Please. And Hughie"—McGarr fit the Walther under his belt—"pull the car down the laneway, so he can't leave from there."

Opening the door, McGarr got out and crossed the road to approach the building from the other side of the street, so he'd appear to be just another old man wending his way back home from a pub.

Reaching into the pocket of his jacket, he depressed the switch on the receiver/transmitter that would allow him to send his voice to the others. "Ruthie, break off with your woman there and cover the door. Sloane's son, the one who thumped Bernie, is out front. He might make a play for the building."

"He didn't thump me."

"Just played knick-knack-paddy-whack on your snowy pate," said Ward.

"You messin'?"

"Yah, I'm messin'. What'll you do about it?"

Seeing a gap in the traffic, McGarr stepped into the street and crossed directly in front of the building, making right for the crowd of maybe two dozen or more. Only when he was nearly upon them did a few take notice. But they did not move.

Pulling the Walther from under his belt, McGarr flicked the barrel at the first one, who put out his hands and stepped back. "Hey, hey—look-ee here. A live one, incoming."

Breaking off their conversations, the front ranks hesitated, their eyes dropping to the gun before stepping back.

Apart from Ray-Boy. One glance at McGarr and he pivoted, an arm sweeping out to shove one of his mates at McGarr, before he bolted toward the stairs into the building.

Where Bresnahan was waiting, a 9mm Glock raised in both hands and pointing at his chest.

Ray-Boy slowed. "You won't shoot me."

"Ah, but I will."

"You won't." He picked up speed, charging right at her. "Bad fuckin' PR. And you're no fuckin' cop."

He was right, she thought. What if she did put him down with a shot? How many additional years would it take her to climb out from under that dark cloud? And here she was with a happy child and a successful business. She shouldn't even be here.

She lowered the gun.

Muttering "Silly cunt," he rushed by her.

Back out at the bottom of the stairs, when somebody stepped in front of McGarr, he did not hesitate. His knee came up, buckling the figure whom he shoved at the others.

Spinning around, McGarr aimed the gun at the forehead of the closest, while holding his Garda ID in the other hand. "Police! Stand back!"

They stopped.

"Back!"

"Fuck that, fuck him. Ray-Boy needs us, lads. He'll only get one of us," said a voice from behind.

"Let that be you," said McGarr. "You with the mouth. You're the one I want."

But nobody stepped forward.

McGarr turned and moved to the door, where Bresnahan was waiting. "Sorry, Chief—I just couldn't."

"Which way?"

"Follow me." They both rushed into the building, McGarr behind her.

Out in the laneway, Ward had stopped his Audi at a chain-link gate that controlled access to the car park in back. Getting out, he had checked the lock and decided that a pry bar would open it easily. But when he returned from the boot of the car to check the lock, he saw headlamps flash on and sweep past McGarr and Bresnahan.

Shots rang out: two, two more, and then three. And the car yawed wildly and caromed off the grills of several others, before straightening out and heading for the gate.

Very much caught in the glare of the oncoming headlamps, Ward glanced back at his car that he had only just bought, before throwing himself toward the corner where the gate met the laneway wall.

Bucking and rocking, the large now-damaged car burst through the gate, which flew over the hood, kissed the side of Ward's Audi, and veered over into the laneway wall that it followed—sheet metal shrieking, sparks flying—before jouncing out into the street.

Horns blared, traffic stopped, and people—Sloane's own mates—dived for cover as the engine whined and the one still-inflated rear tire squealed on the pavement before the car shot forward again.

But there was a figure standing in the middle of the road a hundred yards away with something in his hands.

As the car neared, McKeon raised a 12-gauge Benelli shotgun and pumped six slugs into the grill of the oncoming car. The seventh and final shell he fired through the passenger side of the windscreen, which blew into the backseat, crazing the glass in front of the driver.

Like a torero about to finish off a troublesome bull, he then stepped to the curb and waited for the now hissing and steaming car to lurch alongside him. Whereupon McKeon drew his handgun from under his jacket and squeezed off three additional rounds at the right front tire, which burst with a pop.

As the car pitched forward, the driver tried to compensate and jerked the wheel, causing the back end to rise up. When the front bumper caught on the pavement, the car vaulted into the air, turned end over end, and seemed to hesitate, as though deciding whether to complete the flip. Instead, it slammed down on its top, tumbled sideways and then rolled over twice before coming to rest on its wheels.

McKeon, McGarr, and Ward surrounded the back of the car, with Bresnahan facing the stopped traffic and a gathering crowd.

At length, McGarr nodded, and McKeon and Ward both reached for a rear door handle. Only one—Ward's—would open, and with Beretta raised he slipped in. After a moment or two, he got out and nodded, and McGarr opened the driver's door.

An upper body lolled out, eyes opened, and fell. First a shoulder and then the curly blond head struck and bounced off the tar. The very top of the skull seemed to have been removed and was a red wet crater.

There was a handgun on the seat.

A shout of outrage went up from the crowd.

"Who's that?" McKeon asked.

McGarr shrugged.

"Call the pathologist, Tech Squad, ambulance."

From somewhere in the crowd, a strobe flashed several times. "Yiz is fookin' killers!" a voice shouted. "Fookin' cop fookin' killers."

"And put him back behind the wheel with the door closed."

Slipping the Walther back into his jacket, McGarr turned and walked toward his car, as though mindless of the crowd, whom any acknowledgment would incite, he knew.

"I should have put one in his leg," Bresnahan called after him. "I'll make this up to you, I promise."

"Just continue on with what we discussed, if you would, Rut'ie." McGarr's beeper was sounding, but he switched it off. It was too late an hour, and he had too much to do. For explanations.

The people lining the footpath were regarding them with averted heads and glassy eyes; it was the stare reserved for curious creatures, oddities, killers who could take a life with seeming indifference.

Ward was waiting for him beside the Rover. "Why would they steal the Book of Kells, murder a security guard, then send a ransom tape loaded with all their Druid bullshit, if they did it? Where's the advantage, where's the premium?"

Glancing back at the smoldering car, McGarr thought he saw it. Behind the wheel was a potential martyr, a way of using a death at the hands of the brutal police to attract more followers, to broaden their political base. But could they have planned it like that?

McGarr's eyes swept the crowd, who were still stunned by the sight of the ruined car. All that would change the moment they left.

"No they couldn't have," said Ward, having read his thoughts. "It's Sweeney. It's got to be. When was the last time he was involved in something so vital, and he wasn't into it up to his hips? I don't buy his messenger bullshit. Why him? Why not send it directly to somebody, anybody, connected with Trinity or the government? You or Sheard or Kehoe."

"Where's his advantage?"

"Beyond fifty million quid?" Ward shrugged. "Revenge on you and Kehoe. He'll both score the money and hang the both of you with this thing."

Years past, when Brendan Kehoe had acted as state prosecutor, he had put Sweeney in jail for three years. McGarr had done the same for a lesser period.

"You and I both know how many times he's said it—he never forgets. Or forgives."

Nobody detested Sweeney more than McGarr, but Sweeney could not have foreseen the incident with the television crew. Or this.

And they had involved him because of his ownership of *Ath Cliath* and his conservative Catholic background. Who could beat the drum and make more of getting the books back than Sweeney, to whom they would be precious if not sacred? Why not keep him informed as a check against any government machination or foot-dragging?

TREVOR PAPE'S HOUSE ON THE MOREHAMPTON Road was old, large, and would fetch a handsome price in spite of its condition, which was unimproved.

Unlike nearby houses of the same vintage, its windows had not been replaced with double-glazed, its flag walkway was pitched and heaved, and its long front garden—laid out at the time when that part of Dublin had been a suburb—was a tangle of old, exotic growth, including a eucalyptus tree.

Under it was parked an old pearl-gray Jaguar sedan.

McGarr climbed the ten steep steps to the first-floor entrance and had to reach to twist the disk of a mechanical bell contained in the center of the ornate door. It was as old as the house, McGarr judged, and gave off a weak jingle.

Again and again he rang, until finally he rapped on the frost-glass pane. At length a light flickered on above him, and through the glass he could see a shape approach.

"Yes?" a woman's voice asked through a faded brass speaker.

"Police."

"Yes?"

"Trevor Pape—would he be in?"

"Yes."

There was another long pause.

"May I see him?"

"You are?"

"McGarr. Peter McGarr."

"From the television."

McGarr opened his mouth to object but changed his mind. "The same."

"Then you'd better come in."

The bolt clicked, and the door opened slightly. McGarr pushed it open in time to see a young woman wearing some diaphanous shift with nothing more than a thong below.

Moving quickly to the stairs, she said over her shoulder, "He's in there." Her hand swung to a lighted hallway that led further into the building.

McGarr could not keep himself from noticing how her breasts, which were visible in their entirety through the shift, juddered with each step. Seeing him stare, she glanced down at herself, then back up at him and smiled. It was not an unfriendly smile.

The hallway was long and narrow with a tall ceiling and—could it be?—carved mahogany wainscoting that extended past McGarr's shoulder. The sliding doors of a dining room appeared on one side, a darkened sitting room with a marble mantel and Hepplewhite furniture next, and finally a well-lighted study that proved to be a long room, lined with bookshelves and containing several library-length tables, reading chairs, and a fire glowing in a patterned brick hearth.

Near it, Pape was sitting in a leather chair with copper rivets, staring at a television screen that pictured a pride of lions on a parched savanna with Mount Kilimanjaro in the distance. It was something like a screen-saver; nothing—the grass, the lions, the clouds—was moving.

"Dr. Pape?" McGarr had removed his hat, which he held in his hands before him.

It took a moment for Pape's head to move to him, his blue eyes focused on the hat. "You."

"I have something I'd like you to see."

After another pause, Pape's eyes flashed up at McGarr. "I've seen it on television. You as thug and lout. You're well suited to what you do, it's plain. But flogging a few journalists won't get you your bloody book back, I hope you're learning."

His eyes moved up from the hat; they were bright, glassy, the pupils nearly absent. His hands were gripping the arms of the chair.

"I'd like to show you something. Is that a video player?"

Pape's head dipped down and then up.

McGarr scanned the tables on either side of the chair and then the room. Pape seemed slightly drunk or in some other way . . . absent, but there was no sign of a glass or bottle.

"I assume it's operated like other players."

"Give it to me—I'll do it," said a voice behind him.

McGarr turned to find the young woman, who had put on a purple V-necked jumper and jeans. Her feet were bare.

"When was the last time we caught a flick with the cops, Poppy?"

The pale skin around Pape's eyes wrinkled, his mouth opened, but no laugh came out.

"I assume that the thing is rewound." Bending to the machine, she had to fork her long blondish tresses away from her eyes, and McGarr followed the smooth, tanned skin on the back of her hand. Few hairline wrinkles, no trace of geriatric sheen. Late twenties, he estimated, at most early thirties.

"There we are." Turning, she handed McGarr a remote. "You play."

Her smile revealed long teeth and stunning dentition—a fetching woman with a well-structured face and full lips painted some deep shade of purple to match her eye shadow and jumper, the V neck of which was cut deep. Her jeans were white.

A hand came out. "Gillian Reston. I live here with Poppy." Her tones were British, privileged but slightly slurred.

"You're his—?"

"Houseguest," Pape roared. "Get on with it. Get on with it now and get out. I've half a mind to ring up Jack Sheard and report you. It's nearly eleven of the bloody evening, and here you are, of all people, coming round with a bloody video, of all things. Give me that."

Half a mind exactly, McGarr thought, ignoring Pape's outstretched hand and activating the player.

"Drink?" Gillian Reston asked.

McGarr shook his head and allowed his eyes to drop down her body. She was nubile, to say the least, with a narrow waist and a pleasant flair of hip, and the breasts that he had glimpsed earlier now peaked the cashmerelike material of her top.

"Come, sit." She patted a cushion of the sofa. "You must have been on your feet at least since your encounter with the press earlier, no?

"Oh, how nice—music too, Poppy. And there I thought it would be some dreary drunk-driving exemplum."

Pape coughed or cleared his throat. Then, "Whiskey!"

"Poppy's taking the entire matter of the theft and the murder of the guard too awfully hard," she said, getting up.

While the tape came on, McGarr looked around—at the bookshelves that lined three walls, the long windows for daylight, the library tables with colored-glass reading lamps, rather like one of the reading rooms that McGarr remembered from his several excursions to Trinity with Noreen some years past. But furnished for comfort, not scholarship.

There were tall, healthy-looking potted plants in two corners, an immense Oriental rug on a gleaming parquet floor, and the pleasant grouping of large, leather-covered seats around the entertainment center and hearth with its carved—could it be?—rosewood mantel.

The farthest wall from McGarr was filled with a glass-fronted case behind which was a collection of pottery and stone objects that looked to be Celtic or at least ancient in design. Perhaps three dozen items in various conditions from intact to mere shards were kept there.

The crystal whiskey decanter, from which Gillian poured Pape's drink, was nearly full. If Pape's odd demeanor was due to drink, he had not drunk much from the decanter.

Delivering the glass to Pape, the young woman bent at the waist and brushed her lips against the side of his face, whispering something McGarr could not hear. Straightening up, she regarded McGarr, her dark eyes defiant and—he only now noticed—as bright as any he had ever seen. She returned to the sofa.

"My word," Pape said over the lip of the glass. "Do we really have to watch this? I'm no student of history, but this is just . . . drivel."

Gillian Reston turned to McGarr, her smile still complete. "Sure I can't get you something?"

The invitation was complete with a dark, arched eyebrow. Again, McGarr considered her eyes, which sparkled. As though having to gather herself—like Pape had, only less conspicuously—she turned back to the television, arms folded under her breasts in a way that emphasized their splay.

Pape's chin rose, and he sat up when the hooded figure came on. "Is this the chap?" he asked.

"Chap, Poppy?" she asked, an edge of concern in her voice.

"The chap who murdered Sloane and stole the bloody books, what other chap would I mean?"

"Perhaps if we listen, Poppy—"

"Don't take that tone with me. You're here at my behest."

McGarr increased the volume. "A Judas book. And expendable," said the hooded figure with the voice-scrambling audio device covering his mouth.

He waited until the flame of the welder's torch was held to the page before pushing the pause button. "Now, there. Is that a page—can you tell?—out of the Book of Kells?"

Pape held out a hand, then pulled himself up in his chair. The woman quickly moved off the couch toward one of the tables where she retrieved Pape's spectacles.

"Now, go through it, no stops."

McGarr did.

"And again."

McGarr complied.

"Well, it surely appears to be a page from Kells, a text page. But I should imagine your Garda laboratory will be able to blow up the image, the better to judge."

"What about the possibility of what we're seeing there being paper?" the young woman asked.

Pape's head swung to her. "Gillian—leave the room."

"From one of the facsimile—"

"Out! Now!"

"Why."

"Because I'm telling you to."

"I require a reason. Certainly nobody in his right mind would burn—"

"Now!" Pape as much as bellowed.

Color had risen to her cheeks, and she had again folded her arms across her chest, this time defiantly. "I won't."

Removing his glasses, he made sure his eyes—agatized both

from age and from whatever it was that had narrowed the pupils—
met hers. "Oh, yes, you will. Now. Without another word."

Her head swung to McGarr, her humiliation obvious. Yet she
rose to leave.

"Facsimile?" McGarr asked. "Facsimile, what?"

"And you too. Get out. I didn't invite you in. I'll discuss that"—
Pape cast a hand at the screen—"and anything else with Jack
Sheard, who has the background to appreciate the finer points of
incunabula. And take your bloody gyre of vulgarity with you."

Pape tried to rise from the chair, but neither arms nor legs were
up to hauling his tall, thin body to a stand. With a grunt, he rocked
back heavily into the cushions. "I've told you all I know, and I'll only
speak to Jack henceforth. Am I understood?"

Hitting the eject button, McGarr stepped to the tape player
while calling out to the woman, "Hold on, please."

"Do I have to ring him up?" Pape asked.

She was nearly at the top of the stairs by the time McGarr got
into the hall. "Poppy's collection, the one behind the glass cabinet—
Celtic, is it?"

"The Beaker people," she said without turning her head to him.

Who had been a wave of Celtic immigrants, McGarr seemed to
remember.

"Facsimile—what? What did you mean by that?"

She kept climbing.

"What's OxyContin feel like? Is it pleasurable?"

She hesitated, turning only her eyes to him, before stepping into
the shadows at the top of the stairs.

Treading the expanse of heaved flags on the walkway of the front
garden, McGarr used his cell phone to add Gillian Reston's name to
the list of principals in the investigation that Swords and the Murder Squad staff were working on.

"Anything besides the name and her association with Pape?" Swords asked. His voice sounded tired.

"I'd guess she's British."

"Oh." It wasn't much of a lead. "Jack Sheard get hold of you?" McGarr waited.

"Been on the blower here . . . oh, a half dozen calls, if one."

Only McGarr's staff knew his cell phone number, and he had switched off his pager. "Say what he wants?"

"The business at CU headquarters. It's on the wire in triplicate."

Also blinking was the call monitor on the radio in his car, but he ignored that too.

8

Apart from the tinted windows and the battered body, Ruth Bresnahan's decades-old Opel GT was the perfect surveillance car because of its superior sound system and seats that reclined all the way back.

As long as she was careful not to fall asleep, the oversize rearview mirror, which, like the radio, Ward had installed, gave her an unobtrusive perspective on anything behind. And leaning back as she had been for—she checked her light-up Swatch—nearly two hours, it was impossible to tell if anybody was in the car.

Truth was, Bresnahan had thought never in a thousand years would she miss this kind of surveillance work, stuck in an alley across from Celtic United headquarters waiting for the woman, Morrigan, to come out. But it felt as comfortable as slipping on a pair of old shoes, as was said.

Even the grimy brick walls to either side, the orangish light, the smell of baking bread or buns or biscuits from the factory in back of her were welcoming. Paltry though it was, this had been and should still be her work. Like a corpse, she did not turn her head to the vans that kept threading the narrow alley on their way to a loading dock.

Computers, manipulating databases, hacking into government, bank, and medical mainframes may be the name of the security game at present and was how Bresnahan & Ward, Ltd., made its money. But it was not one that she cheerfully played. There was no humanity, no inherent joy attached to crunching numbers to reveal that target X spent far more money than he ever earned or Y had once been arrested for indecent exposure.

This, however—sitting in the shadows of an abandoned building and wondering how Morrigan (aka Sheila Law of Antrim Town) could have become involved with CU and the New Druids—was another cup of tea altogether. Morrigan was university educated, pretty in a blowsy way, and possessed of an angular shape that she had kept trim right into her early forties.

Perhaps it was sex, as one of Ward's touts had mentioned. But Bresnahan would not allow herself to believe that any woman would center her life around sex, although in a way she herself had.

When Ward had as much as thrown her over for Leah Sigal four years earlier, she had seduced him, got massively pregnant on purpose, and now the three of them—no, actually, the six of them when the children were counted—lived together most contentedly, she believed, in what Sweeney's *Ath Cliath* had called "pagan, orgiastic bliss." For love, not sex. Although there was that too.

As a good country lass from a Catholic background, Bresnahan had spent her adolescence and early adult life in rural Kerry ignorant of sexual delight. But once exposed to it, she could not imagine ever being without a man like Ward, who played her body like a pianola, as was also said. Maybe her life was just one big cliché.

In fact, on stakeouts such as this, Ward and she engaged in nearly constant and unremitting sex, each taking turns maintaining the watch while the other was beyond the plane of view. Phew— where was she getting these thoughts? She hadn't fantasized like this since . . . well, since she was last on a stakeout that mattered, over two years earlier, before Ward and she were sacked because of Sweeney.

Sweeney. With him now involved, it made what they were about all the sweeter. Because he was in the thick of it, she was certain. Sweeney was like a disease, a scourge, a pestilence. If he was present in any way, he was the problem. It was his MO.

But the lights now began to go out in the CU building across the road. And there she was, Morrigan herself. Stepping out, checking inside her large handbag to make sure she had everything—most important, the ransom tape, Bresnahan hoped—and locking the door. She looked around before heading down the stairs.

But the woman wasn't halfway to the street when a car door opened and a young man in a half shirt with a roll of tanned, exposed abs approached her somewhat drunkenly.

She shook her head and pushed by him. Looking rather like a beefy Brad Pitt, he reached for her hip, but she slapped his hand away.

"Go, girl," said Bresnahan in the darkness of the car. You've got an altogether different bun in your oven tonight. Sex can wait.

Damn, she thought, I must concentrate.

THE LIGHTS WERE ON IN WHAT MCGARR guessed was Kara Kennedy's apartment. With legal parking nonexistent, he pulled the car up on the footpath and lowered the Garda ID that was attached to the sun visor.

The cold front that McGarr had felt earlier had arrived, with a sharp wind angling in from the northeast. Above the rooftops in a cloudless sky, the stars were layers deep, the achromatic light appearing purer because of the orange-colored cadmium vapor lamps that lined the street.

The house was a large old brick Victorian of the sort that had been built by people who thought of themselves as "West Britons" and had re-created the middle-class uniformity of Hampstead or York, this one situated on a corner with a well-clipped lawn and hedges bordered by a spiked iron fence.

Back around the turn of the last century, the houses—in fact, most of Rathmines—had been considered an anonymous tract, McGarr knew. Now, the old brick, slate roofs, and tall chimneys soothed the eye, when set against the urban sprawl of the city.

Comfortable if chilly before central heating, the houses featured four bay windows, two up and two down. The gate squeaked on its hinges as he pushed it shut.

Pressing one of two bells, McGarr waited only a few seconds before hearing a voice. "Yes?"

"It's Peter McGarr. May I come up? I've something to show you, and I need your opinion on a technical matter."

"Really? Fantastic. I've been thinking about you and couldn't sleep."

The buzzer sounded, the hall light went on, and climbing the wide staircase with its carved banister and much dark wood he switched off his cell phone and put his beeper on mute. Too much had gone on, and his next stop was home.

Kara Kennedy was waiting in an open, lighted door at the top of the stairs. "Sorry I had to leave the pub. I just . . . well, I just became anxious, I guess. And I was feeling desolate, there's no other word for it. I had to get out of there. Come in, come in."

In a glance, McGarr took in her dressing gown, the pearl gray silk patterned with deep red roses and a matching sash. On her feet, in contrast, was a pair of aquamarine fleece booties with pom-poms on the toes. Her long brown hair had been brushed back and was tied with a gray ribbon.

"Do you find it too warm in here. I had a chill and—" Like a bright, handsome bird turning an ear to the crowd, she cocked her head slightly and swirled her eyes, as though testing the atmosphere of the flat.

Scanning what appeared to be a sitting room for a television and video player, McGarr shook his head. Pulling off his hat, he swung his eyes to her. "I brought the video. I need your professional opinion about several matters."

"Really?" The smile, breaking through her obvious concern, was dazzling—her jade eyes sparkling, the array of her brilliant teeth drawing McGarr's eyes. Could they be real, he wondered, before noticing that her dentition wasn't exactly perfect, apart from its whiteness. "I hope I can help. I've been feeling . . . powerless and thwarted. In here, please. I don't often watch television, but tonight . . ."

As she led McGarr down a hall past several darkened rooms, his eyes fell from her good shoulders to her narrow, sashed waist and thin ankles in the booties that looked like dust mops; he concluded— as he had earlier—that in many ways she had been "given the packet," as had been said about well-formed people in his youth. And she walked with a rolling, big-shouldered gait.

In a room that functioned as a den/library/home office, he imagined, she stopped and twirled round on him rather dramatically. "This is where I live. Or, at least, where I spend much of my time when not at my work."

There was a teacup on one arm of an overstuffed reading chair, a book splayed across the other. A second identical burgundy-colored chair was set on the other side of a tall and bright floor lamp.

She pointed to it. "Please. Sit. Is that the tape?" She held out her hand. "Let me take your coat. Will you take something—tea, coffee, a drink?"

"The last." Tomorrow was sure to be trying, and he would need his sleep.

"Good. I'll join you. Perhaps I'll be able to sleep."

McGarr sat and looked around: At a table on the other side of the room were framed photographs of a number of people who he supposed were her family; other chairs and tables were furnished in a tasteful Continental style that McGarr had seen before but could not name.

A gas fire was hissing in the grate, and in all, the room, with red drapes covering the tall windows and a thick shag carpet in some light shade, was warm and cozy on the first chilly night of the season.

"I left out the ice, given how you took your drop in the pub," she said, returning with a glass in either hand. "There are the wands. I'll let you do the honor." Bending to hand him the glass, she held on to it for a moment until he glanced up at her and their eyes met. She smiled. "I'm glad you came."

Straightening up, she brushed her hand through her hair. "Whew! It's too hot in here. Let me turn it down." As she passed beyond him, McGarr listened to the swish of silk, and did he imagine that, in fetching the drinks, she had also dabbed on a bit of perfume? He reached for the remote on a low table between the two chairs.

"Now then." Moving quickly, she deposited herself in the other chair and reached for her drink. "Roll 'em, maestro." Her slight Scots burr was noticeable mostly when she pronounced an *r*.

As the music and film came on, McGarr sipped from the glass and let the warmth of the whiskey seep down into his body. It was some dark Scots brand, doubtless a single malt, with aromatic subtleties and just the right amount of bite.

Although usually a demonstrative person, McGarr judged, Kara Kennedy watched quietly, her chin raised and her head cocked slightly as she peered down her long, slightly aquiline nose at the screen.

McGarr waited until the demand had been made and the screen went black before rewinding just beyond the point where the hooded figure appeared. He then replayed a snatch of the narrator's voice, set against the pastiche of sectarian mayhem and grieving families.

"Question—what is the most divisive and destructive issue in this country today? What might Ireland have become, had she cleaved to her culture? Had Christianity not displaced the older Celtic verities of life and Druidism?"

"Know that voice?"

"Aye." She dipped her head once. "Name is Ian Mac Laud. Former host on Radio Scotland before throwing in with the Free Scotland crowd. Got sacked for a lack of impartiality is how it was explained in the press. But he was really just a crank who encouraged other cranks. They had to do something. Since then?" She hunched her shoulders. "Or, as here, he's moved on to the larger issue."

McGarr waited.

"Freeing the Greater Celtic World. Pity, there is none."

"Anything else?"

"Well"—reaching for her drink, she turned her wonderful smile on him again—"where do I start?"

"I'm interested in your impressions."

"Remember, you asked." Over the lip of the glass, her eyes regarded him for a moment before she drank and set the glass back down. "The Celtic period in Ireland? What we know of it isn't much, since theirs was an oral tradition with little preserved and that at a much later date. But it spanned from around 600 B.C. to 1169, when Dermot MacMurrough, the King of Leinster, invited the Normans to help restore him to his throne. But you know that."

McGarr nodded. It was the history taught in school.

"But in no way were the Celts peaceful people, any—no, every— source relates. The entire fifteen hundred years was marked by continual intertribal warfare and strife. And only seldom were the Celts able to unite in the face of an external threat.

"As for democracy?" Kara passed some air between her lips. "If and when observed, it was minimal, intraclan, most probably elitist, and sooner or later boiled down to a democracy of the sword.

"Which is not to say that the Celts in Ireland and Scotland did not produce a culture that was in other ways admirable—the art, as seen in metalwork, gold and silver jewelry, La Tène pottery, stone carvings; brehon law; and the custom of diurnal civility among one's clan.

"But most of what we know about the Celts—from their legend and lore through their history—was preserved and has come down to us only because of the very same Christian monks whom this video castigates.

"In fact, a better case could be made for Celtic civilization having achieved its highest form of expression when it assumed and melded with Christian influences.

"So, in my opinion, almost all of that"—she moved her glass toward the screen—"is self-serving drivel, merely an attempt to justify grand theft and the murder of Raymond Sloane. Has it appeared on national television?"

"Not that I know of."

"It will. Mark my words. Publicity is what they're after. Exposure. To become the bad boy of Irish politics, rather like the IRA once was to its political party, Sinn Fein. Here, the New Druids to Celtic United. They'll have every mixed-up, misinformed, romantic lad in the thirty-two counties beating down their door to join. They could now mail back Kells, Durrow, and Armagh, and they would have accomplished at least a major recruitment effort."

But why, then, make a point of murdering Raymond Sloane and so gruesomely? After having as much as autographed the deed with the videotape.

McGarr fast-forwarded to the burning of the page, pausing where it curled up after catching fire.

"Before I came here, I stopped at Trevor Pape's."

"Oh?" Turning her head to him, she seemed disappointed.

"Gillian Reston—know her?"

Kara's eyes flashed down at her glass. "Yes."

"Who is she? In regard to Pape."

Closing her eyes and averting her head, almost as though from a blow, she pulled in a breath. Then, "His latest bauble."

"I don't understand—Pape, how old can he be?"

"He's sixty-four. Just."

"And looks every day of it, in ways."

Her head tilted, but she did not reply.

"Drinks, drugs."

She looked back down at the glass.

"OxyContin. We'll find that in Sloane's body when the reports come in tomorrow, I'm told. Is it as good as they say?"

Eyes still on the glass, her head shook slightly. "I don't know why you're asking it of me."

"Have you tried it?"

"Yes."

"Is it as good as they say?"

"Yes. It's"—her head came up, and she looked off across the room—"euphoria. A euphoria that you could never know without it. In life."

"Did you take it tonight?"

"No."

"Do you take it regularly?"

Her eyes met his. "I'm disappointed you're asking me these questions. I took it only once."

"With Pape?"

She drew in a breath, sighed, then nodded.

"Which is a problem with him?"

"I don't think he would see it so. But, yes—I think it's a problem. It affects his personality, with it or without it."

"Where does he get it? Who's his connection?"

Yet again she shook her head. "As I said, I tried it only once. And I must say, I feel like I'm being interrogated about drugs, which alone is a criminal matter. Perhaps I should have a solicitor present. Didn't you say you needed an opinion on something technical?"

"At least two. Who were the Beaker people?"

"A little over four thousand years ago, a group arrived here in Ireland who produced a kind of pottery that was much different from the stuff associated with earlier periods. It was delicate with fine lines and much of it took the shape of—?" She cocked her head.

"A beaker."

"There you are."

"It's Celtic pottery?"

"No. It's not even pre-Celtic, although some later Celtic pottery seems to imitate its shape. The very first wave of Celtic immigration about which we have hard evidence came about sixteen hundred years later, around 600 B.C. Trevor Pape collects Beaker people pottery and is proud of it."

McGarr nodded. "Worth much?"

"Tons, if he chose to sell and could get a buyer with tons. Problem is, the institutions interested in that stuff are rather poor—Trinity, the National Museum, and several in other countries. Those that aren't, like the Metropolitan in New York, are poor when it comes to acquiring Beaker people pottery. Acquisition being a matter of priorities."

"But he could sell the collection, if he chose."

"That's the catch. I think he'd rather die, which, I believe, Trinity is waiting for. Trevor may not think much of the Book of Kells, but he's a committed antiquarian."

"Technical question number two—the word *facsimile* in regard to the Book of Kells. What does that mean to you?"

She brightened, as though relieved that the subject had changed. "At last, a technical matter."

Finishing the drink, she set the empty glass on the arm of the chair and then arranged her feet with the dust-mop booties—which so clashed with her otherwise elegant appearance—on the hassock before her. Settling back into the seat, she moved her hand out and touched the back of his wrist. "Well, Mr. Detective—the story goes like this.

"Back in the early nineties, an Irish-Canadian foundation decided to produce a facsimile edition of the Book of Kells so that the cultural glory of Ireland's past could be disseminated to other libraries around the world. They had the good sense to hire a printer who produced nearly faultless photocopies with excellent color and so genuine that even the wormholes in the ancient vellum were included.

"Every one of the facsimile copies was snapped up at a cost then of around eighteen thousand dollars, U.S."

"Vellum?" McGarr had heard the word before in regard to writing paper.

"Yes, the Book of Kells—the original—was produced on vellum. The word comes from *vitulis*, Latin for calf. In most manuscripts of that vintage, the calfskins used were taken from very young calves and treated with lime and other substances.

"The vital difference in the Kells book—and what has aided in its preservation—is that the major pages of decoration were drawn on the skins of calves two or three months old. The vellum is thicker and more robust, as if the monks who created Kells planned for the work to last millennia.

"The sheer amount of vellum necessary for its timely completion reveals much about the religious community that produced it." Her left hand had come up again and was chopping off little blocks of thought. Having raised and tilted her head slightly to the side, she seemed to be speaking to a high point on the opposite wall. And there was a faraway look in her deep green eyes.

"In order to produce that many young, a herd of at least twelve hundred animals would have had to be available on Iona, where most scholars believe the book was created. Which gives some idea of the prosperity of the community there. Little wonder they were a continual target of Viking raids."

"But the facsimile editions of the book were reproduced on paper?"

She nodded. "High-quality paper."

"Then"—he touched the remote, and the video began rolling again—"does this look like burning vellum to you? Or paper?"

Again they watched as the flame of the gas torch was held to the page, which smoldered a bit, burst into an orangish flame tinged with blue, then finally curled.

"Vellum, because of the way it rolled up." Her hand moved to his wrist again and lingered. "Go back."

He did.

"There." Her fingers squeezed his wrist. "See? And did you notice how long it smoldered under such intense flame before igniting? Paper, even new paper, would have caught immediately." Her head swung to him, and her eyes, flecked with bits of brighter green, lingered in his. She smiled. "I'm going for a refill. What about you?"

McGarr held her gaze, her touch making him feel at once uncomfortable and—he tried to sort it out—surely alive to what might transpire between them. He tugged his eyes down to his glass, which was still quite full. "I'm very happy as I am."

"I have a question for you, then." Still, her hand remained. "But it can wait. In the meantime, back the tape to the part when that ransom demand first comes on."

"Is that an order?"

"No"—she smiled in the way that transformed her rather stately face—"just a test. I'm not sure I fancy a willful man, and you bear all the hallmarks of unrehabilitatable independence."

Squeezing his wrist harder still, she lowered the booties and slid off the chair. McGarr's head turned—like a puppet in a Punchinello show, it came to him—to follow the graceful lines of her body into what he supposed was the kitchen.

He glanced down at his wrist, wondering at his own vulnerability—that so little as her fingers on his skin and a flirtatious remark, doubtless sparked by the whiskey, could so transform him.

In a nanosecond, he had posited what it would be like again to have a woman in his life. And such a woman. She was, well . . . charming was the least of it. The most being her beauty and the contrast between her obvious sophistication and her equally apparent naïveté in regard to Pape and perhaps the husband as well.

If McGarr's decades of police work had taught him one thing, it was this: After two years of hearing nothing from a husband or wife—not a note, phone call, or ransom demand—he or she was gone, one way or another.

He backed up the tape.

"Now, you'll notice," Kara said, as she approached her chair, glass in hand, "those medallion-like objects behind our Darth Vader look-alike."

Having been concentrating on the figure and the garbled voice, McGarr had taken only scant notice of the background, apart from judging it a drab interior with a lime green wall and a dingy white door. The objects on the wall were only in partial focus and seemingly distant.

He shook his head.

"Shall we find out?" Raising an eyebrow, she shot him a sidelong glance. "You're supposed to ask how."

"How?"

"Why, by a miracle of modern technology is how." Advancing on the television cabinet, she retrieved another small device. "Trinity supplied me this to study the details in illustrated manuscripts on film that we might acquire. If you spool the tape back to where those objects are most conspicuous, I'll demonstrate."

McGarr complied.

"Now, run forward to . . . there."

Wielding the wand, she both magnified the screen in successively larger stages and focused in on one of the several objects beyond the figure's shoulder.

The larger the image became, the more it began to resemble a human face. But the image sometimes became grainy.

McGarr got to his feet and approached the television.

"The quality of the videos I'm supplied, of course, is superior. But what are we seeing here? Doesn't that look like . . ."

A human head. One that had been fixed with several others, Janus-like, to one side of the door with—McGarr had to squint—what looked like a spike through the hairy skull just at the point where the nose met the forehead. The head of the spike gleamed like a shiny, tenpenny bit.

Lowering the device, Kara turned to him and shook her head. "The Druids—the ancient Druids—believed that if they decapitated their enemies in battle they would not come back for revenge in another life.

"But can I tell you something?—I don't know how much more of this I can take."

McGarr switched off the television and hit the rewind button. With head lowered, she was staring down at the toe of one of the homely booties that she was moving over the carpet.

"Who are these people?" McGarr asked through the whirring of the VCR, if only to distract her. He pointed to the long table.

"Family."

Most of the photos were obviously dated. One showed a handsome couple as young adults who in other portraits added three children, the youngest of whom was obviously Kara.

"Where's home?"

"Mull. Actually, Salen." It was a fishing village on Mull, the large island in Scotland.

"And who's this with you?"

"My husband."

The photo could not have been taken too long before, given her appearance. And whereas her husband's face looked somewhat younger than hers—four or five years—his curly, blondish hair had also begun to gray. He was a tall man, thin and square with regular, if blunt, features of the sort that were called ruggedly handsome. McGarr picked up another of the photos.

Dressed in oilcloth and twill, and wearing a rain hat, he was holding open his shooting jacket to shield Kara from a strong wind that had flattened the heather by their feet. Obviously chilled, she was clutching the collar of her jacket and had leaned her head against his chest. Her smile was wan, but she seemed contented.

In his other hand he was grasping the barrel of what appeared by its shape to be a Purdy shotgun. Noreen and Fitz, her father, had owned several of the expensive guns. "Where were you here?"

"Skye."

"When?"

"Three years ago. We were only married a year before."

He had either left her suddenly, leaving no trace, or had been somehow lost abroad, she had told him. "His name?"

"It was Dan. Dan Stewart."

"Where did you meet him?"

"Here in Dublin. At an opening, in fact." She brightened but then looked off.

He knew what she wanted to say; the opening had been at Noreen's gallery.

"First marriage?" McGarr set the photo down.

"For me. Dan was married before."

Which surprised McGarr—that a woman so fetching, charming, and obviously intelligent would not have married until she was— what?—nearly forty and perhaps beyond childbearing age.

"I know what you're thinking. It's rather late for marriage. But it's not as though I didn't have other offers over the years. It's just that I had never really fallen in love before."

"And you haven't heard from him?"

"Not a word."

"What does his business say? Didn't you tell me he had been away on business?"

She shook her head. "They heard nothing from him either. He flew to Yemen, checked into his hotel, went out for dinner, and was never heard from again. No note, no appointment in his scheduler, not a phone call to the front desk or on his cell phone.

"I hired a private investigator who cost me most of my savings. He said Dan's either dead or he just walked out on his life. And me."

"It must have been—it must be—hard for you, not knowing."

She cocked her head and again considered the pictures. "Oh, aye. At first all I could think of was him—what might have happened, how he might have suffered. And all the news out of that part of the world didn't help much either. I did everything I could— contacted the Yemeni embassy in London, Arab organizations. I even went there to see the hotel and collect his effects.

"I spent two weeks in a Yemeni bureaucrat's outer office being served tea until I decided the joke was on me; I gave them a piece of my mind and began walking out. Only then was I invited in to see the official, who told me they had concluded Dan had run off with another woman—and could he take me to dinner?"

"I'm sure that was difficult," McGarr managed.

"But then, later—know what?" She turned her body to him and waited until their eyes met. "I began thinking of me—how long I would continue to wait, write letters, make phone calls, and console his parents. It was my loss too—the loss of weeks, months, years of my life. I had become obsessed. Nothing else mattered. My work suffered, as we know all too well.

"And then, curiously, I felt guilty about feeling so selfish and finally angry at myself for feeling guilty, if you know what I mean."

McGarr did. The guilt he felt about the deaths of Noreen and Fitz had obscured or at least shadowed every other aspect of his life. He ejected the videotape, then reached for the case. When he straightened back up, he found her standing very close to him.

"If Dan came back tomorrow or finally phoned me telling me where he was, I wouldn't have him back. If he's dead, well, I'm sorry, but I've grieved for him. If he's alive, well, I'm equally sorry, but I've grieved for me.

"Look"—she waited until he looked into her eyes—"you and I are in the same situation. I liked what I knew about you and now, having got to meet you, I rather fancy who you are. I rather fancy you."

McGarr tried to look away.

"No, don't look away. Look at me." With a hand she turned his chin. "When you held me this morning, it made me realize how much I need a man's touch. Your touch. And I can tell you fancy me. Would you hold me again?" She raised her arms. "Please?" She was smiling, and the pupils of her jade-colored eyes were dark.

It was against everything that McGarr believed in about police work. But close, like that, he was breathing in her distinctive perfume—some mélange of . . . he didn't know what. And he was feeling her warmth, her—was it?—excitement. There was a flush in her cheeks. She pulsed her eyebrows once, as though to say, What about it?

Slowly, knowing it was wrong and actually frightened that he could not help himself, McGarr placed his hands on the supple curves of her hips, which felt slick under the silk of the dressing gown, and drew her to him, her lips grazing the side of his face as their bodies met.

Tentatively, at first. Testing each other. Then, as he drew her closer, he felt her shudder, and she moved her face into the crook of his neck.

They remained there like that for a long moment in which McGarr wrestled with and tried to deny the comfort that the embrace was giving him, the desire he felt for her, and the near-heady lust that had welled up in him. In a way, it was making him feel almost ill.

There was how warm and soft she felt, the line of smooth yet downy skin leading from her neck onto her shoulder, the pressure of her thigh that now moved between his legs as she drew her head back from him. "Kiss me."

His eyes moved to her lips, which were full and well formed. Her mouth was open in a half-smile with her eyes on his lips as well. "Go on, kiss me."

When he tried, she moved her head aside. "No, not like that."

He tried again.

"Nor like that. I want our first kiss to be memorable." Slowly, her eyes rose to his and her smile faded.

Like that, with their eyes locked, their heads moved together and their lips met gently at first and then more completely, until their abandon was such that they staggered.

She had slipped her hand between the buttons of his dress shirt and onto his breast. "Come. Come into my bedroom." Her lips darted for his, meeting them hard. "Let me make love to you."

But McGarr, summoning all that he knew about himself and

how he had conducted his life over the years, broke away from her. "I can't, really. I couldn't. I—" With the video in hand, he moved toward the chair, his hat, and the hallway that led to the door.

"You can't because you're afraid," she said to his back. "And, worse, you're in love with your guilt, the guilt you feel because of the way your wife and father-in-law died. It controls you. It rules you and makes you lust after revenge, doesn't it?

"When I'm offering you this. Turn around. Look at me. I'm offering you love and a way out."

At the door to the hallway, McGarr paused, knowing he should just keep on moving, knowing that—if he were to turn around—the turn would be a life turn. Nothing less.

"Turn around," she repeated, her Scots burr now definite. "Like you, I don't do this lightly. Turn for me. Turn for yourself."

McGarr's head went back, and his eyes searched the pattern of light on the ceiling of the hall. Off in the distance, the claxon of an emergency vehicle was sounding, and the wind was moaning through the eaves of the house.

He thought of how complicated his life had become as a single parent and head of an embattled agency. How in all probability it could not accommodate another and without question a most complete complication—no, the most complete complication possible. And how, finally, turning around would amount to turning his back on the decorum that had regulated his life for more than a quarter century.

He did not allow himself or any of his staff to become involved with principals in investigations. Certainly Kara Kennedy, for all her beauty and openness with him, remained that. A suspect.

And yet McGarr could not keep himself from turning around. As though being drawn by a force that he could not resist, he found his shoulders and head, his body, swinging toward her, all while another and different voice in the back of his mind was counseling, If you're going to do this, do it right. If you're going to love her and keep loving her, love her as well as you're able. No half measures.

She had opened her dressing gown and was holding the plackets out at arm's length to expose her body, which was naked and at once svelte but very womanly. "I want you," she said as he approached her, "because you're a good man." And she virtually leaped into his arms.

AT HER FLAT IN COOLOCK, MORRIGAN switched on the lights. With a phone receiver cradled between neck and shoulder she almost immediately lowered the blinds and switched out the lights. She then waited an exact hour before stepping out again, the large handbag over her shoulder.

After scanning the cul-de-sac, Morrigan stepped into her car and pulled away. Because there were few cars on the road at the late hour, Bresnahan gave the woman a long lead before pulling behind her.

9

MCGARR AWOKE WITH A START. THERE WAS A hand on his shoulder. He turned his head and found Kara standing above him.

"You said you had to get going early. It's half nine."

With a tumult of conflicting thoughts and emotions suddenly welling up in him—that he shouldn't be there for any number of reasons, that he should have been home or at least called home before his daughter went to school, that he should presently be at his desk assembling whatever he would need when he presented the videotape to Jack Sheard, the commissioner, and perhaps even the taoiseach—he glanced at the patch of lowering sky that could be seen between the drapes, and then, with one sweep of his arm, drew her into the bed and on top of him.

An hour later he left for home, activating his cell phone and beeper as he moved through traffic. He had over a dozen messages on each of the devices, and he had only slipped the key in the lock of the front door when it opened.

"Where in the name of God have y' been, man?" Nuala asked as he rushed by her. "The phone has been ringing off the hook with this one and that—the commissioner, that fella Sheard, even the blessed taoiseach's office. Bernie said if you didn't surface by noon he put out an all-points on you. I'd ring him up first."

While he was shaving in the toilet off the bedroom that Noreen and he had shared, Nuala appeared in the open doorway, his clothes of the night before in her hands. "Is there something I should know?"

In the mirror he glanced at her. "The Book of Kells was written on vellum, calfskin, not paper," he said, trying to keep the shaving cream out of his mouth. "But there was a 'facsimile edition,' they call it—alike in every way—that was produced on paper, back in the nineties. It could be a page from that that he burned on the tape."

She shook her head. "No—is there something else I should know?"

McGarr began shaving again. "Like what?"

"Like when you started wearing cologne." She hefted the clothes. "She the one on the teley?"

McGarr lowered the razor and stared down into the basin, feeling with all the greater force what he had been stuffing down all morning long—empty, vacuous, devoid of himself, the person he'd abandoned on the night before. But also he felt wonderful, as though he had put aside a great burden. He knew, of course, what it was.

With Kara Kennedy he had moved on, as Nuala herself had been urging him, from Noreen. And it was the guilt he was feeling at having abandoned her that was making him feel so miserable. And in need of a drink.

"She's beautiful, all right, and brilliant, it's said. But next time, tell us. Maddie couldn't take her breakfast, she was so worried."

Turning his face, he applied the razor to the unshaven cheek. In spite of lacking sleep, he looked as well as he had in ages, he judged—clear of eye, steady of hand; there was even a flush in his cheeks. "Said by whom?"

Given her age, Nuala spent much of the day on the telephone or at lunch, and for whole decades Fitz and she had been connected to the very highest circles of Irish government and society.

"The papers, of course. The teley. That Pape bloke brushed right by them without a word. Anyhow, she's much more telegenic."

"What about *Ath Cliath*?"

"Wouldn't you know they're onto their 'extra' editions again, calling it a national crisis that's sure to bring the government down. Given the New Druids gang of thugs being behind it and Kehoe having foolishly brought Celtic United, their upstart party, into the government after the last election."

Having no option but to step down, lacking a majority in the Dail.

"Where'd they get that?"

"Sources, wouldn't you know."

"All by Orla Bannon, I imagine."

"She the pretty little one with the sloe eyes and pukka smile?"

McGarr nodded.

"The very one. They have her picture on the front page, bragging about her 'scoop,' which, if true, sure it is." She waited for McGarr to respond.

He finished the cheek before saying, "Well, you saw the tape yourself."

She tilted her graying head, and her eyes, which were becoming agatized with age, moved to the window. "But later I thought— wouldn't it be a right fiddle to put together that tape, get a whopping big ransom, and blame those poor fools in North Dublin for the entire scam?"

Washing off the excess shaving cream, McGarr reached for a towel and moved out into the bedroom. "When you watch the tape again, look closely at the medallion-like things on the wall."

In his closet he reached for a suit, shirt, and tie. Then he retrieved socks, underwear, and shoes, placing all on the bed.

"Well, go on. You can tell me. Me eyes aren't what they once were."

"They're skulls, human heads. Nailed through the forehead to the wall with spikes maybe eighteen inches long."

"Jaysus, Mary, and Joseph—you don't say."

"But I do. Now, d'you suspect they'd wrussle up human heads just for a fiddle?"

Closing the door, he heard her talking to herself as she moved down the stairs. "The enormity of it, the obscenity. I wonder if Grainne is at home at this hour."

DRIVING INTO DUBLIN, McGARR BEGAN sifting through his phone messages, more than half of which were from Jack Sheard.

Beginning with a friendly bureaucratic mumble—"Peter, Jack Sheard here. We should communicate some time tonight to make sure our pins are in place. At your convenience, of course"—to "Where in hell are you, McGarr? You're making a balls of this thing. What in Christ's name was that second fiasco out at CU headquarters? You're to keep a low profile, do you hear me? This is a Code Four investigation, and the bloody taoiseach wants you . . . us to report to his office in the Dail immediately."

Which was pronounced "eee-mee-jit-ly," as, McGarr supposed, Sheard had been taught at Trinity. McGarr had no idea what Code Four meant, but it sounded serious, like something out of the movies.

He checked the time of the call, which had come in only twenty or so minutes earlier. Ringing up his headquarters at Dublin Castle, McGarr asked Swords to phone Sheard and say he was going directly to Taoiseach Kehoe's office.

"The man has been roaring at me all morning. Says he's filing papers to have my job."

"Not to worry—I'll take care of that. Any luck on the whereabouts of"—McGarr had to pause to remember the names—"Mide, Morrigan, or Ray-Boy?"

"No, but with Sloane's car—the big blue BMW?"

McGarr grunted.

"Bloodstains and threads of clothing were found on the right front bumper and grill."

As though it might have been the car that had bumped off Derek Greene, the Trinity security guard who had died a fortnight before, freeing up Raymond Sloane to walk the rounds. "What about the fella behind the wheel?"

"Kevin Carney by name. Sheet runs to two pages. New Druid enforcer, it's said. Caught somebody's bullet in the back of the head. Large caliber, fired from a rifle."

Which none of McGarr's team had been carrying.

"Speculation is—there was a sniper somewhere abouts. The only other thing we have is Sloane's widow and two daughters, who went straight to the Bank of Ireland on College Green this morning. They were there when the doors opened. We're trying to run down why."

"I gave Bernie a videotape last night. Tell him he can take it over to the Tech Squad lab and wait for the results. He's to call me the moment they come in." McGarr rang off and moved through the rest of his calls.

A message from Ward said, "Pape's house on the Morehampton Road is mortgaged to the eaves. His credit is stretched with maxed-out cards and zero sums in bank accounts with formerly sizable balances.

"Travels extensively—Turkey, Malta, Thailand, and Myanmar recently. Likes women, the younger the better. He was arrested in Malta in 1969 for hashish possession. Four years ago, something in Spain. Ten years earlier it was LSD at Heathrow. Some more drug possessions, then only traffic offenses.

"Nothing unusual on the Kennedy woman that we could find. Yet. But it's not as if she floated up the Liffey in a bubble."

Pulling into the security checkpoint at Leinster House, the imposing Georgian-inspired buildings that were the seat of the Irish government, McGarr wondered if the Trevor Pape whom he had attempted to interview on the night before could possibly be capable of the theft of the books and Sloane's murder.

Drugs, he knew, sometimes caused otherwise sane and intelligent people to attempt foolish things, but Pape had seemed too . . . scattered both at Trinity and later for the complexity of the theft. And even if tall, he was a slight man, surely not the hulking, black-hooded figure in the video.

Nor could Kara be involved, McGarr was convinced. She was just too much the committed academic and too altogether . . . fragile for anything like that.

Everything pointed all too obviously to the New Druids and Celtic United. Yet Sloane's car might have been responsible for the death of Derek Greene, the Trinity security guard—whose corpse was now headless.

Finally, there was Sweeney, who claimed to be merely the messenger of the videotape. But who said he had watched it. And Sweeney was another animal altogether, McGarr knew all too well.

Why would the New Druids have chosen Chazz Sweeney, an avowed member of the archconservative Catholic sect, Opus Dei, to be their messenger? If indeed they had made the video. To ride herd on the police and government? To make sure through *Ath Cliath* that a ransom was paid and the sacred books were secured?

A uniformed valet was waiting to take the car. But before McGarr got out, he rang up Ward, who said, "I know what you're going to say, and I agree. Sweeney. Maybe it's just our experience with him, but anything he's involved in . . ." Ward let his voice trail off.

Manpower was the problem. Because of budget cuts, McGarr had only a handful of available staffers to put on the case. He could ask Sheard for help, but at the price of confidentiality. All his own people were rock solid.

"How could we follow Sweeney and not be known to be following him?" McGarr asked.

"I have an idea."

"Discreet, I hope."

"That, and electronic too."

They did not need any further publicity, especially involving Sweeney with the forum of *Ath Cliath* at his disposal.

"Hear from Ruthie?"

"She said the woman—" Ward responded before being cut off.

"Morrigan."

"Spent the night at the second address near the North Wall."

"She going in?"

"Last night the place was locked tight, and it has alarms everywhere. This morning, when the building opened to let in the employees on the first two floors, they posted a guard on the door."

"They?"

"The New Druids. See the papers?"

"Not yet."

"Don't." Ward rang off.

BUT ALL THREE NEWSPAPERS WERE LAID OUT on a table in the anteroom of the taoiseach's office. Whoever had taken the picture of Kevin Carney, the driver of the wrecked and shot-up BMW, spilling from the car had sold the roll of film to Reuters, who had in turn shopped it to all three of the morning papers.

Ath Cliath's banner headline said COP-OUTING, below which was

MCGARR AMOK. Two paragraphs of story said McGarr had begun a "spree of violence not witnessed from a senior Garda officer in decades with a temper tantrum at the home of the victim in the Trinity theft" and then continued on to Glasnevin where "either his staff or two of his disgraced former Garda followers shot and killed the driver of the car, causing a near riot in the Celtic United stronghold."

Orla Bannon's column, "Trinity and CU Deaths Linked," was teased onto the centerfold jump and surrounded by more car photos. Mainly she repeated what McGarr had leaked to her regarding the ransom tape and its supposed New Druid connection with the addition of three CU officials confirming that Raymond "Ray-Boy" Sloane Jr. was a CU adherent.

Stories by other reporters sampled "Celtic United Outrage" from its Dail delegation to the party faithful to rank-and-file stalwarts, who were pictured shaking fists with tattooed and well-muscled arms exposed.

The other papers, while more restrained in their criticism, still ran several photos of both events.

"Proud of yourself?" a low voice asked through a chuckle quite close to McGarr's ear. "You're one of a kind, really. Little wonder you never called in—off beating the piss out of the press and shooting up a neighborhood. You should read the *Times*. Could it be they're right and you didn't remain long enough at the scene to find out if your victim was dead?"

Sheard would not be speaking in an undertone unless somebody else had entered the room, and in turning he stiffened an elbow and brushed by him. "Ah, Jack—I didn't know you were there." McGarr moved toward the taoiseach, who was standing in back of the commissioner. "The other is me good ear."

"Peter." The commissioner—a former politician by the name of Sean O'Rourke—only nodded, but Brendan Kehoe, the taoiseach, stepped around him to offer his hand.

"Good to see you again, Chief Superintendent. I understand you've been busy since the event. Does all of that"—Kehoe swept his hand at the newspaper on the table—"mean you're making progress?"

"Perhaps." Taking the Kehoe's hand, he made sure their eyes met. "You're to judge. It could be we have a ransom demand." From his jacket he took out a copy of the videotape.

"What?" Chuckling, Sheard's smile lit up his handsome face, apart from his eyes, which were icy and focused on McGarr. Otherwise tanned, the knob of flesh on his square jaw—formed by the smile—was nearly the color of his blond hair. "You're unique, McGarr. Full of"—there was a pause—"surprises."

"Is there a tape player about?"

"Did they send you a video?" Sheard asked. "Kind of them and right up to the moment. Curious, I didn't get one."

"Perhaps they thought you too busy cutting your own footage."

"This way." Kehoe led them out of the anteroom and down a hall to a wing of the building that was obviously used for communications. "Could you leave us, please?" he said to two young men who were huddled over a newspaper.

Eyes moving from Sheard to McGarr and the tape in his hands, they complied. O'Rourke closed the door behind them.

"Before this goes any further, I wonder if Peter could bring us up to speed on his investigation." Sheard's smile was still broad. "As I mentioned earlier, we seemed to be suffering from a communications glitch."

"I think we should watch this first, Jack. Then, if you have questions . . ." McGarr shoved the tape into the receptacle of the player and hit the play button, adding, "The intro is a bit much, but the message is clear."

Once the music came on, he leaned back against a desk and slipped his hands in his jacket pockets, reminding himself that Sheard had the ear of Kehoe and was certain to have filled it with every doubt before McGarr's arrival. And then there were the newspapers.

"Can you tell us how we know this is genuine?" Sheard asked before the film had ended. But Kehoe shot him a glance, and McGarr waited until the picture had faded out.

The three men glanced up at him.

"Credibility?" he asked Kehoe, who nodded. "Well, there's the delivery the very day—or at least the night after the day—of the theft and murder in Trinity. I don't know how long it would take to produce such a thing, but it has the look of having been devised rather earlier.

"Second, there's the disguised voice of the figure who makes the demand. It's similar to one of the two scrambled voices on the Trinity library security tape. Presently, the Tech Squad, which has the original, is making a comparison and also analyzing other aspects of the tape, such as the color of the flame from the burning page."

"What?" Sheard began laughing again. "You mean, this isn't the original? Don't you think you should have brought the taoiseach the original? You're a rare brave man, Peter McGarr." And stupid went without saying.

But Kehoe remained impassive.

"Last night I learned that a facsimile edition of the Book of Kells was produced in the early 1990s. In every way, including wormholes, it resembles the original, with the exception of having been printed on paper, not vellum, which is treated calfskin. Spectroscopic analysis might give us an idea of what's being burned.

"And finally"—McGarr spooled back to find the length of videotape that pictured the decorations on the wall behind the hooded figure—"notice the large platelike decorations on the wall behind your man with the book. Were this tape player equipped with an enlarging capability, you'd see that they're actually human heads that have been nailed to the wall with spikes."

"This gets better and better," Sheard said to O'Rourke. "You can't make this stuff up."

"In fact, one of the heads may well be that of Derek Greene, the Trinity security guard who was knocked down and killed by a car in Stephen's Green more than a fortnight ago. His death gave Sloane, who was in league with the thieves before they murdered him, the excuse of walking Greene's beat in Trinity without exposing himself to further scrutiny.

"Yesterday, Greene's family reported that his grave has been disturbed. His corpse has been decapitated, and the head is missing.

"As for the car that killed him, witnesses described it as a large midnight blue BMW with gold wheel covers.

"We believe that the same car, a large midnight blue BMW with gold wheel covers, was parked behind Sloane's house yesterday and was driven away by his son, Raymond. It's also the car with the driver who refused to stop and fired at us in front of CU headquarters on the Glasnevin Road."

"Where the lad was killed?" Sheard asked in an insouciant tone.

"Aye—killed by a rifle bullet. Took off half his head. The slug is presently being examined by ballistics. Or are you ignorant of that as well?"

Sheard's smile fell, his jaw firmed.

"Fired by whom?" Kehoe asked.

McGarr shook his head. "But not any of my people. We fired handguns and a shotgun only.

"The right front headlamp and grill of the car appear to have been damaged in an earlier accident, with remnants of clothing and blood found there as well."

"What about Sloane's son?" It was still Sheard.

"Nowhere to be found. He got away."

"Ah."

McGarr switched off the television and turned to the other men.

"As for the possibility that the tape is a fraud, I'd say it exists. Chazz Sweeney hand-delivered it to me, saying it came to him by motor-bike messenger."

"*The* Chazz Sweeney?" O'Rourke asked.

McGarr tried to smile. "I hope there's not another."

"And he delivered it to you and not Jack?"

McGarr did not reply. The tape ejected automatically, and he tried to hand it to Sheard.

"I'd prefer the original."

"Perhaps you didn't hear me—you have it in the Tech Squad lab." Where it belongs, went unsaid. McGarr was being as petty as Sheard, but it felt good.

"So, Sweeney had this first?" O'Rourke asked. "I'm surprised he didn't run the image of the page from the book being burnt. I can't imagine him finally stumbling over a bit of discretion."

"Don't discount the man." Kehoe reached for the tape. "Sweeney may be a world-class chancer in some matters, but there's his special brand of Catholicism, of which the Book of Kells and the two others are icons."

That had been exhibited in a secular—and formerly Protestant—institution, it occurred to McGarr.

Turning with video in hand, Kehoe moved out of the room and back into the corridor where, at the desk of his receptionist, he asked for a television and video player to be brought into his office immediately.

There he closed the door behind them and asked the others to take seats. From behind his desk, Kehoe said, "Jack and Peter—I won't take up more of your precious time beyond asking you this question. Then I'll let you go on about your important business.

"From a police perspective, what should happen now?"

Sheard began, "Why don't we begin with what should have hap-pened beginning last night when—"

But Kehoe was shaking his head. "I don't think you heard me, Jack. That's water over the weir. What comes next?" He turned to McGarr. "Peter?"

McGarr would have preferred to speak last. "If the objective is to get the books back and also collar the murderers of Greene, Sloane, and the driver of the BMW, then we should tell them we will meet their terms. We should encourage them to come forward and name the place of the exchange.

"Murderers and thieves always make mistakes of one sort or other, and all that money—if it comes to that—will only make them incautious. Sooner rather than later, they'll supply us with some idea of who and where they are."

"But don't we know who they are?" Sheard asked. "I think their identity is plain."

McGarr's eyes met Kehoe's before both looked away. Could Sheard be that gullible?

"Hear me out. I know what you're thinking, which was my first thought as well. It's all too obvious. But look at it this way—who's their audience, who are they playing to? Their electorate and the other unemployed native Irish who feel themselves challenged by technology or have had their neighborhoods changed by immigrants and other outsiders."

Sheard got to his feet and, slipping his hands in his pockets in a way that was characteristic of Kehoe himself, moved toward the window in the large corner office. "I wonder if it matters that they're ever paid. Actually it's probably better for them if the perpetrators of these crimes are caught and killed.

"Like the early IRA, what they're creating are martyrs to be continually revered and waked in ballad and verse. The theft of the Book of Kells is tantamount to the IRA blowing up Wellington's bloody monument on O'Connell Street in 1966 or the hunger strikes of Bobby Sands in 1981. Their leader, this Mide—he was with Sands. This is his generation's thing, and he'll play it to the max, if we let him. His intent is to propel his band of hooligans into a potent cultural/political force in this country. That's the purpose of the preamble to the demand.

"Taoiseach Kehoe"—pivoting, Sheard swung his powerful body around and began moving back toward them, his eyes on the carpet and the high gloss of his black bluchers—"if you don't show the nation this tape and any others this Mide sends us, he will, mark my words. And they'll be shown to the cheers and approbation of every poor punk, thug, and body-pierced rocker in the country, to say nothing of the other young who'll adopt their vestments and stance just to set themselves apart and piss off their parents.

"It's why the tape was given to Sweeney to pass on. This Mide is a sly one, so he is. He knew—he knows—that Charles Stewart Parnell Sweeney, archconservative Catholic and self-avowed patriot, will have copied it and, sooner or later, when this government does not do Mide's bidding, Sweeney will release it to the media.

"McGarr, tell us something." Standing only inches away, Sheard glared down. "What other bloody objective could there possibly be than getting the stolen books back and trying the murderers?"

McGarr glanced at Kehoe. "I'm in the police business, Jack, not the objective business. Could that be a failing?"

"Of course it's a failing. It's even a failing by the book, to mention books. Which has been evident for the past thirty hours."

McGarr struggled to keep himself in the chair. "Nor am I in the book business. I'm not in that either. But were I, which book would that be, Jack?"

"I thought you'd never ask." Sheard stepped away, a kind of joy in his voice. "Why"—he swirled his hands—"the book of standard police practice. The protocols and procedures that police have found essential all over the world. Do you have any idea what standard police practice dictates in this situation, McGarr?"

Kehoe sighed and glanced at the clock on his desk. "Jack—the point."

"You never pay ransoms to kidnappers or terrorists. It only encourages others to do the same. And in this case, it's not as if they're holding human beings.

"Also, we—the government—do not own the Book of Kells, and if we did, where would we get the bloody fortune to splash out on these bloody scuts? Where would it come from? We'd have to go to the Dail, and you would not want to stand for reelection as a politician who voted to splash out fifty million Euros on the New Druids. It's not as though they're the IRA.

"Also, what did they steal? What are they ransoming? The books of Kells, Durrow, and Armagh, which are far too well known. The thieves simply don't have another buyer. If they burn the book page by page, then they burn their only asset. It will diminish in value with every passing day, along with the public's opinion of them.

"Telling them up front that we cannot pay, we will not pay, then communicating with them—speaking, E-mailing, whatever—is the course we should take. Haven't we got science and technology on our side? They? On theirs they've got a failed culture. Eventually under my plan, they'll make a mistake and reveal themselves—who and where they are. And we'll have them.

"Finally, to get back to who owns the books—some might say it's ultimately the Irish people, but in point of fact Trinity College does. I've taken the liberty of inviting Trevor Pape, Trinity's head librarian, to weigh in on the issue this morning." Opening a door to the anteroom, he called out, "Dr. Pape? Could you join us, please?"

Kehoe rose to greet Pape. "This is Commissioner O'Rourke," said Sheard, who had hold of Pape's arm. "And I take it you've met Superintendent McGarr."

From the tweed suit to the earth-toned tie, Pape looked every part the gentleman scholar from out of Trinity's privileged past.

But his skin was pallid, his eyes were bloodshot, and his long graying hair lank. A muscle on the left side of his face was fluttering.

"Perhaps you'd care to sit down," Kehoe said, drawing another chair into the circle.

"No, I won't be staying long. Jack here asked me to stop by." Having resumed his seat, McGarr noticed that Pape had only a few teeth remaining in front, and they were the color of tea. "What is it you wish to know?"

"Why, as we discussed, Trevor—the Kells book, its value to Trinity, and if there might be a buyer."

As Pape parroted what Sheard had said, adding his own opinion of the book—"a gaudy bauble to be ogled by tour buses filled with bloody Americans"—McGarr wondered if Pape would have had the wherewithal, technical expertise, or follow-through to have produced the tape.

Or would anybody throw in with him on such an undertaking? And allow him to live? In the parlance of street Dublin, Pape was flamin' out, his body now obviously succumbing to years of abuse.

"Trinity and the world could surely get by without the Book of Kells," Pape concluded. "Durrow and Armagh are an entirely different matter, and I'm sick—absolutely sick—about their loss. But I suspect the celebrity of Kells will protect them, until the time Jack has the miscreants in hand."

Kehoe stood as Pape left and remained standing after the door had closed. "Any final thoughts, Peter?"

Which had a ring so ominous that McGarr decided to say what he had been holding back. "Even within groups, it's individuals who commit crimes. And the history of prosecuting groups in this country is sorry, to say the least."

Sheard began chuckling. "And you said objectives were not your business. Perhaps someday you'll show us the white paper."

By the time McGarr got to his car, he was seething. He had as much as given his own investigation away. And could Kehoe, as a politician, resist the logic of Sheard's argument? Probably not.

His cell phone was ringing. "Peter?" It was Sheard. "I don't know how to thank you. Know the saying 'To be predictable is to be controllable'? Consider me your biggest fan. I might even accept your calls, after your retirement."

McGarr had only slipped the phone into his jacket when it rang again.

"Peter, it's Kara"—there was a pause—"Kennedy. I just want to tell you how happy you made me last night."

McGarr muttered something.

"I hope to see you again."

McGarr did not know how to reply, or if he should on a cell phone.

"Will I see you again?"

"Yes, of course."

"When? Tonight?"

"I'll have to see. Can I call you?"

"If you promise you will. Will you promise?"

McGarr muttered something else.

"I'll hold you to your word and haunt your favorite place. But, Peter . . ." She paused. "I'm serious. I'd very much like to see you again."

10

"You awake?" Hugh Ward asked into his cell phone from the vantage of a tearoom and coffee bar across Greater Saint Georges Street in the center of the city where *Ath Cliath* had its newsroom and offices.

"Yah. You?" Ruth Bresnahan was still in her battered Opel parked near the building on the North Wall where the woman, Morrigan, had entered, spent the night, and left early in the morning wearing different clothes. "Tired?"

"Of course." Ward was on his maybe sixth cup of strong coffee, although he'd actually stopped counting. "Call home?"

"Everything's fine, but you better too. Lee has everything in hand, but she was full of questions and was obviously worried."

Leah Sigal-Ward was Ward's other common-law wife; the three of them lived together in a large flat above Lee's antique shop with their three children in an arrangement that, while unusual, had many advantages, including day care.

"What about Sweeney?" Bresnahan kept her eyes on the busy scene before her.

"I'm not sure he ever comes out. I'm beginning to believe he's a wraith, an apparition."

It was well known that Chazz Sweeney was a workaholic, if also a probable alcoholic, and that he had renovated the top floor of the *Ath Cliath* into a flat. During his trial for murder more than two years ago, "Sweeney-watchers" had reported that he did not leave the building for whole days.

"What about Peter?"

"I'm waiting for him to call me. Or Sweeney to appear. I'd hazard he's busy enough without chat."

"Me too. Love you."

"Me, you."

"Call Lee." Bresnahan rang off and checked the rearview mirror, before redirecting her attention to the front of the building.

What had struck her most about the thug—who'd obviously been posted as sentry on the door in the building where Mide, she was convinced of it, lived—was the man's inordinate interest in women.

The age or appearance of the women who passed him didn't seem to matter; the young man chatted them up nevertheless.

Before sunup Bresnahan had attached a listening device to the locked door of the building.

"Mornin', mum," she heard him say. "How's the missus this A.M.?" Or, "Them new clappers on your pretty piggies? They're grand, brilliant, like the rest of y'."

Also, "Ah, darlin' girl—feelin' your oats this mornin', I see," to a nubile young thing whose bosoms were cascading as she sprinted toward a bus. And after she had passed, "I'd feel them oats mornin', noon, and night, I would. Take the fookin' frisky right out of you."

Guys, thought Bresnahan. They never had enough, which gave her an idea when, around half nine, the man got tired of having to wield a key to unlock the door every time somebody entered the building. He simply propped it open.

Still, he stopped everybody and either used his phone to call up to what looked like several offices on the second floor of the four-floor structure or glanced at the laminated ID cards that most seemed to possess.

"You need a new pic' on that card, luv. It doesn't do your film-star good looks justice, no it don't." "When, my dear, are y' going to end me suffering and step out for a jar or two?" "Any time your lucky husband isn't lookin' after y', babe—give me a jingle. I'm free." And he actually pulled a card from the back pocket of his ratty jeans. Worse, the woman took it—for a laugh in the office, Bresna-han hoped.

Combing her hair and fixing her face in the rearview mirror, Bresnahan stepped out of the car and removed her full-length down jacket that had kept her warm the night long without having to run the engine.

It was a few minutes after eleven in the morning, and a strong sun made it feel almost hot, a condition that would not last, she knew, once the inshore breeze off Dublin Bay kicked up.

But for the moment, she could safely remove the Bolero-style jacket she was wearing without looking too much like a tart. The blood-red bull-baiting jumper, while fitting her rather ample form snugly, had sleeves, and her black slacks had been cut to allow movement.

Also, Bresnahan did not even have to look to see if the sentry had taken notice of her. She could feel his eyes on her body as she walked toward him, jacket and purse over her right shoulder leav-ing her left breast—the larger of the two—exposed to uninhibited ogling.

Maybe thirty-eight or forty, tops, he'd slicked back his dark hair that curled in long ringlets down his back.

Thin, around six feet but small-boned, he had nevertheless pumped up his pecs and biceps, which were exposed courtesy of a tank top. The requisite rings were in one ear alone, patterned in ever-decreasing sizes and diameters and folded down like a chevron of silver flight feathers.

"How do you, do you, do you do, me luv. Where have you been all of me loife?"

"Fortunately for you, out of earshot. Do I know you? Your familiarity sounds rather . . . well, familiar." She stopped in front of him, plucked a bit of her jumper between thumb and forefinger, and pulled it in and out. "Phew. Hot. I'm in need of a wet."

Raising her wrist, Bresnahan glanced at her watch. "So—it's a bit early but, hey"—she flashed her eyes, which were the color of gray smoke—"why not get a jump on the future?"

Taking a step away from him, as though to cross the street, she stopped and turned only her shoulders so he had a full view of the rest of her. "It's open, I trust."

He had to wrench his eyes off her backside. "What's open?"

"The pub. For the wet." Before he could answer, she tripped across the street and entered the pub, where a barman was washing glasses.

She had just been served a glass of wine when the sentry entered the bar.

"Van-Man," said the bartender in greeting.

"Jimmer."

"What'll yeh have?"

"Whatever the lady is garglin', and put hers on the table too. D'yeh have a name?" he asked Bresnahan.

"Now, that could be a problem." She lifted the glass off the bar and moved toward the lounge, which, she could see, had no windows. "I never wanted a name, and for the moment would you mind if I remained anonymous?"

"Where are you going? I just bought you your drink."

"In here where it's dark and intimate. Drinking in the sunlight is counterproductive."

Noting the women's loo and also the back door, as she feigned losing her way, Bresnahan was pleased to discover that the lounge was a long, dark room. She had only eased herself against the velveteen of a banquette when "Van-Man" appeared, glass in hand.

He shaded his eyes with his hand. "Nameless, gorgeous, flame-haired woman—is your brilliant form anywheres about? Ah, 'dere you are in all of your splendor." He stepped off the distance to her side. "Why can't we sit out front. It's me bloody job to look after the street."

"Because you must choose, Van-Man. Choose between your bloody job and me. Also, come closer while I tell you—I have something to show you."

Van-Man's expression brightened.

"Sit down."

He complied.

"See these?" Reaching down for the waistband of her jumper, Bresnahan pulled it up and exposed her breasts, which were wrapped in a beige, slightly transparent brassiere. "They feel constrained by the device that you see. And I tell you this—today, right now, I'm going into the loo to remove it. Then, if you're very good and have the courage, we'll have another and a more complete showing. Are you game?"

Van-Man could scarcely nod. "You're . . . entrancing."

"And you're da' man, I'm thinking. Maybe you might have something to show me yourself when I return. Now, don't move." With bag and jacket in hand, she moved quickly out of the room, past the toilet and through the bar.

"That was quick," said the barman. "Usually quiff lasts a bit longer with Van."

"Quiff pro quo?" Bresnahan asked, as the door swung to. "I left the condoms in the car."

She had to wait for a clutch of cars to pass before crossing the street. But the door being open without the attendance of Van-Man, she was quickly in the building and up the stairs.

The first floor was an importing firm, with the second split between a paper broker and a solicitor. The third and final floor offered only a single battered door. From her bag, Bresnahan drew out her 9mm Glock and moved up the stairs.

Ear to the door, she listened for a long minute before knocking. There was no response. And again. Nothing. Reaching down, she turned the handle. The door swung open.

The hall was long and dark, and she could hear music playing somewhere off in the shadows. But she had only moved a few cautious feet down the hall when she heard a heavy footfall on the stairs. "Red! You up there? Red!"

Back behind the door, Bresnahan waited, as the door was nudged open.

"Red?" There was a pause. "Mide? Morrigan?"

Bingo. She had hit it. But she would have to do something fast, in case said Mide now appeared from one of the rooms.

The door opened further, and when the shadow of Van-Man's hand appeared on the hall floor, Bresnahan chopped the barrel of the handgun down on his wrist.

A bark of pain echoed down the hall and, as his body crumpled, Bresnahan grabbed up a fistful of curly mane and pulled him forward, her foot kicking out his legs from under him.

Van-Man fell in a piece face-first on a strip of tattered carpet. With a knee to the small of his back, Bresnahan pulled up his right ankle and cuffed it to his uninjured wrist. "Does Mide live here, lad? Is the man himself about?" With Glock in hand, she moved down the hall.

"Fookin' cunt."

"Ah, now—there you have it at last."

The first room was a kitchen with two tall windows that looked out on Dublin Bay, where a tan Guinness tanker was moving down the length of the long granite breakwater. Seeing her, a song sparrow in a cage began a complicated trill. There was a mug on the table along with a barmbrack loaf and a plate of butter. A low blue flame was warming a kettle on the stove. Bresnahan twisted it off.

The next room contained a threadbare couch, a television, and an old wooden stand-up radio from which a commentator was warbling in Irish. Bresnahan switched that off too. "Hello! Is anybody about?"

Somebody—an artist—had painted images and icons on the walls that Bresnahan, whose knowledge of art was admittedly slight, nonetheless recognized as Celtic.

A bedroom came next, with a mussed bed and an equal number of women's clothes in the closet as those for a short man. Farther on was a study with many books on wall shelves, a loud mechanical clock, and more Celtic art, including a glittering golden—could it be real?—torque. If so, it was worth something.

And finally Bresnahan came to the door at the end of the hall, which opened on a long room with chairs, a dais at one end, and— she pushed the door further open—Morrigan and the man she knew was Mide from photos she had seen of him. Morrigan was sitting in a chair staring at the wall where Mide was in two parts.

A long spear or pike had fixed his head to the wall above a table where his body rested. A saber with a bloodied double blade rested where the head had been.

"I told him he'd created a monster, that he'd taken all his Druid bullshit too far. One of these days, some one or other of the young bucks would put into action all his blather about blood succession and war against the church. And it would come to this."

"You found him like this? When you arrived here last night?"

"Yah."

"Why didn't you call the police?"

Only her bloodshot eyes rose to Bresnahan.

"Who killed him?"

She shrugged.

"What about Raymond Sloane Junior—where's he?"

"Ray-Boy is only one of them. There could be any number or all of them who did this. Mide was terrified of returning to prison and was against anything that might land him there. He'd even washed his hands of the drug thing. Given it right up. 'I've little time left,' he'd say to me. 'And I'm not spending any more of it in the drum.' "

"Like talk of lifting the Book of Kells."

"If they had that talk, it wasn't said in front of me. Or mentioned by him."

"But they're behind it."

"I don't know that either, and I'll not have you saying I do. Why would they as much as indict themselves and give their movement a bad name?

"Drugs. It's fookin' drugs. Everything that sucks about this city and culture is drugs. Booze and drugs," Morrigan continued.

"Where's Ray-Boy? Somebody murdered the driver of that car on the Glasnevin Road, shot him with a rifle. I think it was Sloane."

Morrigan's eyes moved from Bresnahan to the saber and then to Mide's head on the wall.

"I'll tell you where I think he could be, if you help me down with Mide's old head. He didn't deserve this, not at all, at all." Tears had welled in her eyes.

"Can't. This is a crime scene."

"Then I can't help you either."

"But you will."

"Why would I?"

"Because Ray-Boy is one of those who would tear your movement apart. Bad enough when that tape gets broadcast." Bresnahan pointed at the videotape on the floor by the woman's feet. "Right or wrong, people will brand you, if only because of the murder of a young lad at your headquarters and the assassination of your founder."

Morrigan stared down at her hands. Then with tears streaming down her face she reached into her purse and pulled out a notepad and pen. "I'm only doing this as retribution. The right bastards who did this thing wouldn't be anything but scuts without him, and look how they paid him back."

She wrote a North Side Dublin address and handed it to Bresnahan. "But you should be warned: Unlike here with only one worthless guard, that place is a fortress. You should go in number."

Out in the hall, Bresnahan stopped beside Van-Man. "Ray-Boy Sloane—know him?"

"How the fook do I know? I'm in fookin' pain."

Reaching down, Bresnahan wrenched up the cuffs, which caused him to cry out.

"Now, perhaps you don't remember the question."

"Course I fookin' know him. Wasn't he supposed to be on watch last night? When I got here this morning, no Ray-Boy, no sign of him."

"Did you come up here?"

"Not unless I'm called."

Bresnahan reached for her cell phone.

McGARR'S STAFF WAS WAITING FOR HIM IN HIS cubicle when he arrived back at his headquarters in Dublin Castle. Sitting on the several document-littered tables or leaning against cabinets, they looked tired, with day-old beards and puffy eyes.

Bernie McKeon—the patch now off his stitched scalp—vacated McGarr's chair. "Sit, oh chief of amok-ing Injuns." He tapped a copy of a tabloid newspaper that had to be *Ath Cliath*. "The smoke signals are not good. Worse, they appear to be genuine."

SPECIAL EDITION

HEADHUNTER CAUGHT

ON RANSOM TAPE

STORY AND COMMENTARY

BY ORLA BANNON

Which capsuled and satirized the earlier part of the tape about Celtic history, legend, and lore, and the supposed disastrous effect of Christianity on Ireland, "all brought to you by the people still practicing the curious Celtic tradition of the taking of heads."

Bannon included verbatim the demand of the black-cloaked figure shown holding the torch to a page.

In another frame, *Ath Cliath* technicians had attempted to enlarge one of the human heads that were impaled on the wall. In a way, the grainy multicolor image was more ghastly because it abstracted the picture and made the blurred features and morbid shape merge.

Bannon included the information that she had discovered about Derek Greene's grave having been disturbed and his corpse decapitated.

"The family is understandably distraught. But the fortnight lead between Greene's murder, the theft that was accomplished with Sloane's collusion, and Sloane's own murder to keep him from grassing demonstrates the thieves' resolve. As well, it illustrates the level of planning and coordination in this cabal.

"Raymond Sloane Jr.—the dead security guard's son—is wanted

for questioning by the police who raided Celtic United headquarters on the Glasnevin Road last night in an effort to find him. Instead, they turned up what they suspect was the car that killed Greene, an action that resulted in the death of Kevin Carney, a CU supporter and alleged New Druid with a lengthy record of drug dealing.

"Earlier, Chief Superintendent McGarr—while in possession of the ransom videotape—interviewed Dr. Kara Kennedy, keeper of old manuscripts at Trinity, questioning her about the authenticity of the page from the Book of Kells that is burned on the tape.

"There is a facsimile edition of the manuscript that is similar in every way but the material on which it is rendered. The original is on vellum (a treated form of calfskin), the facsimile is printed on paper."

"What's she got," McGarr asked, "crystal ball?"

He wondered if she ever slept and had a life beyond her profession. One thing was certain—now that *Ath Cliath* had published photos of the ransom tape, Kehoe would have to deal with it publicly and make some statement about his intentions.

"Excuse me, Chief. What Orla Bannon doesn't—and can't—know is what we've been putting together for the last two days." Swords smoothed out the sheaf of papers in his hand. "I'd like to run it by you, so a few of us can go home for a while."

Leaning back in his chair, McGarr raised his head, twined his fingers around the back of his neck, and considered the cracked plaster of the ceiling covered with at least a century of urban grime. The peeling paint looked like greening lichen on yellow rock and was filled with lead, he'd been told.

Were he Kehoe, he mused, he would pretend to deal—even if he had no intention of dealing—with the thieves. That way, he would buy time and not be seen as doing nothing. Also, a page or pages of the book might be spared.

"First thing is the OxyContin we asked the pathologist to look for in the postmortem exam. Sloane the elder had traces in his system. Tech Squad says it was in the lining of his jacket pockets, and there was a packet of same found in the glove box of the BMW that flipped on the Glasnevin Road.

"Speaking of probable OxyContin, your man Trevor Pape? He's flamin' out, it seems. Comes from a horsey Kildare family that lost everything just as he was entering Trinity."

"When was that?"

"Ah . . . nineteen fifty-six.

"Met a scion of the Guinness family there, married her. Hence the house on the Morehampton Road, the sweet connected life—money, drugs, women—and his post as head librarian that he wouldn't have got without her family, who were at the time helping to support the college in a significant way." Swords rubbed his fingers together.

"But during his affair with Kara Kennedy, Pape's wife left him, saying to one and all at a reception where Pape and the Kennedy woman were also in attendance, 'It's one thing to bed whores, tramps, prostitutes, and the shop girls you pick up in bars, Trevor. But it's quite another thing to prey upon your staff and students.' That or something like it has been corroborated by three sources."

"You missed your calling, Johnny," said McKeon. "*Ath Cliath* could use you." He glanced over at McGarr, who was not smiling and was in something like shock, he guessed. McGarr could feel that his face was red and his heart was beating faster.

Kara with Pape? How could she? Pape was . . . a ruin of a human being, if there ever had been anything to ruin. Little wonder she had been so sympathetic toward and protective of him when McGarr first interviewed her.

"Since the divorce, it's been all downhill for Pape. Money? He's in debt over a hundred grand. Took a second mortgage on the house to pay off the first but has missed two successive monthlies on that.

"The building society has not only served him papers, they've also placed a lien on its contents, which includes supposedly one of the finest private collections of Beaker people pottery in the world and"—Swords glanced up—"a facsimile edition of the Book of Kells valued at thirty thousand."

"Any word on what was being burned on the tape?" McKeon asked.

"None. As for drugs, the man has a history. He was arrested in Malta in 1969 for hashish possession—bricks that filled a locker on a boat he was skippering—but he was bailed out of that by the in-laws.

"Ditto Heathrow in 1974 and Miami in 1981, where he was sentenced to six months in jail reduced to a twenty-eight-day stay in a rehab. Only two years ago he was arrested here in Ireland after a traffic stop for possession of a variety of substances.

"But he was released when, it seems, Jack Sheard stepped in and convinced a judge that Pape, whose addiction was described as a health problem, had had a 'slip,' the court records say, and needed another go at a rehab. 'Being a valued member of society,' he didn't even have to post bail."

Swords turned the page. "Now then, Gillian Reston—the current woman living with Pape? She's only twenty-four but the sheet from the Yard says she's been busted for drugs and blue movies when still a minor, prostitution, and grand larceny. But no convictions on the last two."

Pape, McGarr again thought, shaking his head. Certainly after one night, McGarr had no claim on Kara Kennedy's affections, and as surely she was entitled to a sex life, especially as a single person. But . . .

"Kara Kennedy?" Swords continued.

McGarr turned his head and looked out the window at a lowering sky. He wasn't sure he wanted to hear what Swords and his team had discovered about her.

"We're still pretty much blanked on her. She was born Kara Kennedy at Salen on Mull, went to university in Edinburgh, and on here to Trinity, where she took a Ph.D. studying under"—Swords held the word for a moment—"Pape."

"Which could not have been a good thing," McKeon put in.

It had been a mistake, McGarr decided. But one that he probably could not have helped, even though without question he should have walked away. Because he didn't think of himself as the kind of man who did things like that lightly. In fact, to be honest with himself, he had been smitten by Kara Kennedy—her looks, her touch, who he had thought she was as a person. And now in the fifty-fifth year of his life he felt like a child at sea. Foundering in a tide of emotions.

Truth was, he knew nothing of the etiquette of sex, the bedroom, how to judge the sincerity or the commitment of the other party to the event. Not only had he bedded a suspect, but he had bedded a suspect who had bedded a suspect. And who knew how many others she had bedded, which he also found more than simply disturbing.

"We still have no record of Kara Kennedy having married Dan Stewart or anybody else in Ireland. If she's married, she was married someplace else and has never declared herself to be so here in Ireland. Same thing with taxes. She's never filed in any way as a married person.

"As well, there is no publicly traded Irish oil import firm or private energy broker that will admit to having an employee of Scottish birth or background who was sent to Yemen fifteen months ago, although several, fearing we were running the search for the Americans, refused to respond in any way. A search of travel records also showed no Dan or Daniel Stewart going there, at least nobody declaring they were headed there from Ireland."

Swords turned that page. "Raymond 'Ray-Boy' Sloane Junior is a known member of the New Druids—drugs, strong-arm and protection schemes all his class of thing. Again, arrests and few convictions—did forty days once—and is suspected of running a ring of younger louts like Kevin Carney, the ill-fated driver of the BMW. The bullet that killed him was fired from a thirty-ought-six rifle.

"We visited *Ath Cliath*'s newsroom to see if they had retained the mailer with the videotape." Swords shook his head. "As for tracking the delivery—the volume that hits the front desk there is staggering even in videotapes, with every TV show and movie sending copies for review."

"How, then, did it come to Sweeney's attention?" McGarr asked, if only to appear to be concentrating on what the team had discovered.

"Woman said the messenger said it's for Mr. Chazz Sweeney. He's expecting this and should see it immediately."

"She describe him? The messenger?"

"Tall. Rigged in motorcycle leathers, helmet, tinted visor. You know the type, they're all over Dublin."

"Arseholes all over the road, changing lanes. I saw one the other day go right up on the footpath on O'Connell Street at rush hour," McGarr said.

"Speaking of vehicles"—Sword's looked back down at his notes—"we don't know if Sloane was operating that BMW the night of Derek Greene's death, but the threads of blue material found on the damaged left side match Trinity's security uniform. DNA of the blood is still not in."

Maybe it was how his emotional life would proceed, McGarr continued to muse, again staring up at the ceiling—a succession of brief . . . congruences with no possibility of regaining the permanence and emotional stability, to say nothing of the depth of love and trust, that he had shared with Noreen.

Up until a few minutes ago, he had hoped he would see Kara Kennedy and sleep with her again—the feel of her, her touch, the entire scene that was still at the forefront of his consciousness.

Yet again, he reminded himself—at least on an intellectual level—that she could no more change her past with other men than he could his own with Noreen and the other women he had known before his marriage. Without question, therefore, he was being juvenile and unfair, but he could not help the feeling.

"So, to recap—we've got Derek Greene bumped off by either Raymond or Ray-Boy Sloane, so the elder could have a credible alibi for walking Greene's beat. What Sloane couldn't have known is that his accomplices had planned to kill him.

"We've also got Ray-Boy suspected of leaving his mother's house in the BMW, fomenting the dustup with the press, and then running from us at CU headquarters, with the result being Kevin Carney's death from a bullet fired by somebody who wanted to make us look like killers.

"There's Trevor Pape, who is—"

"A disgusting piece of work," said McGarr, and the entire staff turned their eyes to him. Never, not once, had they heard him pass a judgment like that during a staff meeting.

"And also a probable bad man," Swords went on blithely, burying his eyes in his report. "Apart from age, his present consort is little different. He—they—need money quickly, and he's reputed to own a facsimile copy of the book that he claims to despise.

"And finally, there's Kara Kennedy."

"Our mystery woman," said one of the others.

"With her mystery husband, his mysterious disappearance, and her not-so-mysterious affair with Pape."

"I believe we've"—McKeon rolled his eyes—"covered her."

Swords pincered his temples in feigned distress. "Did I leave anybody out?"

"Sweeney," McKeon said. "Who is a—"

"Surd," McGarr supplied, just as his beeper and cell phone sounded simultaneously.

NEARLY AN HOUR EARLIER, HUGH WARD WAS out of the car stretching his legs when the gray Rolls pulled up in front of the *Ath Cliath* newsroom building and Chazz Sweeney, moving from the shadows of the doorway, got in, accompanied by a tall man with snubbed features, a tanned complexion, and curly, graying blondish hair. Because of the tinted windows, Ward could not see the driver.

With his back to the street, Ward allowed the car to pass before moving without haste to his Audi, which was parked down an alley about a block distant. After all, he had placed disk transmitters up under the bumpers of the three cars that Sweeney used. And Dublin traffic was . . . well, Dublin traffic.

Switching on the electronic scanner that monitored the Rolls's progress on a grid map, Ward followed the large car as it made its way out of the city along Dublin Bay past Blackrock into Dun Laoghaire.

Several times the Rolls had pulled over—in Booterstown, on Seaport Avenue in Monkstown—and when the car cut southwest and stopped on Station Road in Dun Laoghaire across from the Dublin Area Rapid Transit station, it occurred to Ward what was happening.

The Rolls was following the train, and all other stops had been near DART stations, as though—it also dawned on him—Sweeney himself did not know or was being directed where to stop.

Could it be—if Sweeney were to be believed about the delivery of the first tape—that a second was coming in? After all, Sweeney was nothing if not reclusive, Ward knew, having trailed him off and on for the more than two years since the debacle that had resulted in the deaths of Noreen and Fitz and his and Bresnahan's being sacked from the Garda. It made Sweeney's peremptory evacuation of his *Ath Cliath* office unusual indeed.

When the rear door of the Rolls opened, the other man and Sweeney got out. Sweeney held a cell phone to his ear.

Which was when Ward called McGarr.

"I'll be right there," said McGarr. "Remember—it's not Sweeney we're after here, it's the messenger—who he is, where he returns to. And we'll be there soon to give you an official presence."

"I'm not sure you'll have the chance."

In his own shambling way, Sweeney was walking quickly toward the station, heedless of the stream of others who had just got off an outbound train. He brushed into an elderly man; a woman turned and said something to him.

But hand to ear, with his signature rumpled mac billowing out behind him, Sweeney just kept walking, the other man in his wake.

"He alone?"

Fitting on an unobtrusive headset so his hands would be free, Ward got out of his car and moved toward the station. "No, he's with somebody I've not seen before. Tallish, late thirties or early forties. Light curly hair going gray. Fit and quick on his feet."

Ward heard McGarr mumble something. Then, "Adrian Bailey?" Who was an editor at *Ath Cliath*, Ward remembered.

But Sweeney had nearly reached the platform, and hearing the approach of a train, Ward broke into a run.

With an alarm ringing, red warning lights had begun to flash and the street gate was descending.

"We've got one coming in now."

"Which direction?"

"From the south, headed into the city."

As Ward vaulted the stairs two at a time, he heard McGarr issuing further orders. "The driver of the train . . . phone. Close the doors, keep them closed. And keep coming right into town."

Which Ward now realized would be impossible.

"The engineer, the driver, the . . ." was not the driver at all, but a New Druid lout with his head out the window, his braided hair flying in the breeze, a wide gap-toothed smile on his ring-spangled face. But his eyes were muddy, his nose red, and he looked drunk or drugged.

As the train slowed, he shouted, "Ye're a fookin' bloody cunt, Sweeney. But a useful cunt." Ducking back into the compartment, he swiped his arm and scaled a railway man's cap out the window that skidded across the platform and came to rest at Ward's feet.

Which was when Sweeney recognized him and lowered the phone, saying, "Stu!"

Sweeney's companion followed his gaze, then turned on heel and began making his way toward the stairs.

The train did not stop. Instead, it began picking up speed again.

Some in the crowd on the platform shouted; a boy kicked out at a door and was spun off his feet.

"That's mine," said Sweeney, stooping.

But Ward snatched it up. Fixed inside was a videotape.

The gun that Sweeney pulled out of his pocket was something like a derringer—small, snub-nosed, with two over-and-under barrels. "Give me that."

"The train didn't stop," Ward said into the mouthpiece of his cell phone. "The videotape was inside a cap that the yoke who hijacked the train tossed out the window. I've got Sweeney pointing a gun at me. He has another man with him. His Rolls is parked on Station Road, Dun Laoghaire."

"McGarr!" Sweeney roared, slipping the weapon back into his mac. "I must have a copy of this tape. They rang me up and—risking life and limb—I came out here for it."

"Meet me at Pape's with the tape," McGarr said to Ward.

Pulling the videocassette free from the liner, Ward offered the hat to Sweeney. "At least you won't go home empty-handed."

"I would have fancied you'd had enough of me."

Ward only hoped that day would come.

1 1

THE POLICE PRESENCE AT TREVOR PAPE'S house was already significant by the time McGarr and several of his staff arrived. With a signal difference: The police cars, all eight of them, were parked at some distance from the old Edwardian manse, so as not to alert the neighbors, McGarr suspected.

Directing McKeon to pull right into the long drive in front of the house, he ordered one group to search Pape's Jaguar and the grounds with McKeon and Swords accompanying him into the mansion.

They found Pape exactly where McGarr had left him the night before. But he was a far different man from then, and different from the tweedy don who had appeared in Kehoe's office earlier in the day. Dressed in a black suit that looked as though it were made of silk, he had had his hair cut, pomaded—it appeared—and combed back. His shirt was pearl gray, his tie silver.

On the wrist of his left hand was a fashionable gold watch with a black dial. His shoes were Italian, his cologne French, but his eyes—McGarr had seen eyes like that before—were Colombian.

"I have here a court order to search your house." McGarr tore off Pape's copy and offered it to him. When the man made no move to take it, McGarr dropped the document in his lap.

From in the hall, he could hear Sheard saying, "He's here. Yes. What we discussed—you should speak to him yourself, then."

"Are you witness to his refusal?" McGarr asked McKeon and Swords. "Then proceed with the search." As they left the room, they heard Sheard ask, "What exactly do you think you're about here?"

"Think? We don't think shit, Jack," said McKeon. "Or do I have the syntax wrong?"

McGarr stepped into Pape's line of sight. "Mr. Pape—I understand you own a facsimile copy of the Book of Kells."

"It's Dr. Pape. Doctor, my man." Pape's eyes were agatized—two blue impenetrable bluish orbs with only a hint of pupil.

"Do you own such a thing?"

"The last time I looked."

Out in the hall, Sheard called out, "McGarr. McGarr!"

"Where is it?"

The hand came up from his crossed knees and flapped in the direction of the bookshelves. "It's somewhere about, I should imagine."

"Somewhere—where?" McGarr demanded, taking a step in on him.

Pape's reaction was delayed. "Please don't be so demonstrative. I find it oppressive."

Which touched off McGarr's simmering anger. Reaching down, he snatched up a fistful of Pape's gray shirt. "You sorry piece of posturing and predatory work. Let me tell you what's going on here—when I find your stash, which is inevitable, I'm going to haul your sorry ancient arse in for questioning, and we'll see how you'll define 'somewhere' on day three.

"I'll ask you only once more—where's the book?"

"Jack!" Pape called out. "He's in here, and he's threatening me."

His opaque eyes met McGarr's defiantly. "Now, would you take your bloody proletarian paw off me, Inspector?"

Sheard appeared in the doorway, and McGarr shoved Pape back into the chair.

"McGarr—the commissioner is on the phone."

Stepping past the bookshelves where, he knew, a book worth 30,000 quid would not be stored by a librarian, McGarr brushed past Sheard, who was holding out his cell phone. "He knows my number," McGarr said. "I have work here."

"That may be in some doubt. You should speak with him."

Nearly two hours later, McGarr found the facsimile edition with several dozen other books in a safe in a closet underneath the main staircase. As far as he could tell, it looked as though two pages had recently been removed with a razor and a straightedge, the cut having slightly penetrated to the page behind.

Which was when his cell phone rang.

"Peter? It's Commissioner O'Rourke."

McGarr waited.

"Are you there?"

McGarr still said nothing.

"Taoiseach Kehoe has asked me to take you off the inquiry immediately and for you to turn over any and all reports and evidence to Jack Sheard. I'm placing you on administrative leave of absence, pending the outcome of an inquiry into the incident on the Glasnevin Road."

McGarr was tempted to say, You know as well as I what happened there. Instead, he pressed his palm into the keypad, so that the phone gave off a multitonal bleep. Then he said, "There's something wrong with this connection, Commissioner. I hope you're still there. Did you say Taoiseach Kehoe would like to speak with me? He could do that directly at this number. I hope you're still there. I might try to get back to you soon, if I have time."

"You're a cowboy, McGarr. And I'll have you up on charges" was the last thing he heard before ringing off.

Some time later, Swords appeared by his side with something that looked like the drain of a sink in the palm of one hand and holding a black garment in the other.

"Where's Pape?" McGarr asked.

"He left with Sheard and his gang maybe an hour ago."

It was only then that McGarr remembered Maddie.

MAYBE IT WAS THE SMELL OF CHOCOLATE THAT pervaded the neighborhood in Coolock near the address Morrigan had given her. But Ruth Bresnahan was hungry—ravenous, in fact—and tired too.

And the problem was, whenever she got hungry these days, she got angry as well. When what was called for at the moment was a level head, Ward reminded her. He was sitting beside her in the old battered Opel, staking out the warehouse from the parking lot of the Cadbury chocolate factory, where dozens of cars were gathered.

Ward had just got off the phone with McGarr, who had brought him up to speed on the developments at Pape's house. And where McGarr now believed he stood with the Garda.

The car radio had been covering little else than the story of Kehoe's having appeared on television to show portions of the ransom tape and to announce that he had no intention of dealing with their demand.

"It is an outrage that they have absconded with several of Ireland's national treasures and murdered at least two persons that we know of so far. We are bending every effort to apprehend them and retrieve the books.

"But we cannot and will not legitimize crime by submitting to their demand. It would only encourage further brigandry," Kehoe had said, appropriating a term that Bresnahan had last heard from her aged grandmother before her death years ago.

It was only as a kind of afterthought that Garda spokesman Sheard disclosed that McGarr had been relieved of his command and placed on an administrative leave of absence.

A commentator then came on to say that in his opinion Kehoe "politically or morally" had no other choice but to refuse to negotiate with proven murderers or to pay them a dime when, "after all—and let us remember—it is not as if they are ransoming a person. These are books, albeit important books. But even were it a person, paying them would not be the correct step."

Bresnahan switched off the radio. "It's distracting, is what it is. Like the smell of that bloody chocolate."

The Cadbury chocolate factory, which stood on the corner of the street, virtually shielded the old warehouse from view. There was one alley in, a brace of seven roll-up bay doors on a loading dock, a windowless door with a double lock, and not a window in sight.

"And it's fecking illegal, them being in there," she hissed. "What if there were a fire, what then? How would they get out?"

"Probably open those big bay doors. But would we want them to?" Ward asked.

"Yes, certainly—until we find the Book of Kells and gather enough evidence to get Peter off the hook. It's plain what Kehoe and Sheard are about. With the bloody tape showing a supposed New Druid making the demand and then the bungling—no, my bungling—of the bust in Glasnevin, they'll blame him for anything else that goes wrong and martyr him to Kehoe's continuance in office and Sheard's ambition.

"Nothing short of retrieving the books and collaring Ray-Boy—or whoever is masterminding this thing—will do."

"But why choose Peter? What did he ever do to Kehoe or Sheard?" mused Ward.

"Which is the curious part. Now, Sweeney doing this I'd understand. But Kehoe and Sheard? I guess Peter was—is—just handy. And he had the bad sense to bring us two arrogantly sinful, disgraced, and failed cops in on what proved to be a debacle. Wait until that gets out. We were just what they needed."

"How do you figure that?"

"Because before my cock-up, it was a no-win situation for Kehoe. He would have been damned philosophically if he dealt with them, double-damned fiscally if he splashed out fifty million of public money for something actually owned by a private institution.

"And, on the other hand, damned at least as much if his government failed to find the thieves and allowed the most revered single item of early Irish Christendom to be burned in public by a defiant and lawless group of thugs and louts."

Ward could see the sense in that. But there was something they were still missing; he was sure of it. He glanced back out the windscreen at the warehouse.

"I want to get in there right now and bust the fuckers," Bresnahan hissed.

Ward's hand came down on her thigh with a friendly smack. "Down, girl. You know how these things go. We have to be patient and wait on the situation. If somebody's in there—Ray-Boy or some others of his tribe, they've got to come out sooner or later."

Bresnahan glanced down at his hand, which had inched up her thigh from the contact point. In a heartbeat, literally, she fantasized how the next few minutes would unfold. "You know something I don't."

"Could be. I bet . . . I bet"—the hand moved up while the other pointed toward the windscreen—"there's a skylight or a series of skylights or even a glass roof in that structure."

Bresnahan scarcely heard him. She was concentrating on something entirely different—his hand on her thigh. It was like a pleasurable manacle that had suddenly been clamped onto a most sensitive area of her overly sensitive—she had often thought—body.

"Remember, it was put up when electricity was even more exorbitant in this country than it is today. The owner wouldn't have wanted the expense of rows and rows of lights constantly on."

Being easy with men had never been her way, not even with Ward. She made them work for her affections. But releasing herself to his touch, abandoning herself to the love she felt for him—a love she could and would die for—well, that was something she both could not help and would not attempt to quell.

And what if, perchance, for some inscrutable masculine reason he decided suddenly never to touch her like that again—which happened, as some of her women friends had confided to her about their husbands and lovers. Ruth Bresnahan could not conceive of the absence of his hand on her thigh. It was as simple and as tragic as that.

Bresnahan studied Ward's dark features, which were so regular and proportionate—to her taste, handsome—that at times it took her breath away.

"If we could get to the top of that roof, we might be able to look down upon them. And if your woman, Morrigan, is right and they're there, we'll place the call to Peter. Point is—the place might be hard to get into, but it will also be hard to get out of."

She again considered his hand, which was still on her thigh. "I hope you don't expect me to climb up there." Having been raised on a farm in Kerry that was bounded on the west by a tall sea cliff, she knew her mother's constant admonitions about avoiding the undercut brink would be with her for the rest of her life.

"Only if you want a slice of the glory." The hand moved farther up her thigh.

"And you've planned it out, this move?"

"To a fare-thee-well. You hold your hand like this"—Ward

twined the fingers of one hand through the other—"I put my foot on them, and you boost me up. I even think I might know where the office is located."

The hand fell back on her thigh. "And my plan for what we can do in the meantime—you haven't asked me about that. It's much more readily achievable." Now the hand was moving over the material about as far up her thigh as it could go.

"Out with it."

Ward made sure their eyes met. "When was the last time we made this old car rock?"

Taking hold of his wrist, she moved it away.

From out of his pocket, Ward drew a Cadbury nut bar—dark Swiss chocolate with hazelnut-and-nougat centers.

"Where'd you get that?" She tried to snatch the bar out of his hand, but he was too fast for her. "You bastard, give it me."

Pinching and gouging did not work either. A former international boxing champ, Ward easily parried her jabs. "Do we have a deal?"

Sighing, Bresnahan rested her back against the seat. At least he was still that interested in her after—how long had it been?—at least six years, counting the period he had moved in with Lee, his other "wife."

She lowered her eyes to his lips. "Chocolate, I'm told, can be used as a lubricant. That way one of us can keep watching."

"What about the nuts?"

"You should be worried more about me teeth."

The chocolate bar alighted in her lap.

"WELL, YOU'RE ON TELEVISION FOR A SECOND day in a row," Maddie announced getting into the car. "Only Aisling's father can top that."

He was the anchor of a popular television show.

"Granted, it was a still shot, but there you were, gun in hand, looking down at somebody hanging out of a car and obviously dead.

"And one other thing nobody else's pa will ever equal on TV—getting sacked on the teley. Does administrative leave mean we can go on a long holiday someplace far, far away?

"Not to worry, I won't bawl today. I'm getting rather used to all of this."

"It doesn't mean a thing."

"Then it isn't true." The sarcastic tone was gone, and he could tell she wanted it not to be true.

"No, it's probably true. But it doesn't mean a thing."

"Probably? They haven't spoken to you directly?"

"They've tried, but I switched off my phone."

"So you wouldn't hear the bad news that you've, like, been put out to pasture. And that's why it doesn't mean a thing?"

McGarr could feel his anger mounting, not at Maddie or her tone, which ultimately was one of childish concern, but at those three political scuts who, by choosing the most politically expedient and, in Sheard's case, advantageous tack, would condone a spate of murders and grand—no, the grandest—theft.

To say nothing of making McGarr himself, who was actually working on the case and not just the media, a very public scapegoat in a way that had already disturbed his daughter and destroyed his reputation.

People wouldn't remember any of the arrests he had made year after year; they would remember the photo of him gun in hand with the dead driver dangling out of the smashed car.

"It means that they might think they're putting me on the shelf for a while, but they haven't. And then—" McGarr had to brake for a traffic signal, and he glanced over at her: the retroussé nose and protrusive upper lip, her long ringlets of copper-colored curls. "Maybe it's time for me to pack it in anyhow."

Her eyes widened in alarm. "What? You're a policeman, a detective. It's what you are, what you'll always be. And what would you do with yourself otherwise?"

McGarr shrugged. "Dunno. Maybe join Hugh and Ruthie. Or set up my own shop—special investigations, that class of thing."

Maddie shook her head and looked out the window at the Victorian row houses they were passing.

After a while McGarr said, "All the changes, all the uncertainty in our lives must be hard on you."

"It's not me I'm thinking of, Peter." Now he could see tears in her eyes, but she did not cry.

At home, she went straight to her room. Nuala made eye contact with McGarr before following her there.

Failure. He was now living with it in virtually every aspect of his life: on the job; with Kara Kennedy, who he suspected had too much "history" for him, even the little he knew; and now here with the one person whom he loved more than anyone in the world and whom he could not let down.

But he was doing just that, wasn't he? Even now, before any official inquiry, his own personal history had become a burden for her.

In his den, he slipped the second tape into the video player and leaned back against the edge of his desk. Again, music with a Celtic flair preceded the appearance of the cloaked figure.

McGarr paused the tape and studied the room with its lime green chipped paint and probable human heads on the wall, while trying to remember the rooms he had searched in Pape's house. None was green, but he had remained on the first floor; McKeon and Swords had conducted the rest of the search, which had turned up the voice-scrambling device and the cloak.

The figure appeared to be a large man with wide shoulders and a heavy body. While tall with definite shoulders, Pape was gaunt, although he might easily have worn a jacket beneath the capacious garment. He pressed the play button.

As the music faded out, the figure held up what appeared to be another illustrated page from the Kells book. "Tape two, page two. It will be burned if, by tomorrow, you haven't assembled the fifty million in bearer bonds and delivered it to the drop that will be sent you through the usual source. Have a helicopter ready.

"You'll have two hours to deliver it. If you fail, the drill will continue, only we'll begin burning a page an hour, as documented so." Holding up the sleeve of a videocassette, he began his deep, rumbling, and fractured laugh, until it faded out along with his image.

McGarr wondered if Pape's voice, which, while deep, could be made to carry the Vaderesque timber of the voice on the tape. And where were the horrific heads, to say nothing of the level of planning and coordination seen thus far?

In McGarr's experience, druggies and drunks did not possess or could not summon the clarity to carry off detailed crimes. But then, of course, there was the example of Sweeney, who was an epic toper.

Sweeney. Why Sweeney? How had he become involved in all of this? Because of *Ath Cliath*, where the New Druids or whoever was behind the theft were sure to find a forum for their videotapes, regardless of what the government chose to do?

McGarr rewound the tape, made three copies, and debated what to do—send a copy of the tape which, with all other information about the investigation, would sooner or later be sent to Sheard and O'Rourke?

After all, in tomorrow's paper Sweeney was sure to make public the existence of the second tape, and McGarr did not want to appear any more dilatory than he already was.

Picking up the phone, he rang up Swords and asked him to send somebody round to pick up a copy of the tape.

"What about the file of the investigation so far? Sheard called; he wants that too. 'Eee-me-jit-ly.' "

"Before you do, make copies of everything and store them in a secure place."

"And you?"

"I've got Hughie and Ruth helping me. And, sure, don't we have a few leads?"

"More than Hughie and Ruth," Swords said. "You know that. We're here for you."

McGarr did, but he would not allow himself to jeopardize any of their jobs. Feeling even more the failure, he rang off.

IT WAS DARK BY THE TIME McGARR ARRIVED at Kara Kennedy's flat in Rathmines. But there were lights in her windows.

Again not finding a parking space, he drove his Mini-Cooper up on the footpath and lowered the visor with a police shield attached to the reverse side.

Pulling himself out of the low car, he felt ancient, battered, and old, and fully not up to the task at hand, which would be to distance himself from perhaps the most profoundly moving personal experience since the death of his wife.

He had been so vulnerable that he had found Kara Kennedy entrancing, and her attentions had felt to him like a revelation, ushering in a spate of complex emotions, including the possibility that he still might be able to have an emotional life beyond his duties as father to Maddie and devoted son-in-law to Nuala.

But, of course, her attentions had been practiced, he told himself

as he arrived at the gate and reached for the latch. And—could
it be?—he was too shallow a human being to get beyond that. Or
too immature in the ways of sex. He did not climb into a woman's
bed lightly, although, it appeared, she had accepted those who had.
Like Pape.

But he had only closed the gate and turned around when Orla
Bannon stepped in front of him. "Where the fook have yeh been,
McGarr? I've been waiting for ye now for a month of Sundays.
Whatever happened between Pape's and here? I hope you're not
drinking on duty."

She was dressed in a leather bomber jacket and designer sunglasses even now in the darkness—her long braided pigtail wrapped
around her neck like a scarf, a cigarette poised by her lips.

"You saw me leave Pape's?"

She nodded.

"Then you saw Pape leave as well?"

"I did. Sheard took him off. I figured for the drugs he probably
dug up there. My take on it all? Sheard will use Pape as a backup
patsy in case New Druid factionalism and your continuing war on
them doesn't pan out. Rumor has it Mide was murdered, decapitated, and your woman Rut'ie was the one who discovered the body.
Apart from Morrigan, of course.

"Care to comment on that?" Flicking the cigarette into the yard,
she pulled off her sunglasses and stepped in on him. "Where'd you
spend last night?" She jerked her head to mean upstairs. "Good for
you. But, you know, as I said—you could do better."

McGarr looked down into her upturned face with its pixieish
features and jet eyes. "Where do you get all of this?"

"Ah, thanks. You've just given me me column for tomorrow."

"Why would Sheard need a backup patsy?"

"Because your mate and goombah Sheard isn't really investigating the matter. He's got his blokes poring through tax records and

missing persons files, and I don't know why, which is killing me. Maybe he doesn't know how to proceed.

"On the other hand, perhaps he already knows who's responsible. And it's Pape, and he's already got him. But where would Pape assemble the organization, and who would throw in with him? And the entire thing from the heist in Trinity to the fookin' tapes reeks of a gang effort or, at least, more than one prick in the pot.

"Finally, there's your mystery woman upstairs. The same holds for her.

"Did I tell you I think I know where Ray-Boy is holed up? A warehouse in back of the Cadbury chocolate factory in Coolock. Before this all came down, he was out on the street nights, making deliveries. From now on, he'll be keeping himself inside on orders from above, according to my source."

"Does above have a name?"

She shook her head. "Don't I wish."

McGarr reached for Kara Kennedy's bell, but Bannon pulled down his hand and held on to it. "Wait now. Jaysus, haven't I been freezin' me shapely and available arse off the evening long, and you have nothing for me? Not even a measly quote saying what a bunch of right bastards Kehoe, Sheard, and their crowd are, hanging you out to dry when they know—since the pathologist told them too— that a bullet fired from a rifle killed the driver of the BMW out on the Glasnevin Road, not a round from one of your guns.

"A wee 'They are' will do." When McGarr moved his hand up for the bell again, she cried out histrionically and tugged on it with both hands. "Christ almighty, forgive me, but I thought it was a fookin' two-way street, so I did."

McGarr lowered his arm. "Two-way—when you've got something I don't already know."

"How about the name of the firm your woman's missing husband worked for—Dublin Bay Petroleum. Private brokerage operation headquartered on Cayman Brac. Irish principals, I'm told. Now, you play."

McGarr reached into his jacket and pulled out a tape cassette. "Second tape. Be ready with the equivalent of fifty million Euros in unmarked bearer bonds drawn on the Republic of Venezuela and flown to a location they'll notify us of later when we're already in the air."

"You're fookin' jokin'."

McGarr pushed the button.

"Will you let me have it? Or a copy? No, I'll copy it, I swear, and bring it right back."

He slipped it back into his jacket.

"But I need art to run with the story."

"You and Sweeney have art. You splashed it all over the paper today. Keep splashing."

"But I need fresh art, you know, to do the journalist thing. People see the old art, they'll think, nothing new, when in fact—thanks to you, darlin' man—I'm scooping the entire fookin' world."

"You should be happy with that."

"If I were a man, I'd thump you bloody and take it right away. But come closer while I tell you." When McGarr turned to her, she threw her arms around his neck and kissed him. They staggered into the door.

"Hello?" Kara Kennedy's voice said through the intercom. "Hello? Is somebody there?"

"You're brilliant, you are, McGarr. The fookin' Man himself altogether and without equal. When you tire of librarians and want a real woman, give me a jingle."

"Hello? Hello? Is somebody there?"

Digging her cell phone from her jacket, Orla Bannon stepped quickly toward the gate.

McGarr leaned into the intercom. "Kara, it's Peter McGarr."

"Oh, Peter, I'm so glad it's you. Haven't I been watching what Kehoe had to say about the books, and then Sheard about you. Both are outrageous. Don't they realize that one Monet sold for over fifty million pounds some years ago? And not a very good Monet at that.

"But don't stand out there. Come up, come up."

The lock buzzed, and McGarr pushed open the door. As he climbed the heavy, carved staircase, he heard her saying from above, "I'm . . . I'm over the moon that you've come back to me tonight."

She then appeared at the top of the stairs, looking more beautiful than he had remembered. Again she was wearing the pearl gray silk dressing gown patterned with deep red roses.

Perhaps it was the sash, which she had cinched tight about her narrow waist and emphasized the flare of her hips; or her deep brown hair, which had been permed and flowed in waves onto her shoulders; or the heelless open-toed pumps that had replaced her moplike booties and added a few inches to her height.

But she was resplendent with what McGarr thought of as a million-quid smile lighting up her features: her high forehead and high cheekbones, slightly aquiline nose, and definite chin. Her jade eyes were sparkling.

Instead of moving when he got to the top of the stairs, she remained in front of him. "Sure, it couldn't have been a worse day for either of us, I'm thinking—both humiliated, both sacked.

"But your being here—well, you don't know what it means. Come." She reached for his elbows and, stepping back, drew him onto the landing with her and kissed him. "What's wrong?"

McGarr had not raised his arms to embrace her. "You say you were sacked?"

She nodded.

Stepping around her, he moved toward the open door of the flat. "Who sacked you?"

"Trevor Pape."

"When was this?"

"Today at work."

"Can he sack you? Does he have the authority?" McGarr sat on the couch.

"Whether he does or not, he did it in a most unprofessional and, as I said, humiliating manner." Closing the door, she reached for a glass that was sitting on a table. It was half filled with what looked like wine. "I was in the Treasury where, finally, the police—your Mr. Sheard—had allowed us to clean up. And there must have been a half-dozen others about, helping in the effort.

" 'Kara,' he says from the doorway. 'Put down that broom and get out. You're sacked.' I didn't think I'd heard him correctly. 'You're sacked, fired, terminated. How can I make it clearer? Pack up your personal belongings and get out immediately.' "

Her jaw trembled as she raised the glass to her lips, took a sip, and set it down. " 'Why am I being sacked?' I asked. 'Because all of this is your fault. You're supposed to be the keeper of old manuscripts, and during your watch we now have far less to keep.'

" 'But it was you who instituted the new security procedures,' I complained. 'I wasn't even consulted, and I have it on good authority that Raymond was in league with the thieves.'

" 'Whose authority?' he asked, and I'm afraid I mentioned your name. I hope you don't mind. And he said, 'Him? He's an incompetent scut and a liar, who is to be sacked himself. You make a likely pair.'

"With that I'm afraid I began to cry, and I said something to the effect of 'How will I ever get another position? First the books are stolen and then I'm sacked. Who will have me? It'll look like I'm responsible.'

" 'Which is not an inaccurate perception,' he said, turning on his heel and leaving.

"After I composed myself, I told the others that I had no intention of leaving, that it would take guards and a letter from the provost to make me leave. And do you know what? I still can't believe it."

McGarr waited.

"Nobody spoke up. Nobody came over and put an arm around me, not even my assistant with whom I thought I was on the best of terms. In utter silence they just continued the cleanup."

"Fearful of losing their own positions," McGarr said, standing and moving past her into the kitchen where she kept the liquor. "May I ask you something?" Opening the cabinet above the sink, he pulled out the bottle of malt he had been served from on the night before. "Why ever did you have anything to do with Pape?" McGarr splashed the amber fluid into a glass.

There was a pause before she said, "So that's it. Your digging has unearthed my lurid past."

Glass in hand, McGarr turned in time to see her jaw tremble and tears burst from her eyes. She lowered her head and other tears splatted on the tiles by her feet.

The three toenails on each foot visible through the open shoes looked recently painted with a lacquer that matched the deep red shade of the roses on her housecoat. McGarr drank from the glass.

As much as it troubled him to bring her pain, as much as his urge was to reach out and comfort her, he also wanted an answer.

She raised her head and then the glass, regarding him sidelong through tear-blurred eyes as she drank. Then, "I don't know— maybe I'm just a woman who can't do without a man. If anything, the past year or so has taught me that. And Trevor came onto me when I first came here to Dublin and had broken off a relationship I'd had in Edinburgh, knowing that the distance between there and here was simply too challenging to continue.

"Trevor was here, he was my mentor, and at the time he could actually be charming and warm when he was himself, which wasn't always. And he was married, which made him safe for me, a poor research student who didn't have the luxury of actually falling in love. You know"—she glanced up at him again, as though appealing to him—"he was somebody to hold."

McGarr wondered if that's all he himself had been to her as well. "And how many somebodys have there been?"

"After Dan, you and you alone. And I don't think of you as a somebody. I hope you understand."

Stonily, McGarr regarded her. "And before your husband?"

She swung her head away and reached for the wine bottle on the sideboard. "I admit that between my undergraduate years and returning to university, I went through a period of what I think of as 'wandering,' and there were several somebodys. But always, always, I engaged in affairs, not . . ."

One-night stands, McGarr thought she meant.

"And may I say"—she poured herself another glass—"that, while I understand your need to know everything you can about me, that it's really unfair to us—who we could be as a couple. And I hope it already hasn't spoiled any chance we might have had to find that out." With the back of a hand, she wiped the tears from her eyes. "I hate crying. Why do I have to cry?"

Finishing the drink, McGarr placed the glass in the sink. "What happened with Pape?"

"Well, I think you know. We were all the gossip. Everybody in Trinity and, you know, the arts community in Dublin heard about it, I'm sure.

"After his wife confronted him at a cocktail party, he told me he would leave her, and we would marry. Which I squelched immediately. I had no intention of marrying a much older man with a definite and difficult problem."

"His addictions." She nodded.

"Also, I had come to know Trevor, and marriage to me—to

anybody—would never suit him. Whether it's the drugs or something in his personality, Trevor is promiscuous by nature. And in spite of what I've just divulged about myself, I didn't want any part of that. I don't—I've never—considered myself promiscuous."

"What did he do?"

"Just what he did to me this afternoon—made my life difficult in the extreme. After I requested a change in tutors away from him, he tried to poison my new adviser against me, even wrote to the outside readers of my thesis in Britain, telling them he had washed his hands of me because my scholarship was suspect.

"Called on the carpet for that by the provost, he remained unrepentant. When the keeper's post opened up and I applied, he did everything he could to get me rejected, and only the provost—God bless him—came to my defense. And I'll admit this also: It could be that my winning the position was a kind of punishment of him, since he has tenure and while married was connected to the Guinnesses, who still support the college handsomely."

McGarr folded his hands across his chest. Although unpleasant, the questions were necessary. Mainly, for him. "Tell me again about your husband—where did you meet him?"

"Here, in Dublin."

"After Pape?"

She nodded. "Perhaps a year later."

"How'd you meet him?"

She shook her head and gave him a disbelieving look. "I've already told you that—at an opening in your wife's gallery. Perhaps you don't believe me. You could go back and consult her visitors' logs, if you still have them. As I remember, she asked everybody to sign in."

"Tell me again the company he worked for."

"I won't tell you again, I'll tell you for the first time, since you never asked—Dublin Bay Petroleum, Limited."

"And he was . . . ?"

"A broker. An oil broker, and quite successful—flat on Merrion Square, a big Volvo, holidays in the Maldives, shooting on Skye, fishing in Norway. Art, he bought a lot of art."

"There's no record of your marriage, nor did you file your taxes as a married couple."

"We were married on Cayman Brac, where Dan was a resident and paid his taxes. But he was and—I hope—is real enough. I'll tell you what"—she reached for the phone on the wall—"why don't we ring up his parents in Scotland? I call them daily, since he was an only child and they have nobody but me. They'll tell you."

McGarr shook his head. "It's not necessary."

"No, I insist." She began dialing a number.

When McGarr attempted to walk out of the room, she seized his wrist and pulled him into her, where he breathed in the mélange of aromas—her perfume, shampoos, soaps, and other emollients—that had so enticed him on the night before.

"Bridie? Could you do something for me—speak to the man standing by my side. He's a detective who's investigating the Kells theft, and he has some questions about Dan."

"Who is this?" McGarr asked, taking the receiver.

"Fionna Stewart."

For the next five minutes, McGarr spoke to the woman, whose heavy Scots burr made her nearly unintelligible. She hoped he could do something for Kara—"who's the darlingest girl and has been so loyal to our poor Dan"—and perhaps launch a separate investigation into the disappearance of her son. "After all, he had a flat there in Ireland, and his firm sold heaps of petrol and oil there."

When McGarr hung up, Kara was gone. He found her sitting in the main room, arranged—it appeared—on the couch. The housecoat was now open to expose a nightgown different from the one she wore the night before; it had lace and was the color of lilacs with a lemony gauze behind.

Which blended rather well with her skin, lightly but definitely tanned. The olive tone rather complemented her umber hair and jade eyes.

Christ, he thought, she might well be the most beautiful woman he had seen in . . . he had not actually been looking at beautiful women during the intervening years. But now her beauty actually stopped him. He came to a standstill and regarded her.

You can't even remember when you last had food, he thought. You just had a stiff drink; she is the first woman you've been with since the loss of your wife. And she is a suspect in the most sensational and now important case in your career. The one that will define you in the mind of the public you've served for nearly thirty years.

On the other hand, you spent a night with this goddess, and she is surely magic both to look at and be with. How lucky are you that she has decided you are—what was the phrase that Orla Bannon had used?—"da' man."

"Sit." Smiling up at him, she patted the cushion next to her. "Or are you still here in an official capacity?"

From his jacket McGarr pulled the second ransom tape. "Number two. I'd like you to see it and tell me if you think it could possibly be Pape."

"Really?" Rising from the couch, she stopped in front of him. "Know what? I hate leaving things unsettled. I want you to kiss me, so I know you care."

McGarr brushed his lips against hers.

"No, a real kiss." Stepping in on him, she kissed him softly at first but then with evident pleasure, her eyes closing, her body folding into his.

"Yah," she then said into his ear, refusing to part from him even though the grip of his one free hand was light on her back. "You're the one. For me.

"Does that scare you?" She craned back her head to regard him; her pelvis was pressed tight against his, her eyes studying his face. "I can tell it does. But part of you doesn't seem to mind." She moved her hips slightly. "You'll stay with me tonight." It was not a question.

"Check the hands," McGarr said when they had settled themselves on the couch. Kara moved closer to him and placed a hand on his thigh.

"But they're gloved."

"Perhaps if you magnify them, as you did . . ."

Reaching across him for the device that operated that function, she smiled down on him as her breasts brushed his chest and he was enveloped in that same mélange of aromas that he knew he would never forget.

And he couldn't help himself. Taking her in his arms, he laid her body across his and kissed her in a way that made him dizzy and left them rather breathless.

"What about the tape and the hands?" she asked, as he slipped one of his own under her nightgown to play his palm around her nipple. Lightly. Teasingly.

He hefted her breast; she tugged at his belt.

". . . assembled the fifty million in . . ." the curious voice was saying.

"Later," McGarr whispered in her ear as, miraculously it seemed, she had him out and then in her—the epiphanic glide of skin against the softest, most lubricious of membranes. Intimacy at its most particular.

Later, in the darkness of the bedroom, they were roused by the ringing of Kara's telephone.

"I can't imagine who that could be," she whispered, reaching for the receiver on a nightstand. After listening for a while, she held the phone out to McGarr. "It's for you."

Orla Bannon, McGarr thought; she was the only one who could possibly know where he was. He held the receiver to an ear.

"McGarr? Chazz Sweeney here. I've got the money."

McGarr had to think—what money?

"The fifty million."

McGarr lowered the phone and pushed himself up against the headboard.

"McGarr, you there?"

He grunted, trying to piece out if Sweeney could possibly mean what he said, and how and where he might have assembled that kind of money.

"Sure, didn't I put together a group of right patriots with deep pockets. With the emphasis on *right*, don't you know. Like a consortium, with one of them a banker who had no problem getting hold of Republic of Venezuela bearer bonds. Did I tell you they're the preferred currency of drug dealers and gun runners? But you doubtless know that.

"Now then, we've got the money, and I've heard from them again. Them New Druid fooks what done the dastardly deed."

The language and the abrupt way Sweeney was talking made McGarr wonder if the man was drunk. Or drunker than usual. "You have fifty million Euros."

"That's what I said. Fifty fookin' mill in Venezuelan bearer bonds and not a farthing less."

"Your own money?"

"No, Jaysus—I put in only two. Where would I get that kind of money to throw around? But you know that."

McGarr did not. Nor did anybody else know of Sweeney's assets. After the deaths of Noreen and Fitz, McGarr had tried to learn everything he could about Sweeney. To no avail.

Through a web of shell companies and trading entities both in Ireland and abroad, Sweeney had concealed his wealth, such that a finance expert hired by McGarr could determine only that Sweeney owned *Ath Cliath*, a small merchant bank with one other employee and limited taxable assets, and several pieces of city center property. But in no way did his holdings add up to 50 million Euros.

"And your fellow patriots are who?"

"Just a bunch of yokes I toss jars with and who wish to remain anonymous."

More and more, it was sounding like drunken blather. "But you have the bonds in your possession?"

"Would I lie about a matter like this? We'll get the books back, but we need your assistance, McGarr. You . . . you know how these things are done and how to handle them New Druid cockbites and druggie chancers, all tattooed and pierced. Aren't you, after proving it out there at their HQ in Glasnevin? I'd fookin' pierce them meself so they'd know it. But, Janie, isn't that another story?

"And, and, and—come closer while I tell yeh—wouldn't it be a bloody fookin' coup, you coming back with the goods, given how shabbily that godless culchie cunt Kehoe and his gobshite sidekick Sheard have done you? There you are with your arse swinging in the breeze, man. Think of that. How does it feel?

"We get the books back, you get vindicated and the chance to see who the thieves are up close and personal. It's what you want, I know you well enough for that. One sniff, and you'll have the miserable mithers.

"And I, what do I get? I fookin' get to make sure that none of those posturing, Protestant, bluenose pricks in that sieve of a place called Trinity College never ever again get to look after those sacred books.

"They will be lodged in the care and the safekeeping of the Holy Roman Catholic Church where they belong, if I and me fifty fookin' million in negotiable securities have anything to say about it."

There it was, McGarr concluded. Sweeney à la Opus Dei. The books of Kells, Durrow, and Armagh were out there, and Sweeney, who was nothing if not an opportunist, had drawn upon that significant power base to assemble the ransom price.

"Why me? Why not Sheard?"

McGarr now heard liquid being poured into a glass.

"I told you what I think of Sheard—an arse-lickin' yes-man if ever there were one—and in a matter such as this he could only play the fool. No clue in this class of thing, none whatsoever.

"And there's another wee problem—we'll need a helicopter and a pilot, like the choppers the Garda possesses and your man McKeon. They want us up in the air before they'll tell us where the drop is."

McKeon had been a helicopter pilot with the Irish army during the peacekeeping operation in Lebanon and still maintained a license.

"I couldn't get access to a helicopter, not now. And Bernie, he—"

"Ach, don't give me that, man. You're still a senior Garda officer in good standing and without question the most respected man on the force, no matter what Kehoe, O'Rourke, and Sheard have tried to do to you. This is an emergency with a tight time frame. One bloody short window of opportunity. And, as far as I know, McKeon wasn't placed on administrative leave. He's fully qualified to fly, if only to maintain his hours."

"How do you know the demand was genuine?"

"It was the voice, the fookin' voice, man."

"And what did it say?"

"We should ready a helicopter. When we get everything together today sometime, they'll tell us what bearings to take after we're in the air and traveling north northwest out of Swords." It was the location of Dublin Airport.

"We're to contact nobody else. If they detect anybody else in the air around us, the deal's off and they'll destroy the books."

Kara, who had been listening while recumbent, now sat up beside McGarr, the warmth of her arm and shoulder settling against him.

"You only have to say the word. And, sure, we'll be up, up, and away, only to return in a trice as brilliant heroes with the bloody books for all the world to see."

Which was also classic Sweeney. For all his secretiveness about his personal finances, the man was a publicity monger of the first rank, and here was the possibility of garnering what would surely be great glory using mainly the money of other people. With the publicity certainly worth the two million he said he was putting up. To him.

Gone would be his reputation as a probable murderer, convicted thief, and cynical manipulator of the worst sort. The first thing—the great and brilliant thing—that would spring to mind when his name was mentioned would be "the man who splashed out millions to save the Book of Kells." Philanthropist, patriot, and churchman.

Perceptions. Didn't it forever come down to that? McGarr mused, considering his own present situation, in which he could well now become known as the man who let the possibility of retrieving the Book of Kells slip through his fingers. Because of his own pride.

"I'd have to speak with them directly."

"Them who?"

"The"—McGarr had to pause for a term—"ransomers."

"Ah, shite—how the fuck d'you think I'm going to do that?"

"How did you notify them that you'd assembled the money?"

"I didn't. They contacted me."

"Well, I imagine we'll just have to wait. I must speak with them directly."

"Christ fookin' almighty, you're going to blow this thing, McGarr. I can just feel it."

"And your principals—I need a list of who put up the money. I'll speak with them as well."

"All fookin' fifty fookin' yokes? It'll take fookin' years."

McGarr let the silence carry his resolve.

Finally, Sweeney sighed. "Well, the bastard did give me a beeper number."

"Which is?"

"Ah, none of your shenanigans, McGarr. I won't have you pullin' the cop thing on me."

Again, he heard Sweeney's throat work.

"And one other thing, you prick you. You should think of bringing your bed partner along to verify the books are what he claims. Wouldn't we be the fools if the entire exercise was nothing but a bloody big fifty-million-Euro scam." With that, Sweeney began a drunken laugh that devolved into a hacking, wet cough.

McGarr waited until he had quieted. "How did you know I was here?"

Sweeney passed some air between his lips. "You should know by now I'm omniscient. But, sure, I've never been one to hold the odd session against any man, even when the woman is another man's wife.

"Later." He rang off.

Orla Bannon, McGarr thought. In spite of her reported contempt for Sweeney, the man signed her paycheck, and like him she was a manipulator of some skill. He wondered what she had got from him in return.

After he explained to Kara what Sweeney had proposed, she used both hands to brush her hair back behind her ears, so that the profile she presented with its nearly equal angles—forehead, nose, and chin—was regal and commanding.

"I don't like it, Peter. I don't like him nor the sound of what he

intends for the books, if he manages to recover them for that outrageous sum. And the way it will be gone about is fraught with danger. What's to prevent the thieves from taking the money and
blowing you out of the sky? Just for the"—she swirled her hands—
"New Druidism of it, and to foil any police presence?

"That said"—she turned to him and took his hand—"if you decide it's something you should do, I'll go along with you, as
Sweeney suggested. As your expert."

In the darkness, McGarr pulled her to him, and they sank down
in the pillows.

AT NEARLY MIDNIGHT ON THE NIGHT BEFORE,
one after another of the seven bay doors of the old warehouse had
opened and a different type of vehicle had driven out. First came a
Ford van with a "Castrol Oil" logo on the side; next a Mooney's
bread van. Bays three through six issued large cars of various makes,
and the last a stretch limo.

"Notice anything similar about those vehicles?" Ward asked
Bresnahan.

"Apart from their size? No."

"Tinted windows, each and every one of them. And what do you
fancy is in them?"

"Drugs."

"And who do you fancy that is, based on mug shots we saw at
headquarters?" Ward jerked his chin at the sixth bay door, where
the limo was pulling out and a tall, square, but thin young man was
waiting in the doorway, his hand on a switch to lower the door.

"Ray-Boy?"

"Could be." Ward reached for the binoculars that lay on the
backseat, but by the time he raised them to his eyes, the door was

descending and the figure obscured. "My theory about there being skylights in that building?"

She nodded. "Now would be the time to test it out—with the darkness and the others gone."

Ward opened his jacket, pulled out the Beretta handgun he kept there in a sling, and checked the clip.

"But remember, it's reconnaissance alone. We have no authority, and isn't Peter in enough trouble as it is?"

It was nearly midnight, yet there were two beads of bright headlamps along Coolock Road, which the laneway of the warehouse joined. Weaving between cars parked in the chocolate factory lot, Ward noted the line of dense wintry-looking clouds that were about to obscure the moon and had the look of a storm front.

Waiting for a moment in the patch of shadow that divided the two properties, Ward and Bresnahan again scanned the environs before moving to the end of the building farther from the road.

What they found there was a narrow, litter-filled gap between the sooty brick wall and a chain-link fence topped by razor wire.

"Ah, Jaysus—just our luck."

"Nonsense. It will make it all the easier. Hands."

"Remember—I don't care what you find, I'm not coming up." Bresnahan twined her fingers and lowered her hands.

Ward raised his foot toward them. "Now, on a three count, launch me as high as you can." Bouncing on the count and thrusting down on her foot on "Three!" he shot his arms as high as he could, grabbed the fencing, and climbed to within inches of the razor wire.

There he paused a moment, as if to gather himself, and in one motion, with an athleticism that Bresnahan could only admire, he both spun around and threw himself at the building, his hands managing to grab hold of the upper edge of the wall. Then, on sheer strength he pulled himself up far enough to hook a leg onto the roof.

All those hours in the gym, thought Bresnahan enviously, while she was at home with their child. Well, she made mental note to demand some exercise time for herself and a more equally divided child-care schedule. Also, it wasn't fair, the way men were built for such things, while there was just too much of her to get in the way of climbing most anything, to say nothing of a sheer wall.

Rolling himself onto the projection, Ward found just about what he had expected—a roof that was more a series of glass chevrons to capture light. Several were open; two rows were lighted.

Standing, Ward heel-and-toed his way down the length of the outer wall until he was standing by the lighted skylights, the glass of which was so grimy and pitted that it was translucent at best. But he could hear music and voices, and, moving a bit farther toward the corner nearest the bay doors, he found an open window that revealed a cluttered desk, a chair, and a filing cabinet below. Cigarette smoke and heat wafted up at him.

Because of the music, he could hear only a word or two of the voices. But twice he heard the name Pape, and a young blond woman dressed in a black tank top and a short black skirt passed by the desk before sitting down and putting her feet up, which exposed yet more of her upper thighs.

"Gillian, you right bitch—turn that fookin' yoke down. I can't think."

"You? Think? Now, there's a laugh." But she lowered her legs and reached out of Ward's sight and lowered the volume.

Ward then heard: "But how fookin' secure is it?"

There was a pause.

"And a back way out?"

Another pause; obviously the man was on the phone.

"What's he want for it? Ah, Jaysus—he's holding us up. Don't he know who we are? Then you should fookin' make him aware, straightaway. Give me the address again. Twenty-four . . . what? You're breakin' up. Span . . . what? Spancel Court. Never heard of it. Ranelagh. I know every laneway of Ranelagh, and I never . . ."

Then, "Oh. Oh, yeah. Right. Good. Good, lad. You too."

Then the woman—Gillian Reston, Ward assumed—reached into the shadows, and the music swelled.

Ward caught only snatches of the conversation between the man who had been on the phone and another man, whose voice was nearly inaudible because of the music. Whole minutes went, and more than once Ward thought he heard the word *ransom*.

Christ, he thought, have we stumbled upon the thieves?

At the very least, the woman Morrigan thought the gang inside was responsible for the murder and decapitation of Mide, the New Druid founder.

It was then that legs of a man appeared near the desk, and the woman, glancing up, now rose and stepped aside, so he could sit. All Ward could see of him were his head and shoulders. But when she settled herself on his lap in a way that turned six inches of buff cleavage nearly into his face, he looked up and smiled appreciatively.

It was the "Stu" who had been with Sweeney on the railway platform in Dun Laoghaire when the second ransom tape was delivered from the hijacked train. The man whom Sweeney had warned by saying "Stu," which caused him to flee:

Late thirties, early forties. Curly blondish hair that had just begun to gray. Handsome in a rugged sort of way, in spite of a rough complexion and a noticeable scar on one cheek.

He said something to the woman, and she rose up a bit and slid her hand under her bottom and down on him.

"Pssst!" Bresnahan whispered from below the window. "See anything? I'm freezin' me fanny off down here."

Reaching up, the woman below—Gillian—pulled her top off one shoulder and the other just to the edges of her nipples, then leaned back to rest her head on the shoulder of the man beneath her. Stu.

Who muttered something to her, before picking her up with both arms, turning and spreading her across the top of the desk, out of Ward's direct line of sight through the open window. And when he positioned a knee on the desk and climbed up, all Ward could see of her and him were their shoes.

But combined with the movement of their shapes through the grimy, vaguely translucent glass, it was enough to understand what they were about. Especially when her ankles crimped around his and she gave out a little cry of what sounded like pleasure.

"Hughie! I swear, I'll go back to the car, if you don't come down."

Which was loud enough to stop them.

"You hear that?" the man, Stu, asked.

She mumbled or moaned again, and there was a pause before their four feet began moving again.

Very slowly and cautiously, Ward moved to the edge of the wall. There he sat and eased himself over, allowing his body to stretch to the max before releasing his grip. Even so, he would have fallen in a heap, but for the fence that kept him upright.

"So?"

"I'll tell you in the car."

"You mean—we're not going in?"

"We—you and me—can't go in"—no longer being Gardai, he meant.

"It hasn't stopped us yet."

"Yes, but it's not just you and me. It's Peter, who's in enough trouble as it is."

"Because of us, you mean? Because of me? I can't believe you just said that."

"I didn't say anything of the sort. And it's you who's only after saying it yourself."

"That's different."

"How's it different?" At the corner of the building, Ward surveyed the warehouse loading dock, before stealing across the laneway to the trees that separated it from the parking lot of the chocolate factory, with Bresnahan behind him.

"It's different because you're supposed to love me and support me."

Ward twisted the key, and the doors of the old Opel popped. "Didn't I say it was shite? What are you supposed to do—shoot the bastard with a gang of maybe fifty behind him? You did the right thing."

"You're sure."

Exasperated, Ward only looked off through the trees toward the warehouse.

After a while, Bresnahan settled herself back against the seat. "So, what are we going to do? Nothing? When here we sit at the location of a major—perhaps *the* major—drug distribution center in the city, to say nothing of being the safe house of suspected murderers who also decapitate their victims, and—"

"There's nothing that we can do. We can't storm the building, not with at least three of them in there most likely well armed. The squad can't help us, now that Peter's been removed from the case, not without risking their own jobs and careers. And any call for official help will only bring Sheard."

Bresnahan sighed. "And we don't want that."

Ward reached over and tried to place a hand on her thigh but she fended him off. "You're tired."

"No, I'm not—I'm exhausted."

Ward then told her what he had seen through the open skylight window. "It's this Stu who interests me."

Earlier in the day, when the large car had pulled up in front of the *Ath Cliath* news office, Ward had seen Sweeney's companion leave the building with him.

And whose car was it? Sweeney's? As far as Ward knew, Sweeney, who had lost his driver's license after multiple drunk-driving convictions, was now chauffeured around town in one of three Rolls that he owned.

With tinted windows and the wheel of the car on the curb side, the driver was obscured.

Finally, on the DART commuter train platform, there had been Sweeney's warning to the man—"Stu!"—who had then fled.

Had this Stu been in the *Ath Cliath* building with Sweeney? Or was he, as if now seemed, an ally or part of Ray-Boy's group? And where was Ray-Boy? Discretion could be the better route. Why make Sheard look good?

"Why don't you go home, get some sleep. Later, you can spell me."

Bresnahan shook her head more in resignation than disagreement. "In the old days, we would have stormed the feckin' place and extracted them and the truth, one way or another."

But the old days on the Squad were gone forever, mainly because of Sweeney.

Ward reached for his cell phone to call Bresnahan a cab and ring up McGarr. In that order.

12

McGarr left Kara Kennedy's flat early,
around half six, taking note of how she slept with seeming abandon—
one arm thrown back over her head, the other having been resting on
McGarr's chest when he awoke.

In such a pose, she looked almost juvenile—her breasts raised
and splayed to either side, her stomach concave, her thighs slender
and spread with one knee cocked to the side. Like that, he judged
her to be a handsome woman—not traditionally pretty, but just well
made in a way that was at once classical and exotic. And sounded
something deep in him.

Kissing her gently on the smooth curve of her forehead, he said,
"You sleep. I'll call you later when I know what I'm about."

"Oh, no," she said sleepily, reaching for him. "Aren't you going
to stay with me just a wee bit longer?"

But he was too consumed with thoughts of Sweeney's phone call.
Somehow, it all seemed too good: Sweeney's having the money, the
possibility of getting the books back largely intact, and—when he
had checked his phone messages in Kara's kitchen on first getting
up—a call from Ward saying that Bresnahan and he had located not

only Ray-Boy but perhaps Gillian Reston and the man who had been present at the drop of the second videotape, the one who had arrived with Sweeney.

Moving down the staircase from the flat to the front door, Mc-Garr phoned Swords at Murder Squad headquarters. "What—no sleep?"

"Who needs it?" Swords replied. "Sleep is boring. Not like the newspapers. One thing we can say about Sweeney—he's an entertainer. I'd read you today's installment of *Ath Cliath*, but it's something you should savor on your own."

"May I add to your burden?" In a way, McGarr felt guilty about how he had passed the night, when compared with Swords and the other staffers who had worked through another night, sifting through documents. But being with Kara again made him understand how much of life he'd been missing.

"Could we find out just what automobiles are owned by Chazz Sweeney and/or *Ath Cliath*?"

"Sheard's been by. Twice. Once for the file, the cloak, and the voice scrambler from Pape's. Second time, it was to tell me he's taking over the squad. Had a letter signed by O'Rourke. He ordered us out, then switched off the lights and locked the door. We adjourned to Hogan's and came back after closing."

"Good man." McGarr rang off.

A heavy pounding rain had begun overnight, and it had scarcely eased as McGarr hurried to his car, where he found Orla Bannon's business card under the windscreen wiper with the advisory "Other women get horny too."

On the short ride home, he stopped at a newsagent and had to pull the three papers out of their bundles at the early hour, slipping the money through the mail slot. Neither Nuala nor Maddie had arisen, so he carried the papers into the kitchen, where he readied some coffee.

Ath Cliath's cover story was BANNON: RANSOM TAPE II. The story jumped to a two-page spread where she also covered the decapitation-murder of Mide, the New Druid founder.

In premier tabloid form, she speculated that "perhaps the theft of the Book of Kells prefigured a power struggle between the New Druid founder—who possessed an actual, if suspect, ideology—and recent recruits attracted by the New Druids' seeming monopoly of drugs, money, and street sex in the major cities of the country."

A third story without a byline was more interesting to McGarr. It dealt with Sheard's announcement that Pape was cooperating with Garda investigators and there would soon be "a breakthrough in regard to the theft of the books and the murder of Raymond Sloane."

But as for the possible return of the books: " 'There's been no movement on that front, nor is there likely to be,' " Sheard was quoted as saying. " 'As Taoiseach Kehoe has said—the government will not truck with thieves, murderers, and their ransom demands, no matter the consequence. It would only encourage further such criminal acts.' "

And of the three papers, again it was only *Ath Cliath* that reported a possible reason for the hijacking of a inbound DART train at Killiney and its abandonment in Sandymount. "The hijackers, seen brandishing handguns and assault rifles, were dressed in the regalia of New Druids, according to an eyewitness, with a hijacker tossing out something onto the platform at Dun Laoghaire."

McGarr glanced up over his kitchen sink, where he was standing, and looked out at his garden, which because of high walls had only just come into clear view in the early morning light.

Hadn't Ward said to him it was a hat that had been scaled to him, and only after he picked it up did he discover that it contained a videotape. Only he and Sweeney had debated who would take possession of it.

Could Sweeney now be writing for his own paper? Why not? But he had always claimed an Olympian distance from all but the editorial page, Bannon's independence being proof of his objective stance.

"An earlier ransom demand for the ancient manuscripts stolen from Trinity College Library took the form of a videotape. The second tape was picked up by an bystander who Garda officials hope will come forward with the packet."

Carrying his coffee out into the garden, as first light was melding into dawn, McGarr moved slowly around the flagged walkway, which was still damp from the rain during the night, and tried to understand just where he stood in all that had happened.

Could he beat the charges about the car and the shooting death at New Druid headquarters? Ultimately, if all the evidence were brought to light. But it would take time, especially if Sheard chose to drag out the process, and he would be branded—even more so than he already was—by the event, to the detriment of his family, any career that he might still have left, and his reputation.

Why had Sheard gone for him?

Why not? There was Sheard's obvious ambition, and, once Mc-Garr had provided Kehoe a way out of the blame that inevitably would have been visited on him, it would not have been difficult for Sheard to convince him of the politic course.

Now they could blame the New Druids or some larger conspiracy involving Pape and claim Sheard had lost the opportunity to collar them because of the Glasnevin Road incident. And even if and when, later, the postmortem report were issued, the political fallout would be far less. After all, it would be the public's perceptions—formed by *Ath Cliath* and the other media—that would count.

Suddenly, McGarr felt the presence of somebody near him and looked up to find Nuala.

"How be ye?"

He nodded.

"That Sheard is a bastard. You haven't heard the last of him yet."

McGarr nodded again.

"Raising himself up with his boot on your neck."

McGarr looked out on the soil of his unplanted garden.

"What will you do?"

He shrugged.

"You have to do something. Like this, he's burying you, and all the good things you've done over the years won't matter a jot."

Some time went by. A pied wagtail kited down onto one of his barren raised beds, turned an ear to the ground, and plucked up a fat worm.

"There's the form for you," said Nuala. "Bravo, me budgie."

After another little while, during which they heard a neighbor departing for work, "Not to add to your problems, but Maddie?"

McGarr turned his head to her.

"She says she doesn't want to go to school this morning."

"Ill, is she?"

"No. She's not ill. She just says she doesn't want to go for a while."

"Because of me?" McGarr stood.

"I would suspect."

McGarr had to knock on Maddie's closed door.

She did not respond.

"May I come in?"

Still nothing.

McGarr turned the handle and opened the door. She was in bed with a pillow over her head. "What gives? Nuala tells me you don't want to go to school. But you're not ill."

She did not move; the pillow remained over her head. He reached down to take it away, but she held on to it fast.

"I think you can hear me, and I should imagine this has something to do with my situation. Am I right?"

McGarr sighed and sat on the edge of the bed. "I'd like you to go to school, but I'll leave that decision up to you. For today.

"Things . . . can be made to seem worse than they are. That fella who spilled out of the car? He had shot at us. But the bullet that killed him? It was fired from a rifle and maybe by one of his own, for reasons we don't quite know.

"Television, the press, reports, even being there—people can come up with distorted views of what happened. But the important thing is to do everything you can to discover the truth, not just as you want to see it, but as it is."

There was still no response from her. And no movement.

"Second thing? Even if what's being said about me were true, you're not responsible for that in any way. All you have to know is that I try to do my job as well and as fairly and legally as I can.

"And think of this—what would your absence from school suggest to your classmates? That you're ashamed because I did wrong? I think so. When, in fact, you should only be ashamed of whatever you do wrong. And then, I actually did nothing wrong.

"I'll leave you now, but you should know I love you."

Standing, McGarr found Nuala in the doorway. "They say Sheard's about to give another press conference. Perhaps you should see it."

While Brendan Kehoe was not standing with Jack Sheard at the brace of microphones, McGarr recognized the anteroom in Leinster House, which stamped the occasion with the imprimatur of the taoiseach's office.

Reading from notecards that he held in the palm of a hand, Sheard was saying, ". . . on charges that he conspired with security guard Raymond Sloane, Sloane's son—Raymond Sloane Junior—and unknown others to steal the Book of Kells and those of Durrow and Armagh. It is not known why Sloane the elder was murdered during the commission of the crime, nor if the death of one Derek

Greene, another Trinity security guard, a fortnight earlier might be connected to the theft. But we know this.

"Greene was knocked down and killed by the same car that, two weeks later, Raymond Sloane Junior was suspected of driving and was discovered behind the headquarters of Celtic United on the Glasnevin Road. In an attempt to question Sloane and examine the car, Garda officials and some others—who may have been helping the police—fired upon the car, resulting in the death of Kevin Carney. Evidence was discovered providing scientific proof that the car had been involved in the death of Greene."

Opening a lapel of his tan suit jacket, Sheard slipped the notecards into a pocket and paused dramatically before lifting his eyes to the cameras. "The owner of the costly car—a large and rather new BMW—had been Trevor Pape, the head librarian of Trinity College, before he virtually gave it to Sloane senior.

"But there is another link in all of this—the scourge of drugs. Not only were traces of a variety of drugs discovered in the boot and backseat of the car, Dr. Pape's drug problem is long-standing, as was that of Sloane senior. Additionally, Sloane junior is a suspected drug dealer and New Druid enforcer. As we know, a ransom demand was made by a man who hold the beliefs of that group.

"How Pape, the Sloanes, the car, and perhaps some element of the New Druids actually worked the crime will remain a matter of conjecture perhaps until Sloane junior or some other of the conspirators are apprehended. But two items of physical evidence linking Pape to the ransom tape were discovered in Pape's abode. For health reasons, Pape has been removed to a hospital detox unit."

Sheard took a half step back from the microphones. "Questions?"

Which were shouted at him: Do you have any idea where the stolen manuscripts are? Has Pape made a statement? How ill is he? Do you know where Ray-Boy Sloane is at the moment, and are you close to making an arrest? Is there evidence other than the car linking him to the crimes? New Druids control the drug trade in Dublin, New Druids appear on the ransom tape—is it the government's intention to crack down on their activities and/or have them declared an enemy of the state, as is the IRA?

To nearly all of the questions, Sheard said he'd divulged all that he could at the moment and would not presume to speak for the government. He was simply a policeman doing his job, but there was progress.

As ever, he appeared confident, competent, and in command of the situation.

Until Orla Bannon asked, "What about the mix-up on the Glasnevin Road? My sources indicate that the driver of the vehicle was not killed with a Garda weapon but rather a bullet from an assault rifle of the sort not in the armory of the Garda Siochana."

Sheard's features glowered. "A rumor like that was floating around. But as announced yesterday, the matter is under investigation with the offending . . . the commanding Garda officers having been suspended.

"But I should like to say this—police investigations cannot be allowed to become witch hunts, just because a senior officer feels some personal animosity toward one group or another, based on their suspected crimes or public appearance and deportment.

"By the day, this country is becoming more pluralistic, more democratic, and—it is to be hoped—more tolerant. I'm not certain all of the country's native-born communities can accept the new paradigm, but they must be made to conform to law and democratic practice. By whom I mean at the present time: both the New Druids on the one hand and rogue elements of the police on the other. I'm certain the government backs me in this stance."

"And bad cess to you and your miserable minions," Nuala said to the screen; she was standing in the doorway. And then to McGarr, "That ambitious man, without question acting with Kehoe's complicity, has as much as burnt you, buried you, and pissed on your grave. Whatever will you do?"

McGarr's cell phone had begun ringing. He shook his head; he did not know. It was Sweeney. "They'll be ringing up any minute now, as soon as I put down the phone."

McGarr tried to estimate how long it would take him to get into town to Bresnahan and Ward's digs in the Coombe, where they had set up all their electronic gear. "I can't talk now."

"But aren't you talking to me?"

"Make it quick."

"McGarr!" Sweeney roared. "You're making a balls of this thing. They will talk to you now or never."

"Anything else?"

It took a second or two for the man to gather himself. "I've also got those names for you—the ones who've joined me in putting up the money."

Traffic would still be heavy now at midmorning. "Forty-five minutes at the inside. Make it an hour."

"They told me you'd say that and it was a no-go. What in the name of sweet Jesus could you be doing that's more important than this?"

"Family. You know that about me, Sweeney. My family comes first. They're never out of my thoughts." McGarr rang off.

THE COOMBE LIES IN A HOLLOW THAT RUNS down to the banks of the Poddle; once a center of textile manufacturing and weaving, many of its old commercial buildings had been converted into lofts and offices.

Bresnahan, Ward, Ward's other wife, Lee Sigal, and their three children lived in a rambling series of buildings that also housed Lee's antiques business and looked out over the narrow stream.

The bell on the door, which had been a feature of the shop for more than a century, scarcely produced a sound any longer, but a buzzer that sounded in the living quarters soon brought Lee.

"Well, Peter McGarr," Lee said, advancing on him with her hand out. "Aren't you all the news these days? I hope you're keeping on."

"Have I any choice?" McGarr accepted her hand, and they embraced.

"No—none whatsoever. That Sheard is a bloody piece of self-serving work, so he is. And we must right the record. I take it you've come for Ruth. Hughie is on stakeout, but I suppose you know that."

Turning on her heel, she moved through rows of furniture, architectural appurtenances, and other collectible items that stretched off into the shadows of low, crowded rooms, which changed into a bright and airy apartment with tall windows the moment they passed through a heavy curtain.

Only then did McGarr notice that the dark, pretty woman was pregnant. "Well, this is news. Why am I always the last to know?"

With finely formed features and dark eyes, she smiled, dimples appearing in her olive-toned cheeks. "I suspect Hughie thought you've had enough on your mind."

They found Ruth in a large work area filled with computers and other gadgetry. Quickly, McGarr filled her in about the possible call from the ransomers, adding, "If they're prompt, it should be any minute now."

Bresnahan phoned Ward, and they decided upon a strategy that would enable them to learn the number of the incoming call and perhaps even learn its location.

One of the machines that Bresnahan and Ward used for surveillance was also able to detect the location of the wireless service sending the signal, and from there it could track back to the place from which the call was being sent.

Learning the number of the phone was more complicated. "But

the point is to keep him on the line as long as possible." Bresnahan tucked a strand of her auburn hair behind an ear and typed several codes into a computer. "You should sit here for the best reception."

McGarr had scarcely taken a seat by a tall window when his cell phone bleated. "Yes?"

"You're McGarr?" the same fractured voice from the video-tapes said.

"I am, yeah. And who might I be speaking with?"

"The money. The helicopter. Once you're up we'll be in contact with you."

"How do I know this is real? That you're in possession of the books?"

"The objects on the wall in the videotapes? I should add your pate to them with an eighteen-inch nail." He rang off.

"Shit. Not enough time by half," said Bresnahan.

McGarr's cell phone rang again.

It was Sweeney. "So? You think he's coddin'?"

McGarr didn't know what to think; because of the *Ath Cliath* headline and the Orla Bannon article, it was now public knowledge that the ransomer collected heads. But the eighteen-inch nails had not been mentioned and would have been apparent only to some-body who had a copy of the tape and the capability of magnifying the image, like Kara. "You have those names I asked for?"

"Got a fax?"

McGarr asked Bresnahan for the number and within minutes it appeared, nearly fifty names long with phone numbers and contri-butions in Sweeney's barely legible scrawl.

Moving to a desk, McGarr began working through the list, not getting through to at least half the contributors because of secre-taries or assistants. "The blighter phoned me at half-two in the blessed morning, so he did," said one well-known Dublin developer who had ties to Kehoe. He had coughed up 5 million. "With nary an excuse nor an apology. Strong-arm all the way, and I hope Peter McGarr sees to it I get my money back."

Another said he was threatened; yet another said it amounted to blackmail, "him with whole teams of snoops on that rag of his."

Not one pretended to be happy about giving. The most sanguine statement was "Well, it's all for a good cause, and I hope, if it's got back, it's kept in some more secure setting. Sweeney's right about Trinity—an object of such value should never have been kept in a library."

McGarr thanked Ruth and said good-bye to Lee and their babies, who had arisen from a nap. He drove home and was just walking through his front door when his cell phone bleeped.

"No common detox for Pape," said McKeon. "He's in intensive care—suddenly, inexplicably having lost consciousness in Sheard's patrol car, and it doesn't look good for him. But for Sheard? Shit, with Pape's brain scrambled or dead, well . . ."

The political fix would be in—exculpating Kehoe, the Garda as an institution, and Sheard from blame in the loss of the treasures. The onus would be put squarely on McGarr and Ray-Boy and his gang of louts.

Even Kehoe's tenuous alliance with Celtic United might be maintained. After all, Mide and Morrigan had been thorns in Kehoe's side, with their carryings-on about the Celtic past. Younger New Druids simply wanted to maintain their hold on drugs and other illegal trades.

"There's been a second tape and Sweeney says he's put together the ransom money." McGarr glanced at his watch; it was time for Maddie to be getting ready for school, if she were going.

"You're jokin'."

In more than a few ways, McGarr wished he was.

"How did he do that in such a short time?"

"It appears he worked through the night."

"But is the demand genuine?"

"Apparently so." But McGarr wished he could be more certain, since what he was about to ask McKeon might certainly end his career too, even if they were successful.

Moving through the upper hall and down the staircase, McGarr paused on a landing with a tall window that looked out on his back garden. What would be agreed between them would, he imagined, set the course of the rest of their lives.

Explaining how Ward had intercepted a second ransom tape, he then detailed Sweeney's news that he had put together a "group of patriots" who would pay to retrieve the book but not return it to "that sieve of a place," Trinity College.

"Some Opus Dei zealots or others, I'd hazard."

"But the demand mentions a helicopter."

McKeon waited for the other shoe to drop.

"And I thought we might provide the service."

"You and me."

"Well—you, me, Sweeney, of course, and the keeper of old manuscripts at Trinity."

"The Kennedy woman."

"So it's not—"

"A pig in a poke we're left with. I understand."

There was another pause, during which McGarr moved down the cellar stairs.

McKeon sighed. "Don't you know, it's curious you should bring this up. Because I'm only after thinking, with this Sheard yoke always on the teley blowing his horn that it was time for me to pack it in, join up with Ruth and Hughie, and make a few quid for once in me life.

"But then the missus tells me that with the kids now gone she thought I'd give up the work altogether, and at last she'd have a companion in me.

" 'Companion?' says I. 'Not sure I like the sound of that. A companion to do what?' And didn't she drag out this grocer's list of places around the globe she'd like to go courtesy of something called Elder Hostel? And me neither an elder nor hostile in any way."

McKeon waited for McGarr's reaction, but there could be none. The situation was too serious for comedy, no matter how well intended.

"But"—there was another long pause during which McGarr unlocked the cabinet he was now standing before—"maybe I can learn."

"I hope—and it's just a hope—that you won't have to. But I'm only offering up a suggestion here." McKeon had raised a large family, who in many ways still depended upon him; McGarr, on the other hand, had only Maddie and Nuala to care for, and having to make a living was probably no longer an issue for him. "I want you to think about it before deciding, perhaps talk with Grainne."

Opening the cabinet door, McGarr switched on a light and looked in at what made up a small arsenal of weaponry.

"What's to decide? Didn't we toss our lots together—how many years ago was it, Peter?"

"I don't know. Over twenty-five, I guess."

"No sense in breaking that now. I'll ring up the airport, tell them I need to keep up me hours."

Which would without question end up in at least a suspension, once he strayed from his flight plan. "You're sure?"

"If we're going down, let's do it properly. Flames. Crash and burn. Figuratively speaking, of course."

AFTER SWITCHING OFF THE TELEVISION THAT he kept in a far corner of his safehouse/headquarters in Coolock, Raymond "Ray-Boy" Sloane Jr. remained seated in the near darkness while he tried to sort through his emotions and summon his instinct for survival.

It was what had saved him in the past. Through gang violence as a lad and drug warfare as a man, it had kept him alive, told him when to split, who to hook up with and who to unhook. It had even got him clean without much fuss, enabling—there was a good word, he thought—him to dominate the chancers, gobshites, and other assorted cocksuckers around him. Enabling him, in essence, to get where he was.

Which was? Sloane shook his head and stared down at his sandals, which were lit by a wedge of daylight angling in from an open skylight above him.

Fucked, altogether. Thoroughly, totally, terminally fucked with no way out that he could see beyond cutting the balls off the bastards who had betrayed him.

How had he not seen there was no way people like that would split with the likes of him? After—"Fucking after!" he now shouted at the walls—he'd done his part.

But he'd promised them, hadn't he, when they'd decided to go ahead with it. He'd held up his hand and pointed at each and every one of them in their turn. Then he'd said, quiet like, "You know what I've agreed to do, what none—not one of yous—could or would do ever, no matter the scene.

"All I ask is yous do yous part. But yous should know this. Fuck with me, fuck with me in any fucking way"—he had brought the blade of the broadsword down on the council table—"I'll not just kill yous. No. I promise yous here—and yous should know—I'll kill each and every one of your family from your granny to the youngest scut that bears your name."

Now jerking up a leg, Sloane kicked a sandal off one foot and then the other, before reaching for his boots by the side of the cot.

Maybe that was the way out. He'd take his revenge and all the fucking money, if by then they had it in hand. He knew where they were and where they'd be. Or, *or,* he'd wait until they got the money. Then he'd take his revenge. And so forth.

When they decided to cast him off without making sure he was dead, they had to know there'd be a major dollop of . . . and so forth. They'd brought him aboard for just that, he'd been told from the start.

Which was a plan, Ray-Boy decided. But first he had a bit of business to take care of. Because nobody dissed him, especially not "Hawaii Five-O." They all had handles, real names being an unnecessary hazard.

"Oh, Dan-Oh Boy," he began to sing, reaching under the mattress of the cot for his broadsword. "Ah, cripes, ah, cripes—yer mawlin' me."

Which weapon was well and good for the third century but would not do in the twenty-first. From under the cot itself, Ray-Boy also pulled out a shiny Ruger .457 magnum that weighed about four pounds and was packed with hollow-point bullets that could punch an exit wound through a person the size of a blood orange.

And had, he reminded himself. Surprised by the size of the one he'd plugged through a druggie thief, Ray-Boy had spent maybe a whole precious minute marveling at the hole, when the fucking cannon had made so much noise he really should have split right away.

Now fitting the gun under his belt at the small of his back, Ray-Boy strapped on his Celtic breastplate, pulled on a leather jacket, and moved out into the middle of the warehouse, which was lined by rows of floor-to-ceiling shelving, some containing old plumbing supplies in crumbling cartons. He had bought the place as is, then registered a dummy company with the Commerce Board.

From the small office near the bay doors, he could hear a radio playing, and he wondered if the station had broken off to cover the cop press conference. And if the two in the office knew how he'd been done.

He could also hear Five-O saying, "Great." A pause. "Smashing." Another. "Yeah, I'll take care of it." Obviously speaking into a phone. "See you soon."

"I wouldn't count on it, Five-O," he muttered. Not for a moment. "Oh, Dan-Oh Boy," he sang again, waving the broadsword from side to side with the lyrics. He'd reached the open door of the office, from which heat, cigarette smoke, perfume from the woman, and the stink of sex was flowing out into the otherwise unheated building. "From pen to fen, and down your monstrous side."

Tapping the broadsword against the frame of the door, he reached the blade into the room and wiggled it back and forth, as though it were the one doing the talking. "Are yiz decent and not engaged? Are yiz home for company? Bad enough I have to ask, me who's footin' the bill for these brilliant digs, me with all these inches to spare. Would yiz look at me sharp form of forty-eight fucking nasty inches."

In the reflection off a picture on the wall, he could see the woman reclining on the sofa with her head on a hand, a cigarette dangling from the corner of her mouth. One pudgy tit had lolled out of her open blouse, the nipple spread over the milky flesh like a big pink bruise.

"With nobody—woman nor man—brave enough to put me where I belong."

Five-O had to be seated or standing somewhere behind the door, which was not good. Ray-Boy reached back and felt for the butt of the handgun.

The woman had raised her other hand and was beckoning with her fingers. "Come. Come 'ere, baby," she said woozily.

But Ray-Boy had not got where he was by shagging poxy

bitches. And the thought of how they'd sandbagged him a second time sent a bolt of white rage coursing through him.

Raising a foot, he kicked open the door to find Dan-Oh sitting at the desk, feet up. He was staring down at something in his right hand, which he raised and pointed at the woman.

Bang. Her arm shot out and her head fell with a crack against the wooden arm of the sofa. There was a small dot, like a bindi, on her forehead, and the cigarette had fallen on her bare breast, where it lay smoking.

As though the report of the small gun was disappointing, Dan-Oh examined it for a second before swinging it at Ray-Boy, who had to tug to free the barrel of his Ruger.

Too late.

Dan-Oh squeezed off four quick shots, all of which struck Ray-Boy on the breastplate, as he wheeled toward the door, gun now firmly in hand. A fifth shot was high and whizzed past his ear. But the sixth was low and caught him in the thigh, the impact causing him to squeeze off a round as he lurched out the open door.

The blast was stellar in the small space, and he fired twice more as he dragged his leg, which felt numb, into the darkness. How many shots could Five-O have in a peashooter like that, Ray-Boy wondered.

And knowing he still had four left in his own weapon, which more than outgunned the other man, Ray-Boy dropped the broadsword and spun around in time to see Dan-Oh's hand strike the lift button on the bay door closest to the office.

The motor engaged, and the door began its rattling rise.

Aiming with both hands now—ba-boom!—Ray-Boy squeezed off another round that splintered the frame of the door behind which Dan-Oh was hiding. Three.

Would Dan-Oh reload? Sure, if he'd thought to carry another clip, which Ray-Boy doubted. They were heavy, bulky, and unnecessary for the surprise hit and a quick escape that the prick had obviously planned.

Raising the gun, he aimed at the black smudge near the top of the rattling door and squeezed off a round that bucked into the lift motor, which exploded in a shower of brilliant sparks and stopped the door.

But Dan-Oh, having seen Ray-Boy lift the gun, now bolted from cover and, firing once more, dived under the narrow opening at the bottom of the door, with Ray-Boy—bam! bam!—touching off his last two remaining slugs.

One went out the open door, the second ripped a fist-sized gap in the corrugated metal door and sprayed the yard with shrapnel, Ray-Boy hoped.

Moving as fast as he could with the slug in his thigh, he dragged himself to the next bay and punched the button to raise the overhead door. But nothing happened; it didn't work. Nor the next nor the next.

The motor that he'd shot must have shorted out the circuit breaker. But it didn't matter much, he realized, since he knew where Dan-Oh would go to ground. Eventually.

What did matter, however, was Ray-Boy's crew, who could no longer return to the warehouse.

After phoning them, Ray-Boy picked up the broadsword and limped toward the office, suspecting he'd need a little something for shock value. If only to keep them on edge.

After he plastic-bagged and boxed his trophy, Ray-Boy returned to his room, where by the light of a pocket torch, he removed the breastplate and his clothes, bandaged his leg as well as he was able, and put on the set of street clothes he used when visiting his bank— a conservative gray pinstriped suit, white shirt and pearl gray tie, black brogues, with even a hankie in the pocket.

In the mirror, he removed the ring from the septum of his nose, which caused it to bleed a little, as always. He then gave his brogues a few swipes with a polishing rag and tossed the mattress off the cot, which covered a small armory of weapons.

What would he need? It was hard to tell, but certainly the rocket launcher and two charges just to get out of there, and the rifle that he'd used so agreeably the other night on the Glasnevin Road. It would be his weapon of revenge.

And also something to match his suit of clothes. Say a Beretta .222—smallish, light, but not without a killing punch. Slipping it into the pocket that the tailor had fixed under the left-side placket, Ray-Boy limped down the length of the building with his weaponry in tow toward the office.

There, Ray-Boy placed the scrambler in his mouth and made the final call, he assumed, from the building that he'd called home for nearly two years.

It made him feel a bit nostalgic as he moved through the darkened building to bay seven, where he kept a Land Rover for just such an emergency.

Raising the launcher to his shoulder, Ray-Boy loosed a charge that blew through the door with a stunning report and created a gap just large enough for the Rover. Which he considered an omen of such note that he decided to place the launcher beside the rifle in the well by the back gate of the vehicle.

Slowly and carefully he backed the car out into the laneway. A flat would not do now, not here where the explosion had already drawn the attention of two people in the car park of the chocolate factory. They had walked to the edge of the lot.

But what was the chance of a punct with thick, new, knobby tires on a car that could take him just about anywhere?

The thought cheered him, since it hadn't been the money, really, that made him agree to the proposition that had ended his father's sorry life and might also kill him too. No. It was the doing of it, and doing it right.

Like the heads. The heads were a brilliant touch, just the thing to make all the other Celtic bullshit, which otherwise would have been incredible, work.

Of which Ray-Boy still had a bit to do himself. But he knew where that would happen, planning being his forte. In everything.

OUT IN THE CAR PARK OF THE CHOCOLATE factory an hour earlier, Hugh Ward had watched the bay door begin to open. He saw a man bolt from under the narrow aperture, then twist around to fire a small handgun back inside before rolling to the edge of the loading dock platform. There the blast from the exploding door blew him off into the laneway, where he lay for a moment or two, before scrambling up and sprinting right at Ward, who only then saw it was the man Sweeney had called Stu on the railway platform. The tall and thin man with blondish gray curly hair. In his forties, but fit and tanned.

As he came closer and closer, Ward slumped down farther in the seat, debating what he should do—take him down or follow him.

And Ward saw he was hurt, as he bolted past the Opel. Blood was pouring down one side of his face, his ear, his neck. His eyes, which were some light shade of blue, were a bit glassy.

In the rearview mirror, Ward watched him use an electronic key to enter a rather new Volvo sedan. The lights flashed on, the car sprinted forward, then wheeled toward the road.

Ward reached for the ignition key, not the lights, and he waited until the car had bolted out into traffic. Only then did he move forward.

13

and Kara arrived at the Garda heliport near Dublin Airport.

Sweeney—McGarr could see from the large car that was pulled up beside the dispatcher's shed—had already arrived. As arranged, McGarr dialed in Sweeney's number and waited for him to answer.

"Took yiz fookin' long enough."

McGarr did not respond.

"And there you had the dead cert part. Me? I'm at sixes and sevens, I am. Every last bloody cent I could get me hands on in short notice, and every marker, favor, and good deed I've done in the past was called in. McGarr, you there?"

McGarr made a noise in the back of his throat.

"Relatives, friends, and—I'll admit it, the church—put what they could into the pot. And then, then, I had to get me hands on bloody bonds, which took some bloody doing on short notice, I'll have you know. Fifty fookin' million quid in bearer bonds, the kind you, me, or your poxy granny could take to Switzerland, the Republic of

Eire"—he pronounced it "err"—"or the Cayman Islands and have it accepted with due groveling and no questions asked.

"Where's the fookin' chopper? I'm getting out."

"Don't," said McGarr. "We'll wait until Bernie's filed a flight plan and gone through the motions inside."

"Yiz haven't done that already? Christ, you're making a balls of this thing, and we're not even off the ground."

McGarr would later remember glancing down the runway toward the west, where a lowering sky was obscuring the sunset, and thinking how ominous that sounded. Which was his last-second thought. "Have you spoken to them again?"

"I have, yeah?"

"Did they give you some idea of a direction. Bernie will need a heading for the flight plan."

"Nah, shit. They're a bunch of gobshites and wankers altogether. The most I could get out of him was head northwest, and once they see us in the air, they'll give us a bearing.

"Wait." McGarr could hear Sweeney strain and then the rumpling of paper. "It's twenty-three degrees northwest, which means nothing to me."

McGarr repeated the number, and McKeon got out of the car and approached the dispatcher's shed.

From the backseat, Kara reached out and caressed the back of McGarr's neck.

"What the fook do I do now?" Sweeney asked.

"Hang on."

"Janie, do you see that fookin' sky. Have yiz not heard the reports? We've got to get this sideshow up, up, and away. Instanter."

Leaning back into her hand, McGarr wondered how much Sweeney had drunk. Or if he had been drinking at all. Could he be always on the qui vive, like this? Was there a real Sweeney?

"Who's that with you? The person in the back with her hand on your . . . neck?" he demanded.

McGarr ignored his deep wet laugh and the unmistakable pop of a cork from the neck of a flask.

Inside the shed, McKeon found the dispatcher at his tea in the storeroom behind the office. They had timed it perfectly. "Seamus Flavin, old man, how be thee?"

"I'm in great form altogether, Bernard." His hand swept the table, which was set rather formally with an actual plate, stainless-steel utensils, and a cloth serviette. There was a microwave off to one side, and the dish appeared to be some thick beef or mutton stew. Steam was rising from the teacup. "What can I do for you?"

"I won't keep you from your tea, but didn't I dig out me hours this morning and see I'm getting low. And wouldn't you know the minute I'm found wanting, they'll be needing me services with me no longer qualified."

The man's brow glowered. "But have y'not checked the weather, Bernie? It's closing in. We've a falling barometer and predictions of fog. And it's late." He glanced at the clock on the wall, which said half five. "Can't you take her up tomorrow?"

McKeon shook his head. "It's all the better—instrumentation, night flying, the whole megillah. More like the real thing." He turned to the office, where the flight plans were kept. "The Sikorsky's gassed up, I assume, ready to go."

"Like all of them," Flavin said defensively. "All of the time. It's my job, and don't say I didn't warn you. In fact, I'll note it down." He began to rise from his chair.

But McKeon held out a hand. "Tuck in, tuck in—I'll do it for you."

Flavin looked down at the dish, nodded once, and sat. "And safe out and back."

"Please, God," said McKeon, who moved to the door and signaled to McGarr, before reaching for a flight plan. "I'm putting it right here under the conditions, Seamus—'Warned by dispatcher foul weather and darkness.' "

"Good lad."

Out on the tarmac, McGarr said into his cell phone. "Okay— we'll get out now. Quickly. And have your driver pull away."

McGarr got out and opened the back door for Kara, who was wearing stout boots, slacks, and a waterproof anorak with hood. "Just in case," she'd said.

Which had caused McGarr, who hadn't thought about the possibility of having to deal with the elements, to dress similarly in his oilskin fishing jacket, half boots, and fishing hat, all waterproof.

Sweeney, however, was as always wearing the rumpled mac. Pulling himself out of the large car, he shambled around to the boot, which had popped open, his gait at once pigeon-toed and bowlegged, which caused him to lurch from side to side.

His head was slightly bent, as though having to tote around his massive body was a burden that he felt with each lumbering step. Or that he was constantly glancing down at his feet to make sure they were following the choreography that he had devised for them. Which was, McGarr knew all too well, intricate and Byzantine. Or perhaps Celtic? There was no way to know.

McGarr tried to see into the car, but all the windows, including the windscreen, were obscured, and the interior lights had not switched on when the door opened.

Reaching down into the boot, Sweeney grunted and pulled out a packet about three feet by four feet but only four or five inches deep. Spinning around, he had to put a foot to the side in order to steady himself. "Here 'tis. Fifty fookin' mill. Take it, please." He thrust the container at McGarr, who did not raise his hands.

"Then you." He swung the packet around to Kara, who with a smile of surprise accepted it. "Now you'll be able to tell your kids you once had your hands on fifty big ones."

Reaching back, Sweeney pulled out a metal case into which, McGarr assumed, he would fit the bonds. When the lid of the boot was closed, the large car rolled away. "And haven't I heard about you, darlin' girl, and not all good. But then again"—Sweeney swung the meaty features of his pocked and rumpled face to McGarr— "I hear about myself constantly. Daily. The scandalous things people"—he jabbed a finger at McGarr's nose—"presume about me are patently outrageous when, it's now turning out, we've been on the same side all along."

"Speaking of presumptions, Mr. Sweeney," Kara said, resting the packet by her feet. "I've seen and held cartons before, but I've never glimpsed just what a bearer bond looks like."

"Ach, why not. We'll do it in the ship. I've always wanted to do it in a ship."

There were fifty sheets in all, each composed of ten U.S. $100,000 notes with perforated edges that could be torn off and redeemed, or converted into another form of currency by the bearer, hence the name. Their color was green.

"Lightweight, easily transportable, and utterly negotiable," said Sweeney. "Fools though these Druid cunts may be, they're a savvy lot when it comes to ransoms. Though, I'll hazard, they'll fall out with each other the moment this arrives in their possession."

They watched as McKeon, who had entered the cockpit, now toggled several switches, adjusted his headset, and activated the solenoid of the starter motor.

"Sure," Sweeney had to shout, "with this lot and a good"—he held the word for a moment, his rheumy eyes glancing up and fixing McGarr's—"woman, why even you might consider retirement. A world tour. The Costa del Sol.

"Are you armed, man?"

McGarr only regarded him.

"With you along, I left mine at home. But, of course, I can't be armed, villain that I am. Drink?"

From his mac, Sweeney removed a large silver flask and offered it to Kara, who had turned her head and looked away.

At the corner of her jade-colored eye, McGarr could see a tear forming.

"You?"

McGarr shook his head.

"And you—you're drivin', and get on with it."

As the helicopter lifted off into the overcast and now windy night sky, Hugh Ward watched the man called Stu lower the binoculars he'd been holding to his face before tossing them into his car and walking briskly toward the busy airlines passenger terminal that was lit by banks of brilliant lights.

Ward debated what to do—follow him or wait until he returned to the Volvo, which was parked illegally and would get clamped or towed, were he not to return soon.

After five minutes, Ward got out and checked the number of the tax stamp of the car, not daring to enter the rather new car that a small sticker on the driver-side window said was equipped with an alarm.

Back in the old Opel, Ward called Swords, who ran the number through the Garda database. "You won't believe this. The coincidence. It's owned by an outfit called the Kells Corporation, one of eight vehicles including a light truck."

"Address?"

"Thirty-seven Coolock Road."

It was the location of the warehouse.

"What about the large car, any luck with that?"

"Some. The list of possible owners runs to four pages of small type. What we'd need would be the tax number."

A tall, uniformed Garda dressed for the worsening weather now approached the Volvo, turning his head to the side to take in the license plate, then training the beam of his torch on the tax stamp. Looking into the car itself, he shook his head, evidently upon seeing the binoculars on the seat, Ward supposed. They were an open invitation to the smash-and-grab thieves who frequented the car parks of the city.

The Guard checked his wristwatch and moved on to Ward's car. "Sorry, sir, you'll have to move along. No parking here."

"What about that car—somebody special?"

"I'm giving the driver five minutes."

"What about five for me?"

"And not a minute more."

Ward explained to Swords then. "The Kells Corp. What can we find out about it—ownership, the principals, capitalization, etc."

"If it's Irish, everything." Which was the advantage of no longer actually being in the Garda, where such a search—through government commerce and tax files, which could be hacked into—would be improper and illegal without a court order. And just not done by anybody wishing to hold on to a job.

Then after some small talk, they rang off.

Moving back out into traffic, Ward turned the car south toward the warehouse off the Coolock Road.

DUBLIN AIRPORT, FROM WHICH THE GARDA helicopter took off, lies fewer than ten miles north of Dublin city center and three miles west of the Irish Sea, where, the moment that the helicopter moved out over the water, they encountered a thick fog.

"I don't like," said McKeon to McGarr, who was now seated beside him in the cockpit. "I'm fully qualified to fly by instrumentation, but I can never get used to it." He pointed at the Plexiglas bubble of the helicopter canopy, which, in spite of the airship's powerful lights, was an impenetrable gray mass that only once in a while broke to reveal just how fast they were flying—145 knots by a digital display on the control panel.

"Any luck with a heading?" McGarr asked Sweeney, who had abandoned his safety harness and was kneeling on the cabin floor a foot or so behind them. Kara had remained in a passenger seat.

"Just comin' on, I'd say. Hello, hello! Fuck! You're breakin' up. Hello." There was a pause, then, "That's fookin' better." He listened some more. "What does that sound like?" Sweeney held his cell phone to the roof of the cabin and the rhythmical beat of the rotors.

Then, back on his ear. "You happy?"

Yet another pause. "What? Iona. Iona's in fookin' Scotland, arsehole. How can we get there?" Cupping a hand over the speaker, Sweeney asked McKeon, "What about Iona? How far is that?"

McKeon shrugged and reached for the mouse on the computer display unit. Clicking through several screens he found an area map with radius bands in fifty-mile increments from their present position, which was indicated by a glowing phosphorescent dot. "The better part of two hundred miles."

"Can we make it there and back?"

"Punch in Iona, Peter." Using the keyboard, McGarr complied. McKeon clicked on "Fuel," and the screen came up with 91 percent. "Just. With little leeway for a headwind or dicking around."

"We'll leave that to your man." Sweeney's head tilted to McGarr, who turned his head to Sweeney.

"I'm not going to say this again—keep your innuendo to yourself."

"What's that supposed to mean?"

"Mind your tongue."

"Ah, Jaysus—relax, man. Chill. Here we are on the adventure of our lives, something we'll recall to our grandchildren—how we saved the fookin' book of fookin' Kells—and you've gone all prickly on us. With the sound of this thing, nobody"—Sweeney jerked a thumb to mean Kara—"heard nothin'."

Having determined a heading, McKeon now swung the helicopter on course, as indicated on the computer screen, and they beat on into the fog for whole minutes without words, Sweeney maintaining his vigil between them. Flying north-northeast literally up the middle of the Irish Sea between Scotland and Ireland, the ship now and again broke through banks of gauzy tufts, like phosphorescent cotton, that appeared before them for a second, only to melt into the fuselage.

McGarr twisted around and tried to look past Sweeney at Kara.

"She's fookin' fine, man. Sleeping, like we all should be." Sweeney had his flask out again, and the acrid-sweet stench of malt filled the cockpit.

More minutes of silence ensued as they clipped on into the dense darkness. Finally, Sweeney said, "Who d'yiz think is behind this? Particularly? Was it that Mide bloke what lost his fookin' knob? Or maybe his squeeze, the woman Morrigan. Hasn't she got a pair of bloody bumpers to be proud of? Likes 'em young, she does, I'm told. Ray-Boy Sloane, for instance, and her. There for a time they were inseparable, joined at the fookin' hip."

Neither McGarr nor McKeon said anything.

"He's my bet. Him and his old man, Ray the former. And Pape and his child bride, Gillian . . . what's her wonderful Brit last name? Rest-on. Perfect.

"Your man, Sheard, through dumb luck or whatever, he got it right, I'm thinking."

The flask appeared between them. "A wet? G'wan, it'll loosen yous up. Fook, we're stuck here, may as well make the most of it. I don't mind sharin'. And, in fact, I brought another, just in case."

After a while, Sweeney withdrew the vial. "Well, fuck yiz and the bloody pukkas you rode in on." And he returned to a seat in the cabin of the helicopter.

More minutes went by until McGarr, who had closed his eyes, heard Kara's voice. "May I ask where we're going?"

"Iona," McGarr said, reaching for her hand.

"Really? It's rather fitting, isn't it? Since it was probably where the Kells book was conceived and at least some of it produced. Have you been there, Peter?" She returned the pressure on his hand.

McGarr nodded. It had been with Noreen during the spring, when there had been few other visitors there, and he had found—in spite of his doubts and his disbelief in the holiness or serenity of a place—that the peace and tranquillity of Iona had impressed him. They had taken a walk and got lost in the fog, like this, nearly blundering into a bog.

"Well, we're here," said McKeon, slowing the chopper and looking down at the display. "But where they are is another matter altogether."

Which was when a bank of lights switched on nearly below them and illuminated what looked like four industrial pallets arranged in a square. Next to each outlined in paint were letters or numbers: "K-1," "K-2," "A," and "D," indicating the two Kells books and the books of Armagh and Durrow, McGarr supposed.

Off beyond a hedgerow sat another helicopter with aerodynamic lines that made it look newer and faster than the Garda Sikorsky.

"Fookin' brilliant, isn't it?" said Sweeney, shouldering Kara out of the way. "One thing—you've got to hand them—they sure know how to throw a party."

As McKeon began a slow descent, a solitary figure stepped out from the shadow of the other helicopter; dressed in a black cloak and mask with the strange, drainlike device covering his mouth, he was holding something that looked like a rocket launcher on his shoulder.

"Janie, Mac." Sweeney wiped sweat from his brow. "Now that I don't like, not one fookin' bit."

Sweeney's cell phone began ringing; he held it to his ear. "Yah?" He listened further, then, "Wait a minute, wait. Wait! What's your yoke on the ground all about, the one with the fookin' bazooka?"

He listened some more. "What? Don't you fookin' threaten me, you cunt, or we'll piss off out of here, and then where will you be?"

Sweeney hit the mute button on the phone. When he glanced up, his ruined eyes seemed worried. "Bastard says he's got us, and we're to do as he says. Heat-seeking missile, says he." He shook his head. "I don't like it, I don't like it at all, at all."

He turned to McKeon. "What's the chance of us avoiding that thing?"

"The missile? Fired from that short distance, the heat-seeking element doesn't matter a jot. It would be pure targeting, and we're a mighty big and slow target."

"I don't give a shit. I'm for leaving." The collar of Sweeney's shirt was damp with sweat. "So we set down and begin making the exchange. The money? Fuck—if they know anything at all about bearer bonds, they'll understand in a heartbeat they're real.

"But the books is another matter altogether. Authenticating them will take time. Look at the way they're wrapped. What's to stop them from taking the money, blowing us to bits, and leaving with the whole megillah and nary a live witness in sight?"

The phone bleated; they had hung up and called back.

Sweeney hesitated before answering. "My vote is to take our chances and leave. Now. Feint toward their landing site and just keep on going. If we stay low enough—"

McKeon shook his head.

The phone kept sounding insistently.

"I don't see him missing, and did we think they'd choose a venue they couldn't control?"

"Remember, now—I was against it." Sweeney answered the phone. "Yah?" He waited, again shaking his head. "We're to drop the money here, then set the chopper down where he's pointing."

Raising his free hand, the figure indicated another light that now switched on at the far corner of the field from the illuminated pallets.

"Only after they collect the money and leave do we get out of the helicopter. Otherwise, he blows us away."

Again scanning the neat, illuminated layout below them, McGarr hesitated. Now he too was worried. Something was awry down there. Why bother to create such a spread when a simple exchange—the money for the books—would suffice in soupy conditions in the dead of night.

But they had gone too far to turn back. "They can do that anyway. But they won't until they have the money in hand. And we've come all this way. Perhaps we should see what they've got first."

Sweeney's outsized head was wagging. "No-go. We examine the goods, only then do you get the bloody money."

A blinding flash bolted up from the launcher, and a rocket spun past them, mere feet from the churning rotors.

"Yeh cunt, yeh!" Sweeney roared. "Why'd you do that."

Even over the pounding of the rotors and the noise of the engine, McGarr could hear laughter coming from the phone.

"I'm still for splittin'. What's the chance they'll risk destroying money that's irreplaceable?"

Like the books, thought McGarr.

Slowly McKeon wheeled the lumbering craft toward the second patch of illumination.

"He says, drop the money, proceed to the landing site, and then send the woman out. He'll examine our packet while she looks at the books. Simultaneously. Any bullshit, and he sends a second round up our"—Sweeney glanced back at Kara—"britches."

He then nudged McGarr. "You'd better give me a hand with the delivery. It's a weight in that metal sleeve, so it is."

Passing by Kara, McGarr extended his hand, and she took it briefly. In the achromatic glow of the phosphorescent flares, her face looked pale, masklike, and she was plainly frightened.

"You don't have to do this," he said, sliding open the bay door. At once, the roar of the rotors was deafening, and the damp night island air swept into the cabin.

Sweeney bent over the metal case. "And to think—I've begged, borrowed, and as much as stolen the last sou I'll ever get me hands on." He raised his outsized head to her. "It's got to be genuine, the real thing—get me?"

She nodded and then looked back down at her hands.

"On the count of three," said Sweeney to McGarr. "One, two, tallyho fifty fookin' million smackers." And they launched the packet out the bay door.

With a thump it hit the ground. And McKeon swung the helicopter back toward the patch of light, where he landed, making sure that the cockpit presented a view of the other helicopter. "How's he going to lug that packet over to his chopper and—" McKeon raised a pair of night-vision binoculars to his eyes. "Ah, shit—it's already gone."

"What did I tell you?" Sweeney rushed toward the cockpit. "Give me them things." Then, "Kara—get out there, girl, and tell us if the goods is real."

Sweeney's phone began ringing again.

She glanced at McGarr, who jumped down onto the spongy turf and raised his arms to help her off.

"McGarr. McGarr!" Sweeney roared from the cockpit. "He says only her, not you."

McGarr pointed her forward, then moved off at an angle that kept most of him obscured by the body of the helicopter and the deep shadows of a hedgerow. He had a feeling that the cloaked and masked figure was alone; if others were present, they would have shown themselves bristling with armament, the further to intimidate. And with the money now gone from the drop site, the man would be struggling to get it back to his helicopter.

As McGarr moved in that direction, he caught a glimpse of Kara out of the corner of his eye, bending over the carton on the first pallet. From her pocket, she pulled out her cell phone, which she placed on top, then retrieved what looked like a box cutter.

The other helicopter was maybe seventy-five yards distant, and McGarr tried to plot the route that the other man would take to get it over two hedgerows and through a thicket of hazel bushes.

But as he neared the second airship, an amplified voice said from the helicopter, "Whoever else is out of the helicopter is risking the exchange. If you don't return immediately, we'll destroy the books, which are mined."

McGarr stopped where he was, wondering where he had heard that voice before and if it could be a bluff. He was now only a hundred or so feet from the other helicopter, and if one person was retrieving the money, then there was at least one other person aboard the ship.

It also occurred to McGarr that if they had bothered to mine the four pallets containing what they represented as the stolen books, then they evidently had no intention of actually returning them. Or whatever was encased there was not genuine; in spite of their New Druid rhetoric, would they chance blowing up an asset of such value?

No. Once they had the money securely aboard their helicopter, they would touch off the mines, perhaps even catching Kara still going about the time-consuming business of examining each of the four pallets.

But would they leave without the money and also chance destroying that too? Probably not.

McGarr heard footsteps off to his left; dropping down, he caught sight of the silhouette of a hunched-over person struggling with the large odd-sized carton that he had rigged with a sling over his shoulder, so that the weight was resting on his back.

And it struck McGarr even then, as he dropped down and waited for the figure to move closer, that there could not have been enough time to open the carton and examine the contents. In fact, how had he known to equip himself with a sling just the length and design to accommodate the packet?

Now with only a few yards separating them, McGarr rushed forward and lunged at the figure, one shoulder striking him squarely at the knees. The sling and its contents fell from the man's hands, and he went down hard.

Scrambling to his feet, McGarr began to raise his Walther when the deep island night exploded in successive balls of orange flame. The concussion of the first blast drove him right over the other man, who was still on the ground.

And three successive blasts kept toppling him farther still. Finally, when he managed to move, he found he had lost the handgun somewhere in the now-pitch darkness. And even one of his shoes.

He was dizzy, and something was wrong with his hearing. In shock or pain, he could not summon the strength to raise himself up.

Kara could not possibly have survived those blasts, unless somehow, for some reason—maybe the warning the pilot had issued—she'd returned to the helicopter.

And as from a distance, he was now hearing faint voices.

"Are you all right, Stu?" asked the voice from the helicopter, the one he thought he had heard before.

"Aye. Muckle fine, if only I could walk. Where is he?" The accent was Scots.

"Forget him. We've got what we want, and now it's time to get out. Without delay."

"Pass me your light—I'll put a bullet in his head."

"No, you won't. You know his preference in this, what we agreed to as our part of the bargain. We're to keep him alive."

"Him? Why the fuck is it always his preference that matters. With this money, it's now us who've fuckin' got the hammer."

"Yes, but we don't quite safely have the money, do we?"

Not long after McGarr heard the whine of a starter, followed by the thump of rotors accelerating, and he shielded his head from the blast of the helicopter lifting off.

Once it was clearly away, he again tried to stand. Something was burning his back.

A beam of light playing over the brush now found him. "Peter, be still. Your jacket's smoldering." It was McKeon.

It stung more severely, as McKeon used his own jacket to press out the burning material.

"Do you think you can stand?"

He nodded. "Help me. Where's Kara?"

McKeon hauled him to his feet.

"What about Kara?"

"Let's take care of you first."

"Take me to her."

"Ah, now, there's not much we can do for her, I'm afraid. Sweeney rushed out to pull her away, and I'm afraid maybe . . ." His voice trailed off.

No, McGarr thought, not a second time. Maybe thirty yards away he could see small brushfires scattered around the area where the pallets had stood. Glowing, smoldering debris was scattered everywhere, it seemed: snagged in the low trees and bushes and littering the ground of open field. Wood, textile, cardboard. Like snow, a confetti of paper tufted the grass.

McKeon had trained the ground lights of the helicopter on the area where the pallets with their packets had been. And there stood

Sweeney with Kara limp in his arms, staggering, one side of his face streaming with blood.

He swayed and took two tentative steps in the direction of the helicopter. Instead of falling, as though careful of his burden, he spun and sat almost gracefully.

McGarr could see she was dead, her back was clearly broken and ripped open to the bone with one leg nearly severed. And she too was burned, her long umber hair scorched to the scalp.

"Janie, didn't I try to pull her away?" Sweeney said, his deep voice suddenly gone high. His right eye was plainly damaged, both the brow, the cheek below, and the orb. "But I only just got to her when the fuckin' thing went up, and blew her into me. She"—he raised a hand and touched a bloody cheek—"never fell. Know what?"

McGarr squatted down to take Kara from him.

"I can't quite make you out."

"I'll take her now. Bernie will help you up."

Telling himself that if he just dealt with what had to be done at the moment, moment by moment, he'd be able to make it through, he lifted her out of Sweeney's arms.

What struck McGarr is how perfect she still looked, in his mind unchanged from the woman who had jumped off the helicopter only minutes before.

But carrying her through the field, he felt so desolate and bereft that he truly wished he had been blown apart there as well. To think that Kara had as much as said she thought the attempt foolhardy but would accompany him because he had asked, and then to have her beautiful, innocent person utterly destroyed like this—well, it was an enormity of which McGarr himself alone was guilty. Done to salvage his reputation and failing career.

Having to strain to lift her into the helicopter, McGarr found himself suddenly dizzy. But he managed to scramble into the high bay door near where he found a litter and several emergency blankets to cover her.

"Peter—there's a ladder to the right," McKeon said. "And if you could give me a hand with him. We should get out of here. The blasts . . ."

Would have been heard and probably reported, and the last thing they needed was a run-in with the local police.

"Ah, Janie," Sweeney kept saying. "Janie Mac, it smarts. Is there someplace I can lie down. I feel a little woozy."

Opening a second litter, they helped Sweeney lower his body into the canvas sling. "Thanks. Thanks, gents. What a debacle. A complete and utter fuckin' debacle."

It was only after McGarr took a seat and they were airborne that he again became conscious of the burning pain in his back.

Yet in one very significant way the steady sear was necessary—at least in some small way he too had been injured and had participated in her agony. Which mercifully had to have been brief.

Instead of appearing abandoned, the old warehouse and its laneways were teeming with police and emergency vehicles, cherries splashing the building with lurid swipes of red, halogen alley lights focused on two shattered bay doors—the one that was only open a yard or so, and another with a gaping hole fringed with shattered strips of metal.

Getting out, Ward advanced quickly on the low door, which was not being guarded. He slid under and moved toward the office where a small crowd of Gardai and emergency personnel had gathered.

They had only just arrived, he could tell, and were still in some shock at what they had discovered.

Playing the beams of strong handheld lights above them, they were staring at the headless corpse of a woman who had been strung up, like the carcass of a sheep, from one ankle. Her other leg and arms were hanging akimbo, and her two large breasts had lolled out from under her blouse. Dark, old blood had pooled everywhere, it seemed.

There was a note pinned to the garment at crotch level. In large letters with a Celtic flare, it said, "Oh, Dan-Oh Boy."

A uniformed superintendent turned to Ward. "Hughie—what are you doing here?"

Eyes scanning the rest of the office, Ward said nothing.

"You shouldn't be here, you know."

"Have you looked around yet?"

The man shook his head. "Just got here."

"Mind if I take a peek? I have an idea who did this."

The man thought for a moment, then, "Only if I come with you."

In the far corner of the building, they found Ray-Boy's Celtic paraphernalia, along with the green walls, the skulls, the battered door, the video camera—everything out of the ransom tapes.

"I'd say, bingo. But we would have found it anyway."

"The person who called it in?" Ward asked. "Strange, gravelly, Darth Vadar–like voice?"

"The same."

Ray-Boy Sloane, Ward wanted to say. Guilty of patricide, at least three other murders, participating in the theft at Trinity, and now this.

But he had also noted the surgical gauze, bandage plasters, and scissors on the floor near the cot, the sheets that were stained with other rather fresh-looking blood. Four indentations on the breast-plate that had probably been made by small-caliber bullets.

Ray-Boy had been injured in his exchange with the man, Stu— or, rather, "Dan-Oh Boy"—and Ward wondered where he would seek shelter.

Home to mum and the two sisters? Perhaps, if only briefly. One of them was a nurse, Ward remembered from the information that the squad had assembled.

After that, maybe 24 Spancel Court, Ranelagh.

"Thanks." Pivoting, Ward made for the door.

"Where're you going? Do you know who this is? Hughie, you're not telling us everything."

Ward quickly moved toward the blossom of brilliant, achromatic light flooding through the shattered bay door.

14

"Drink!" Sweeney kept shouting as the old Sikorsky limped home. The roar of the engine firing up had awakened him. "What a fookin' debacle. A debacle!"

McKeon told McGarr where the medical kit was, but even after three tablets of a painkiller/sedative—the maximum allowed, according to the instructions on the vial—he was still giving out.

"You lost me fookin' money, me fookin' eye, I'm sure. And the fookin' books to boot. Whatever got into you, man, to think you could rush them? What we wanted, needed, had to have, was a clean exchange, nothing more, nothing less. We should have left when I said. But there you had to fookin' go and play fookin' cowboy."

McGarr was sitting near Kara or, at least, near where her remains lay.

"I'll tell you here and now—I don't know how any of us is going to get over this," he continued. "But I'm going to try, and let the chips fall where they may."

It was then Sweeney discovered whatever was left of his second flask. Throwing back his head, he finished the last drop, then squeaked the silver cap into the top. "And another thing, McGarr—"

McGarr leaned across Kara so he wouldn't have to shout over the beating of the rotors, the roar of the engine. "I want you to listen to me now, and I won't say this again. Don't say another word. Not one."

"Who the fuck do you think you are," Sweeney began saying, "to talk to me like—" when McGarr slammed the barrel of his Walther into the side of the larger man's temple.

"I should shoot you now and drop your body into the sea. That would be better for him"—McGarr swung the barrel toward McKeon—"and me. And her." He meant Kara. "It was your idea, we helped you, but—like her—you did not survive." McGarr waited a moment. "Got that?"

Sweeney looked away drunkenly, his head swaying. But he did not respond.

McGarr's sorrow, his guilt, his remorse—no, his bloody anger— at Kara's death was boundless, infinite, world-darkening. Now he did not care what happened to him in the particular; that Kara, like Noreen, had died because of their mutual involvement with him made him fearless.

What had Bernie said? Crash and burn? He would crash and burn, but he would bring whoever had slain Kara and made a fool of him down. It had come to that.

Dawn was breaking by the time they got back to Dublin Airport, and the moment the helicopter touched down, three men stepped out of the Garda office there and approached the aircraft.

"Open the fookin' door," Sweeney said groggily. "And help me up." Once down the ladder and onto the tarmac, Sweeney had to steady himself before setting off on a stagger toward the terminal building.

Said McKeon to McGarr, "You've enough trouble already. Get yourself gone. I'll deal with this, and, remember—I'm with you. Maybe you have an idea?"

McGarr raised his hand; McKeon's met his firmly.

At his car, McGarr gathered himself. He tried to remember everything he could about the blast and its aftermath—what the two from the helicopter had said, one wanting to kill him and the other saying that wasn't in the cards, that they'd agreed to keep him alive. Why? Agreed with whom?

As well, one had called the other Stu, as had Sweeney the man with him on the railway platform at the delivery of the second ransom tape. Kara's husband was—or had been—named Dan Stewart. He was Scottish; the Stu on Iona had a Scots burr.

Could Stu be "Stew" instead? it now occurred to McGarr. Could Kara—with her husband, Dan Stewart—have been in on the theft and murders all along? And could what McGarr thought he had shared with her have been nothing more than an element of the scheme? For a share of 50 million quid many people could be made to do just about anything, he knew all too well.

But why, then, would the husband plan and carry out her execution in such a barbarous way? And why the need to bait and entrap McGarr himself?

Yet the Stu at the meet in Iona had not thought it necessary to check the ransom payment, and he had equipped himself with just what was necessary to carry the bulky packet. And obviously all along, the two of them had planned to blow up the books anyway. Or a facsimile edition of the books. McGarr now remembered the confetti of paper around the meadow.

Where to begin? Twisting the ignition key of his Mini-Cooper, McGarr thought he had an idea. The small, fast car, accelerating, forced his back into the seat, reminding him that he should tend to whatever wound was there, and perhaps get some rest.

Pulling up in front of Kara's flat not far from his own house in Rathmines, McGarr reached into Kara's handbag, which he had thought to take out of the helicopter, and found her keys.

But he had only closed the gate and turned around when he found Orla Bannon in front of him.

"I know, I know—like a bad penny, and so forth. But I was—am—worried about you, McGarr, given how you seem to be the target of the government, the New Druids, and certain dangerous women, meself included." It was a cool early morning, and she had dressed accordingly in black leather slacks and jacket that was tight on her torso and seemed to mound her breasts, which were swathed in a white cashmere jumper in the open top. She had her long dark braid in her hands.

"I mean, your HQ is shut down, and you were not at home, Nuala told me—we had a nice long chat in the kitchen, looking out at your garden. So I figured the only other place apart from Flood's you might wash up is"—she swung her head to the house—"and here you are looking haggard, I must say. Where've you been?

"And what's that smell? Cordite? Or have y'been near a fire?"

McGarr looked up at the windows of Kara's flat and suddenly felt as desolate as he had on the helicopter. That he had again exposed somebody he cared for to the lethal dangers of his profession—and she, not he, had paid the ultimate price—was so . . . upsetting that . . . "I'd like your help."

"Name it."

"Would your paper have file photos of Pape, Gillian Reston, and your man Sweeney?"

"He's not my man in anything but pay packet. And who knows for how long."

"Could you get hold of them and meet me at Foyle's? It's a pub—"

"Sure, I know where it is. The deceased Raymond Sloane frequented the place, I was told."

"Can you do it in"—McGarr checked his watch—"two hours?"

"*Mais oui.*" She smiled in a way that made her jet eyes sparkle and dimples appear in her cheeks. "It's a date. Yet might I wonder—is there some small chance that there's a story in it for *moi?* From the killer look of you, I'm thinking there is."

McGarr stepped by her and moved to the door with the key out. "Be there. I won't forget it."

"I like your purse. Is it new? I have a key for you too, keep in mind. Whenever you're ready."

Climbing the wide staircase with its carved banister reminded McGarr of the two other occasions on which he had received the love of she who had been very special to him, no matter what he might discover about her. And he now hated himself for having doubted so much about her.

The door to her flat, however, was partially open, and the photos, which he had come for, had been removed from the long table against the wall in the den. Or, at least, all those that pictured her husband, Dan Stewart.

It took McGarr about an hour to search the apartment without finding another representation of the man. Pouring himself a malt, he moved into the bedroom, where, standing before the three-way mirror of her dresser, he pulled off his jacket, which had a large scorch in the middle that had also burned through the shirt and left a perfectly round patch of darkened skin in the middle of his back, a black spot the size of a fist.

Was it a sign? And what to do about that? Nothing without going back to his house, and McGarr did not think he could do that unless and until he exculpated himself in some way. Nuala might understand, but what could he possibly say to Maddie?

He had noticed several men's shirts in the hall closet, along with three jackets, slacks, and shoes in a size far larger than his own. He could roll up the sleeves of a shirt, and one of the jackets might be close enough in fit.

Perhaps it was the alcohol and the fact that he could not remember when he had last had food, but as he stepped away from the closet, the sense of loss and his own gross incompetence welled up and stopped him in the middle of the sitting room.

Tears burst from his eyes, he hung his head, and he remained like that for whole minutes, not knowing how he could possibly carry on. But it was essential, before he was further humiliated by being locked up.

As he raised his head, his eyes fell upon the purse, which was blurred through his tears. In the wallet, he found a surprising amount of cash, more than 5,000 Euros, along with a snapshot of Dan Stewart, the husband, and—even more surprising—a photo of McGarr himself, which had been clipped from a newspaper.

But when? Before the theft of the Kells book? Or after? McGarr did not read everything written about him, and he was usually un-interested in any of it.

After, he could only think. It had to be after.

In the toilet, he bathed, shaved with a razor he found there, and donned the shirt and jacket, which proved longish in the sleeves and tight on his arms and shoulders. In the car, he remembered, he had a hat.

But what to do about his eyes, the gray color of which made the abiding red all the more apparent.

With Kara's keys in his pocket, McGarr locked the door behind him and moved quickly down the stairs, remembering suddenly, as he approached his car, the artist's rendering he'd ordered of the man who had met with Raymond Sloane in Foyle's fortnight before the theft. A man who had been seen with a complementary woman who McGarr hoped had not been Kara Kennedy.

He reached for his phone.

It was fully midmorning when McGarr pulled up in front of Foyle's, where the door had been propped open. The footpath was wet, and Annie Foyle, wearing a bib apron and heavy black shoes, was sweeping it down.

McGarr pulled into a no-parking zone and lowered the visor with a Garda shield attached to the back. At least he still had that.

The damp weather of the night before had passed, and overhead the sky was freighted with a line of high white clouds rolling in from the north. Otherwise, the fall sun, rich and golden, was warm where it fell.

"I wouldn't trust that sky. There's been an edge to the wind for days now," she said, without looking up from her work. Her eyeglasses were nested in her steely hair. "The others you sent for is in at the bar, Orla—a darlin' girl if ever there was one—among 'em." She glanced up at McGarr, taking him in. "And one of us. Have y'not had your breakie?"

McGarr tried to smile.

With broom now over her shoulder, she tilted her head at the open door. "Come in, I'll get you a nice fry and a cuppa. Make you a new man for a new day."

Which was something his mother had said.

Stepping in from the sunlight, the pub was dark, and McGarr could barely pick out the three lone figures in front of the taps. The only light was from a television over the bar.

Orla Bannon and Ruth Bresnahan were sitting on either side of John Swords. Only Swords had a drink, explaining, "Been up all night, Chief."

McGarr nodded, then, "Ruthie?"

"Rang up John here an hour ago, said I'd like a quiet word." Her eyes swirled to O'Bannon. "He said he was coming here to see you, and since it's only around the corner . . ."

There was a long moment and then, "We think you've been keeping something from us, Peter," said Bresnahan. "Where's Bernie?"

"And Kara Kennedy?" Bannon put in. "Without her purse. May I make an observation?"

Beyond tired now—exhausted, really—McGarr waited.

"Your tailor should get his eyes checked. Or maybe he has a higher opinion of you than is necessary." Her dark eyes smiled up at him mischievously.

Said Swords, "Sheard's been asking after you, and there's a report of a Garda helicopter having gone missing overnight, only to return banged up with a body inside."

"Here now's your tea," said Foyle. "I've got the niece on the fry, so I'm all yours. You've something to show me, Orla says?"

"Well, I only assumed."

McGarr moved toward the tea, which she had set on a table away from the bar, and the others followed. "Tell me, have you ever seen either of these people before?" He placed photos of Kara Kennedy and her husband, Dan Stewart, before her.

Sitting, the old woman pulled down her eyeglasses and fitted them over her nose. She turned them into the light from the doorway, then held them at various distances.

Finally, "She's only ever been in here once. She was with the infamous Chazz Sweeney, which was the only time he ever darkened our doorway as well. And that fella was with them too." She pointed at the photo of Stewart.

"With Sweeney drunk and saying to the other two, 'Ah, sure—aren't you two the best son and daughter-in-law a father could have.' He even sang feckin' 'Danny Boy' with nobody but me daring tell him to shut his bloody big gob, the little good it did."

The others stepped closer to get a look at the photographs.

"When was that?"

"All of a year ago. No, I'm probably wrong about that—it's two, I'd say. Or more. Time ramblin' on as you get up in years, don't you know."

McGarr nodded. He knew, and he wanted to know, that it had been at least two years ago. "They were here to meet Raymond Sloane, the Trinity guard?"

She pursed her lips and glanced out into the street. "He could have nipped in, like, since the door is closed apart from me checking for drinks. But he wasn't among them that I recall."

"What about the man and woman you told me about, the two who came in here two weeks ago and met with Sloane?"

"Him it was, for sure. The one who was in here with Sweeney." She pointed to the photo of Stewart. "The woman, like I said, I saw little of, since it was Raymond who ordered and carried the drinks in. But the artist you sent round? Two of the lads said they got a look at her, which I don't doubt, gawkers and stalkers that they are. And what he came up with wasn't too much unlike her."

Swords opened an envelope and slid the artist's mock-ups of a man who looked not unlike Stewart. The rendering of the woman, on the other hand, bore only a vague similarity to Kara and could more easily have been Gillian Reston.

"What did she drink?"

"Wine. All the upmarket lassies drink wine these days. I'll have to remind meself to get more in, now that we've been discovered." She winked at Orla Bannon.

McGarr's eyes passed across the bottles in back of the bar. Far from tea, he could use something stronger, although what he needed, he well knew, was absolute clarity. He had the feeling he'd been in over his head from the start without knowing.

"What about these?" Orla Bannon pulled two photos out of her purse and placed them before Foyle.

"Them two are in here near weekly, the Duke and Duchess we call them. Gin for him, vodka for her. Bitter lemon, the both of them. And the Duke, he can get nasty. We hear him right through the door, lashing into her with his tongue. One time, I sent a lad in to check on her."

"Sloane join them?"

"I never knew he did until once I opened the door without knocking first, and there he was, standing by them with an envelope in his hands. Like embarrassed. Or caught. Guilty."

A young woman in an apron appeared beside them holding a hot plate in a towel.

"Before you tuck into your breakfast, Chief. May I have a word?" Bresnahan eased off the bar stool and moved toward the door. McGarr followed.

"What about me?" Bannon asked. "Amn't I invited for the rest of the ride? There's gratitude for you."

Turning her back to the others, Bresnahan explained how, on the evening before, Ward had followed the man Sweeney had called Stu from the warehouse out of which Ray-Boy Sloane was running his drug operation to Dublin Airport. "He'd had a falling out with somebody inside. There was shooting, and he was injured enough to bloody his head and face.

"Outside the terminal, Stewart just got out of the car and abandoned it in the street. Hughie checked the registration, which said Kells Corp. So I ran down the name."

McGarr nodded. Even private entities doing business in Ireland had to declare the name and address of a party who would be responsible for any malfeasance. Usually it was a solicitor. Bresnahan handed McGarr a slip of paper. "Number Twenty-three, Fitzwilliam Square. From what I can tell without actually going there, it's a residence owned by"—her smoky gray eyes fixed his—"*Ath Cliath*.

"Also, Hughie believes he has a line on Ray-Boy Sloane." She then related what Ward had discovered when he returned to the warehouse—the police, the blown-out door, the headless corpse most probably of Gillian Reston, Ray-Boy's lair where the ransom tapes had been filmed with the heads on the wall.

"Earlier, when we were there together, he overheard somebody taking down another address that sounded like a fallback position. That's there too." She pointed to the second address.

Which eliminated Ray-Boy as the second man with Dan Stewart on Iona. Dan, who had murdered his wife, who might herself have been a party to his many crimes, although McGarr could still not credit that.

Not that he had ever thought Ray-Boy and his New Druid louts could have been capable of coordinating the theft at Trinity, and even in the making of the film, with its historical and other references to Celtic culture, they'd probably had help. Ray-Boy Sloane was no intellectual.

"Where's Hughie now?"

"There." She pointed to the 24 Spancel Court, Ranelagh, address. "But he's fading. I'm going out to spell him now."

"Best case?" McGarr slipped the paper into his pocket and wondered if he actually knew the best case anymore. "Follow him. He can't be behind this thing, not totally, and for whatever reason—his cut, revenge—he'll lead us to them."

Said Bresnahan, "And then there's the falling-out with this Dan who, I assume, was the husband of Trinity's keeper of old manuscripts."

In averting his eyes from hers, McGarr gazed at the television screen, where, he noted, a camera was panning in on the Garda helicopter that McKeon and he had flown to Iona. There was a large hole where shrapnel from the blast had struck the rear of the fuselage. The audio report had been muted.

"So you don't hear it secondhand . . ." McGarr then told her what had happened on Iona.

Bresnahan was stunned. Her hands moved out to the one he had placed on the bar. "Oh, Peter—how ever will we get you out of this? And Bernie."

McGarr shook his head; it was something he'd have to do himself. It was tragic enough that he'd sent Kara to her death and brought McKeon down; he could not involve anybody else. He had to find out who was behind the theft, the murders, the disaster on Iona with proof and quickly, before Sheard, O'Rourke, and Kehoe made him yet more of a scapegoat than he was already. Made him and his name infamous, which, of course, was Maddie's name as well.

Again he glanced at the television screen, which was showing McKeon being led into a Garda patrol car. "Stay on Ray-Boy is all I ask. And keep me informed."

Sliding off the stool, he looked down the bar where the three others were sitting with the plate of food on the table. "Come et your breakie and have a sup." Foyle pointed to the place setting.

Debating with himself how to proceed, he decided that if the worst happened, he would want his side told in all its particularity, mainly for Maddie. He raised his hand. "Orla." With a snap of his fingers, he called her to him.

"Ah, Janie, no—you can't be thinking of telling her," Bresnahan whispered. "Going public without all your pins in place is . . . suicidal."

Taking the diminutive younger woman by the arm, he led her out onto the sunny, windswept footpath.

"Is this 'your place or mine' time?" she quipped. "Couldn't we wait at least until the sun is over the yardarm?"

At her car, he opened the door for her.

"Jaysus, it is. Well"—she cocked her head and smiled up at him—"I'm a woman of my word."

McGarr closed the door, walked around, and got behind the wheel. "You're acquainted with the phrase 'not for attribution'?"

"Ah, shit. How did I know you'd turn out to be a big, bloody, two-hearted wanker. First, you break me heart, now you're breakin' me back. Attribution is what I do. Without attribution I'm just a sourceless gobshite."

McGarr's eyes flickered over the display of the clock; it was nearly noon. Now that he had an address for Dan Stewart, he would go there. "Listen, first, and you'll know why. This is important to me but more so to my daughter. And eventually you'll have more of a story than you'll need."

She let out a little cry of pique. "I can't believe he's using his power over me to corrupt me principles." Her dark eyes met his; they were smiling. She studied his face, then said, "You tell me what you must, and it'll be safe with me until you say otherwise. You're a good man, McGarr, and I believe in you."

Her hand reached out and gave his a squeeze.

He told her everything—about Kara and him, the ransom process, the helicopter, what they found on Iona, how Kara bravely began examining the cartons on the pallets while he made a rush for the man who had retrieved the money, how that man might well have been her husband, how perhaps she had been in with him all along. "Why? For what?" he asked.

Orla canted her head and looked out through the windscreen at the twin rows of attached and timeworn workers' houses that marked the area. There was not a green leaf or growing thing in sight. Everything looked gray and gritty, in spite of the strong sun.

"The money, of course. Fifty million quid is quite some sum, is it not? But from what you tell me, I'm not sure she was involved—why kill her? Perhaps the husband, this Dan person, got the notion of stealing the books because of what she said, how she enthused about them. He might have been tired of her. He's plainly a bad man." She shook her head.

Orla then turned to McGarr. "The greater question for you and, may I presume to say, for me is—why you? Did circumstances mark you? You just happened to be in the wrong place at the wrong time? Or—"

Now both were staring out at a rather young woman with two toddlers, a pram, and a dog on a leash, who was struggling to negotiate the narrow footpath between grimy row houses and the busy street.

Suddenly Orla turned to McGarr and raised one arm, looping it over his shoulders in the small car. "Come 'ere. Give me a hug."

He hesitated.

"No, come here. Do as I say. Put your head right here." She touched her upper chest.

McGarr removed his hat and leaned toward her, and she pulled him in. She was warm and soft, and she ruffled the curls at the back of his head.

"Credit the possibility that I in my profession—like you in yours—have seen some people in my time. Observed them, questioned them, had to come to terms with their lives in, I hope, honest words. Few get to do that. And don't think I haven't been tracking you.

"Years ago, at your wife's gallery during an opening when I was a wee thing writing obits at the *Times*, I saw you two together and I thought, Now there's the perfect couple. She, this little red doll, and you, at once the hardest and gentlest man in the universe." There was a pause in which she took his hand and made him cup her left breast. "You're a rare, brave man, McGarr, and my greatest hope? That you can get through this.

"Me? I'll put this story on hold. Nor will I run it at *Ath Cliath*. I'm done working for that man."

Closing his eyes and wishing he could sleep there, McGarr listened to her breathing and her heart, and only after a while did the import of what she had said occur to him. "You know something I don't?"

Her breast juddered as she shook her head. "If I did, I'd tell you. And you should know that."

And it occurred to him that life was indeed short and could, as it had for Kara, be snuffed out at any moment. "I should go."

"I know. Shall I come with you? I could help you."

McGarr had to think, because it was plain that something had just passed between them. And it was also clear that whatever it was, it was good.

But he had already been down that road twice before. Fatally.

15

THE ADDRESS WAS FANCY INDEED—FITZWILLIAM Square, one of the priciest streets in the city.

Nuala still owned property there, the large house in which Noreen grew up.

Finding a space virtually in front of the building, McGarr eased the Cooper into the curb and decided against lowering the visor with the Garda shield attached.

Instead he pulled out his cell phone and dialed his home number, which was answered on the first ring. "Peter, where are you? Tell me you weren't a part of this thing they're reporting on the teley. Haven't they collared Bernie McKeon, who, they say, might be charged with murder, to say nothing of stealing a helicopter."

"I'm hoping it will all work out right," McGarr said, scanning the facade of the building where, supposedly, Kells Corp Limited or Dan Stewart or both were located.

"Hoping?" There was a pause. "It's not like you to hope."

"Where's Maddie?"

"In school."

"And yesterday."

"Ditto. You don't sound like yourself."

"Number Twenty-three Fitzwilliam Square—ever been in there?"

"Countless times. Didn't the Burleighs live there, and Hubert, a partner of Fitz's in one thing or another?"

"Was it flats then?"

"No, but it's flats now. Or businesses with one flat in the eaves, I'm thinking. What about this Orla Bannon? She seems too nice to be a reporter, and she's mad about you."

"Three flats?"

"Four, counting the attic, which Adelaide, after Hubert died, converted into a 'pad' for her son, David. You remember him—we had him down in the country often. A great shot, as I recall, but a crashing bore otherwise."

"Would that be 23D, then?"

"If the ground floor is A."

"How do I get up there without going in the front door?"

"Can you get in the back from the laneway?"

"I'll see. Hang on." McGarr moved down an alley that led to the laneway that gave onto the back gardens of the houses on that side of Fitzwilliam Square.

Every now and then a patch of cloud, driven on a strong north-easterly wind, would pass across the face of the sun, making it chill and wintry. There was a door into the back garden of 23 that looked pickable. "I can get in—then what?"

"Get in first."

"I'll have to slip the phone in my pocket."

"I hope you're not doing anything illegal that will embarrass us."

It was a simple barrel lock, and McGarr was quickly inside. "Now what?"

"If you're facing the back of the building, look to the right. See those steps down? When Noreen, rest her soul, was a child, her friend Josephine had a playroom down there large enough to kick around balls and ride bikes. Right outside the interior door, there used to be gates to a lift that they'd spend hours riding up and down."

Catching sight of a head in the window of the second floor, Mc-Garr moved quickly toward the house and down the stairs to the basement door. "Thank you, Nuala."

"When are you coming home again?"

"I'll phone."

"For dinner?"

"I'll phone."

The lock on the basement door proved no more complicated, but McGarr had to shoulder the jamb to open it enough to slip in. He listened for an alarm before closing it.

The room had obviously not been used for any purpose by the new owner and still contained a variety of dusty and dated toys—a rocking horse, a box brimming with batons, balls, even a hula hoop—and the thought that Noreen, as a child, before she met him, had played and laughed and had fun in the room stopped him cold.

It was as though he could feel her presence there. "Noreen," he said to the darkness, "I miss you so, so much."

He waited, hoping that there would be some sign, anything, by which her spirit would acknowledge his attempt to make contact with her. But he heard only the squeak of the floor above him, as somebody walked across the room.

The lift was an ancient affair with an open-mesh accordion safety door. Peering up, McGarr could just catch sight of the car, which was, he guessed, on the fourth and final floor. Nearby there was a flight of stairs with—he aimed the beam of his penlight up into the darkness—a lock.

And then, he imagined, each floor, containing a separate business or flat, would be locked away from the others.

He unbuttoned his jacket and loosened the handgun that he carried under his belt before reaching for the call button. With a crack, the old elevator's solenoid engaged, and the counterweights raced up as the lift descended, rattling and juddering until with a kind of sigh it arrived in front of him. Sliding back the accordion grate, he stepped in and began his ascent.

At the fourth floor, he could see into the flat, which was mainly one long room. There was a large bed positioned under a dormer window looking out into the square with the kitchen area by other windows facing the back garden.

He could hear the steady ticking of a clock, and some other sound, like breathing. He tilted his head. No, more like snickering. But from where?

"Your mother-in-law couldn't have told you about this, now could she?"

Startled, McGarr swung round and looked up into the barrel of a gun and the smiling face of Dan Stewart, who was squatting above an open hatch in the ceiling of the elevator. "More's the pity."

McGarr lurched toward a corner of the elevator, and the shot, which was stellar in the small conveyance, grazed the side of his shoe. A second blast ricocheted around the cabin. And a third and a fourth.

McGarr had just drawn his Garda-issue Glock to fire at the ceiling of the lift when he heard a flurry of shots from inside the flat—some large-caliber handgun. There was a pause, a thud, and then Stewart's arm, shoulder, and the side of his face lolled from the open hatch.

Stewart's hand opened and the gun clattered to the floor. There was a large red hole under his chin from which blood now began to pour.

Swinging his Glock toward the flat, McGarr found Jack Sheard standing beyond the grate, holding a handgun by his side, massive and stalwart. "Ah, McGarr—you make a balls of everything, don't you?" He opened the grate. "You should get out of here before it's made worse. Take the stairs."

"How—?"

"Haven't we been staking out this place from day one? We were hoping Stewart would lead us to the others, if there are any. The books and now the money. Go on." He waved the gun at the door dismissively. "Get yourself gone."

McGarr did not know what to think: Like Stewart, Sheard must have caught sight of him going through the back garden and entering the house. Why had he not waited for night? "I—"

"Don't say anything, please. Just get the fuck out."

There were faces in the doorways of the three landings. And whispers. Did he hear ". . . the disgraced one?" "Yeah, he's suspended," and ". . . up on charges"?

In the shadow of the alley, he paused to gather himself and thought of Maddie, Nuala, Bernie, and all the others whose lives would be affected by the spate of trouble he had just brought on. Because he felt he had been—what was the term?—dissed. His pride had been hurt by O'Rourke and Kehoe when Sheard had been placed over him.

And all along Sheard had been the competent one who'd had a lead on Stewart.

What he regretted most, however, was not having questioned Stewart about Kara, and if she'd been a part of the conspiracy.

In the car, the lack of sleep and food suddenly hit him hard. He glanced at his watch—it was just about time to pick up Maddie. But instead he rang up Nuala and asked her to send a car in his place. After all, she could afford it, and, the truth was, he just wasn't up to facing his daughter and any questions she might ask.

"It's all over the news about Bernie, the helicopter, the dead woman, and you. They have him in custody. They're looking for you."

McGarr did not reply. He had pulled into the curb near the Royal Canal, and he now eased back his seat and closed his eyes.

"Are you all right, lad?"

"Sleep." He rang off but did not fall asleep right away, asking himself: If he had been in Sheard's shoes—the same Sheard who had gone on television to announce that Pape, Gillian Reston, and Ray-Boy Sloane and his New Druid drug gang were behind the theft and murders—would he have hesitated at all in collaring Stewart?

Sheard was already on record saying he'd solved the crime. Who, then, could Stewart lead him to?

McGarr closed his eyes and tried not to think of Kara Kennedy and whether . . .

He awoke with a start. The cell phone, which he had cupped to his chest, was bleating insistently.

"It's me again," said Nuala. "I hope you got some sleep and had something to eat."

McGarr tried to speak, as he leaned forward to bring the seat back up to a driving position.

"Are you near a teley?"

McGarr swirled his neck, which was sore, and the burn on his back was again galling him. Glancing out the windscreen, he caught sight of a canal-side pub. "Could be."

"Should be. Sweeney? They're saying he's recovered the Book of Kells and the other two, but lost an eye into the bargain, to say nothing of fifty-five million. And he'll be damned, says he, if the books ever get returned to godless—he actually said the word on national television—Trinity College, gobshite that he is." Like Noreen, Nuala was a graduate of Trinity.

"Fifty-five million?"

"Aye, you heard right. I think he's drunk. He then went on to say he had to spend another five million, in addition to the fifty that was already splashed out. To get the real books back, don't you know. But he did it without the bungling and life loss of the Garda Siochana.

"Would you like to speak to Maddie?"

No, he thought. He did not want to speak to his daughter in his present mood. "Yes. Of course." He had to wait for her to come on, as he walked toward the pub.

"Peter?"

"Mad'."

"Are you okay?"

"I am, yah."

"What about Bernie, my . . . godfather."

"He'll be fine, don't worry. It's wrong, what's being said. It's all a bit more complicated than people know at the moment."

McGarr stepped into the pub and moved toward the bar, which was unusually quiet, all eyes on the screen.

"I've got to go."

And yet again they repeated the litany of "love-yous" that Mc-Garr found difficult to endure but his daughter obviously required.

Sweeney had chosen the venue, McGarr concluded—the steps of St. Mary's. Pro-Cathedral Catholic Church on the North and working-class side of the city. And it was a live event with the cameras showing Sweeney with a bandage over his eye and his helpers—in white jumpers with *Ath Cliath* in green-and-orange lettering across the front—arranging the stolen books for the cameras, while a voice-over explained that Sweeney had called for the press conference only an hour earlier.

Details of his checkered past were then reprised—as a businessman and convicted felon, his successful suits against the Garda and the government, the circumstances of his purchasing *Ath Cliath* from its founder, who was discovered murdered two days later.

Finally, saying, "Enough. That's enough for the blighters to see. Get out. Out," Sweeney straightened up and and shambled toward the microphones.

An announcer's voice said, "And here is Charles Stewart Parnell—'Chazz'—Sweeney."

Stewart—could it be a coincidence? McGarr wondered.

Sweeney looked into the cameras, his one eye a moil of reddish color. As always, the immense man was wearing the rumpled mac with blue blazer and red tie beneath, and he appeared to be sweating; his rough, lumpy features were shiny and his collar damp. He passed a hand across his mouth and looked down, as for a drink.

A hand passed him what looked like a coffee cup. He drank, then said, "I'm not big on press conferences and blowing me own horn, so I'll cut to the chase.

"I come before you today a sad man entirely. Not wanting the Garda to botch another exchange, kill some other innocent parties, and waste more bloody money on the New Druid scuts what stole the books, I met with them, paid another five million—money I had to beg and borrow—but, and this is the only good part, I got the bloody books back.

"Into the bargain, I lost an eye, the surgeons tell me, seven million quid total, and but for the Garda Siochana—or, let me amend that—but for an already disgraced senior officer of the Garda Siochana—the intrepid Kara Kennedy, truly a keeper of old manuscripts, would still be alive. I suppose we can take solace in the knowledge that she died, God love her, retrieving the greatest single treasure of the Irish people and in that way she's both a martyr and a patriot."

Sweeney again toked from the cup.

"And speaking of patriots, none of this"—his large paw swept the table—"would have been possible without the Christians and patriots who stepped up to finance this great effort. Not for nothing was it done. Never, not if it takes years of toil and litigation, will we allow these icons of the Catholic Church to reside where they were lost.

"And don't think"—he finished the cup—"don't think the cowboys and gunsels of the Garda Siochana won't see me in court. I've a mighty big bone to pick with them." He cast a hand to one side where Jack Sheard had stepped beyond the reporters and was moving toward Sweeney with several other officers behind him.

Questions were barked at Sweeney until one voice was allowed to continue. It was Orla Bannon. "Can you or won't you tell us exactly where and how the exchange was made? And how you were injured?"

"I don't take questions from uncredentialed reporters."

"Here's mine." She reached for the lanyard and photo IDs hanging between her breasts.

"They're no longer valid. You're sacked."

Shocked, the others turned to her.

Although her smile seemed genuine, there was a flinty look in her dark eyes. "I think that would be unwise."

"That's why you're no longer employed—your judgment is impaired."

"At least for me, it's only my judgment, as judged by you," she shot backed, and the crowd laughed.

Sheard had reached the microphones. "This event is over. We're confiscating the stolen property, and Mr. Sweeney will be accompanying us for the purpose of an interview and debriefing."

"I will not," said Sweeney, swirling his heavy sloped shoulders.

Turning to him, Sheard said something under his breath, and the others led him away.

Sheard stepped to the mikes again. "After our interview, Mr. Sweeney will of course be at liberty to answer your questions, should he decide to do so."

"What do you know about . . . ?" the others began shouting, but Sheard moved off after Sweeney. Other Gardai were taking possession of the books, which, McGarr supposed, would be held on the pretext of being evidence, until Trinity sued for their return.

"Shouldn't you be up there?" asked a voice behind him.

It was Ward. "Got something for you." He handed McGarr a sheath of folded paper, explaining that he was on his way to spell Ruthie on the stakeout of 24 Spancel Court, Ranelagh. He'd spent most of the day in his office on the computers, researching Daniel Stewart, Kara Kennedy, and Jack Sheard.

"Why Sheard?"

Ward's smile was more a baring of white, even teeth. "You mean, beyond his being a self-serving prick who's as much as ruined four good careers? Well"—he glanced back up at the television—"haven't you ever wondered where his suits, cars, houses, and so forth come from, when he was not making any more money than we were?"

McGarr had, and more than once. "I heard talk that the wife has money. Didn't they meet at Trinity?"

Ward tapped the papers. "It was only talk. Her father, Kenneth Reynolds, is a retired Presbyterian minister in Larne with a modest house, an old car, and a small pension.

"I'd expected to find reams of account information and mountains of debt." Ward shook his head. "Every so often Sheard gets this wad of cash, or so it seems, and he pays off his debt—over forty thousand pounds' worth in the last six months."

"Stocks, bonds?"

Ward shook his head. "Unless he's doing the Cayman Island thing. But if he owned any European or American shares, I would have found them, as I did for Sweeney and Stewart."

"What about the law? He's a solicitor. Maybe he makes use of his contacts and moonlights that way."

"I thought of that and examined court records and filings. He hasn't submitted a property or title transfer or filed a brief or will in a decade. Conclusion?"

McGarr waited; he had his own idea about Sheard.

"Either he's into graft big-time in one of his supposed 'corporate' investigations that O'Rourke thinks he's so skilled at, or somebody with a lot of money has more than a passing interest in Jack Sheard's prospects in the Garda."

"What about Dublin Bay Petroleum?"

"It's a Panamanian entity, owned solely by Stewart. A brokerage that bought and sold on the spot market, but nothing that would have made him rich."

Not like 55 million quid and getting rid of an unwanted wife. Or was McGarr being naive about the part that Kara had played?

But her story about her missing husband—traveling to Yemen and petitioning that government—had all rung true to McGarr. Also, there was the call to his mother. "And Kara?"

"She had a small amount in her savings account, a checkbook balance of under one thousand Euros, and about thirty-five thousand in a retirement program run by Trinity College. But not one debt that I could find."

"Any joint account with the husband?"

Ward studied McGarr's face before shaking his head. "You shouldn't fault yourself. The husband obviously used her. Why else would he have killed her? They murdered Gillian Reston, tried to kill Ray-Boy Sloane, and were either responsible or complicit in the deaths of Derek Greene and Raymond Sloane. Their entire intent was to leave no potential touts, to pare the take down to themselves alone. And that's Pape, who's the only one left alive."

Perhaps only because he'd been taken into custody by Sheard. And named as a conspirator. "But Pape has a big problem."

Ward canted his head and followed McGarr's gaze to the televi-

sion screen, where, felicitously, Pape was shown debouching from
the Trinity Library right after the theft had been discovered. With
head raised, he was staring down his long patrician nose at the assembled photographers and cameras.

"Even so, I don't think we can doubt for a moment that his men-
tality was beyond hatching the scheme, and we both know addicts
take chances. The drug problem aside, he's not a stupid man.

"Maybe he holds the Book of Kells in contempt, but he spent his
life as a librarian, and he owns or owned a facsimile copy."

Like what was probably blown up on Iona, thought McGarr.
Much of the confetti was brightly colored.

"My bet? If those books"—Ward pointed at the television—"are
genuine and undamaged, Pape was definitely behind the crime."

"Then who just made the exchange with Sweeney?"

"Ray-Boy?"

Not if, as Ward himself and Bresnahan thought, he was at 24
Spancel Court, Ranelagh, and had not come out. Also, it could not
have been Ray-Boy with Dan Stewart on Iona.

THE BUSINESS WAS A STOREFRONT IN A MINI-
mall—nails, tanning, and perhaps sex, Bresnahan had decided after
her first five minutes parked across the busy main street.

Nearly all the customers were male and not of the sort who
looked as though they required a manicure for fine dining or a big
meeting with an important client. Most were working-class yokes,
some of whom looked like they'd had a few jars. The two women
who ventured inside took a quick look round and left.

The only customer who looked like he belonged now stepped out
holding a cell phone to his ear. Tall, maybe still in his twenties, he was
wearing designer eyeglasses, an expensive gray pinstriped double-
breasted suit with a pearl gray tie, and a tall fedora—something a bit

like a homburg. He moved stiffly toward a long silver BMW with gold wheel covers, rather like the car that had been destroyed outside New Druid headquarters on the Glasnevin Road.

A lorry pulled past Bresnahan, obscuring her view for a moment. But when the BMW moved by, she could just see through the tinted windows that he had something like a bit of bandage plaster on the underside of his nose. Which, it occurred to her too late, might be concealing the hole for a ring.

16

SHEARD'S HOUSE WAS NESTLED IN A CROOK
of the Dublin Mountains, part of a rather new housing estate of
pricey homes on large lots with fine views of the city below. Dublin
was fully lighted now at 7:30, as far as the eye could see.

Neo-Georgian in style, the dwelling was a rambling red-brick
affair all on one story with arched windows and a four-car garage.
Parked on the drive was a rather new Volvo and a Maloney's Catering van with two young men in white ties and tails carrying silver
platters of food into the house.

Knowing Sheard could not possibly be home after Sweeney's
press conference about the books, with reporters interviewing him
and all, McGarr slipped the Garda-issue Glock he'd been carrying
under the seat of his Cooper and got out.

Every room was lit, and with the front door open, he simply
walked in, noting the quality furnishings and the bar that had been
set up in the largest room, which looked like the lounge in a select
hotel. The portraits on a hall table were of Sheard and his wife,
Maeve—McGarr thought her name might be—and their three chil-

dren. Towheads all five of them, they looked like a happy family out of a soap opera.

It took him a while to find the kitchen, where the catering team was obviously setting up for a party. And there too stood the blond wife wearing an apron over a form-fitting black dress, directing their efforts.

"May I intrude?" McGarr asked, holding out a card. "You're probably not aware that your husband just saved my life, he might tell you later. It all happened so fast. I'm here to thank him."

She looked down at the card. "Peter McGarr?"

He nodded.

"Well, Jack has always said you were his model, the very kind of policeman he wanted to be. And is. Have you been watching the television?"

Obviously she hadn't, or she would know what her husband had been saying about McGarr recently.

She was a natural blond whose skin carried a buff sheen that seemed to glow. With pale blue eyes, regular features, and an angular body, Maeve Sheard was one of the better-looking people that McGarr had cast his eyes upon in some time.

"Do you expect Jack soon?"

"Oh, yes. Of course. Within the hour, guests are arriving."

"You're having a party, I can see. Your birthday? His?"

She smiled and shook a head bedizened in comely golden waves. "Jack just felt like having the neighbors over to celebrate, don't you know?" Her brow furrowed, perhaps only now remembering what McGarr's experience had been over the last few days. "Would you be having anything? Let me get you a drink."

McGarr smiled and followed her pleasant curves and good legs to the bar in the living room.

"Gorgeous place you have here," McGarr commented, as his

drink was being readied. "With a view to die for. When did you have the house built?"

"Oh, nearly seven years gone now, after the birth of my first son."

"I like the lines, the proportions. Was it architect-designed?"

She nodded and rested an elbow on the tall bar in a way that flared the radical angle of her chest.

"And the furnishings—I admire your taste. It all must have cost a packet."

"Oh." She closed her eyes. "I see what you're getting at. Jack inherited a fair amount of money upon the death of his father about a decade ago. And then, he's so resourceful." Her smile was utterly guileless. "He bought this house from a man who was in legal problems and required representation both in and out of tax court.

"Jack's first preference in regard to work is, like yours I should imagine, the police. But he's also a solicitor." Her hand came up to her pretty mouth. "Oh, dear, I shouldn't have said that either. I hope you're not offended. I only now remembered the difficulties you're in."

McGarr looked down into the drink and shook his head.

"Well, anyway, Jack just arrived." She pointed to the bay windows. Car headlamps had appeared on the driveway, and a large Audi swung into the floodlights by the garage. They watched as Sheard, pulling his large frame out of the car, advanced on McGarr's Cooper and looked down at the Garda shield that was displayed in the windscreen. Pivoting, he made for the house.

"I'd better tell him you're here." She moved toward the hallway.

McGarr waited, hearing, "Where is he?" from Sheard.

She said something inaudible to him.

"I don't care. He has no place in my home." He then appeared in the doorway. "You. What are you doing here?"

McGarr shrugged. "Curiosity. I wanted to see for myself how you live."

"What?"

"You heard me. I wanted to see how you live." McGarr let that sit for a moment. "I'm also interested in why, when you learned where Stewart was, you didn't bring him in immediately. And why you were alone when I got there. No support, no backup."

"Isn't it enough I saved your bloody life?" The wife now appeared beside him, but Sheard raised an arm, as though to bar her from entering the room. "Go see if everything's ready while I get rid of this yoke." Sheard lumbered forward with his big-shouldered gait, the fist of his right hand actually clenched.

He stopped within inches of McGarr, looming over him. "You have great bloody cheek coming here when, you should know, you're now wanted for questioning. You'll be charged, and you're going to prison, count on it."

McGarr smiled and looked down into his drink. "Well, at least it won't be for tax fraud." He glanced up into Sheard's pale blue eyes. "You never inherited any money to purchase this place, and your wife's father is a poor parson in the North. Nor did the owner of this property ever need your legal help. In fact, there's no record of your having functioned in any way as a solicitor in over a decade.

"The more important record is your failure to pay a farthing of taxes on any of the money that floated all of this.

"No." McGarr raised the glass and drank from it. "Miraculously, you just seemed to surface with cash, whenever necessary.

"The Stewart matter? I've got Bresnahan and Ward working on that—phone calls in particular." McGarr watched Sheard's ears pull back and his nostrils flare. "Swords? He tells me there's no record of you or any of your staff reporting Stewart's address or even hinting that he was a part of your inquiry." He held the man's searing gaze.

"I should have let him kill you."

McGarr nodded. "I'd call it a tactical error. But you'd come there to kill him anyway, and street cop has never been your strong suit, Jack. You're more the camera class of fella. And good at it, I'll hand you that."

McGarr finished the drink, set the glass on the bar, and stepped around Sheard. "As those who actually practice the law say, 'Be seeing you in court, Solicitor.' Perhaps you have skills in that direction. For your family's sake, you should hope so."

But McGarr only got halfway across the Oriental carpet.

"McGarr."

He turned to find Sheard holding a handgun.

"Ah, Jack, isn't that a cliché?"

"What have you done with this?"

"Nothing. Yet." He studied Sheard's features, which appeared transformed—eyes widened, brow furrowed. He was perspiring.

McGarr reached into his jacket and pulled out the sheaf of papers Ward had given him. "But it will soon be on its way. Remember my assistant Hugh Ward? The one you insisted be cashiered? You can thank him for this. Irony is, he put it all together, he did, with the skills he's learned since you got him sacked. With the same skills at which you're supposed to be expert—white-collar crime. How does it feel to be hoist on your own petard, Jack?"

McGarr pulled out his cell phone. "Like to give him a call? Need his number?"

Sheard only stared down at the papers, his color now high.

"But none of this need happen. You know who I want— Sweeney." McGarr turned for the door.

"McGarr!" Sheard roared, pulling back the slide of the automatic. "It's not too late for your death. I'll say you came out here and assaulted me. Your hatred of me, your professional envy is well known. I'll say you and your team of lawless operatives have been stalking me for weeks now, digging into my affairs, using the power of your office to conduct an illegal investigation. And when you couldn't find anything, you came here in a rage and pulled a gun. People will understand how that could happen. There's your wife and father-in-law and the debacle over on Iona that got Kara Kennedy killed. And you an old man falling apart."

McGarr stopped in the archway to the hall. "Jack, you're right on all scores. I am an old man, and my wife and father-in-law are dead. Iona was a debacle twice over, since Kara lost her life and the money appears to be gone, although we both know it isn't. What was your share, Jack? How much were you to get out of it?

"And sure, I'll agree—my staff can be lawless, and you should count on it. You could shoot me. But you won't, because you'd be handing yourself a death sentence. And we can agree on something." McGarr waited a moment before turning around.

Sheard had lowered the gun. "Who else knows, apart from Ward?"

"Bresnahan and McKeon, who will also keep their counsel, if you give me Sweeney and proof."

"But they'll always have it hanging over me. I'll always be under their gun." His eyes fell to the object in his hands.

"As long as you remain in the Garda."

Slowly Sheard's eyes moved up to McGarr. "As well, there's himself. And he's—"

"Mortal," said McGarr.

IF ANONYMITY WERE POSSIBLE IN IRELAND, IT would reside in Kinsale, a harbor town in South Cork. Several decades earlier, Continental yachtsmen had discovered its deepwater harbor and neat rows of eighteenth-century houses lining the waterfront.

The ensuing real estate frenzy brought trendy restaurants, boutiques, yacht brokerages, and further foreigners to the quaint maritime community. Before the economic boom of the nineties, it was said few Irish could afford to live there and that the town should be run from New York by the United Nations.

Pubs had been closed for about an hour, by the time Peter Mc-Garr slowed his Cooper and rolled into the narrow streets by the harbor that were nevertheless still busy with traffic and window-shoppers and others on footpaths. Clubs, restaurants, and the after-hours bistros would still be open. Large yachts in the harbor were ablaze with light.

Finding a legal parking place, McGarr nevertheless lowered his Garda shield, not knowing how long it would take and not wanting to be clamped or towed.

Switching off the car, he paused for several moments to steel his resolve. It was not a court of law he would be conducting, neither a tribunal nor an interview. What he was about—he told himself, twisting the rearview mirror to chance a look at himself—was an in-terrogation of the sort that would get at the truth, one way or an-other. After a summary judgment would come the penalty phase.

Glancing at himself in the mirror, he was shocked by what he saw. He was pasty, haggard, and decidedly old, with bloodshot eyes and a grizzled beard. A muscle at the corner of his right eye was twitching. Pulling the Glock from under the seat, he tucked the handgun under his belt, reminding himself of Noreen, Fitz, and Kara Kennedy. He opened the door and stepped out.

It was chilly, with a brisk wind sweeping in off the harbor and the streets damp from a recent shower. McGarr turned up the collar of his jacket and leaned into the blast, as he passed down a line of shops looking for the address Sheard had given him, a residence, he assumed, over a business, which was Sweeney's preferred modus vivendi.

While anything but reticent when honing his personal image, Sweeney was otherwise reclusive in his personal life—sleeping in his office at the *Ath Cliath* newsroom, before that on a cot in a back room of his run-down building on the Dublin quays where his supposed "merchant bank" was headquartered. Or here, in a building that was just off a main business street—narrow, tucked between two more imposing structures. In spite of his millions.

McGarr stepped out into the street and looked up at the facade and its windows, which were shuttered and lightless. If Sweeney were there, he did not want anybody to know.

When McGarr stepped back onto the footpath, there was a figure before him.

"Hiya, stranger—where you been? Come 'ere and give me a hug, I'm feckin' freezin'.'" It was Orla Bannon who stepped into him, wrapped her arms around his body, and placed her head on his chest.

McGarr did not resist. On his cheek, her glossy dark hair felt soft and warm, and he breathed in the pleasant odor of whatever shampoo she had used.

"I'd give you the line, 'I can tell you're happy to see me' "—she tightened her hold on him, pressing herself against the Glock—"but I imagine that hard thing I'm feeling is another animal altogether."

McGarr moved to break away from her, but she held on. "Ah, now—it's only a moment or two I'm asking. At the moment." Her thigh now slipped between his legs. "But he's up there, I can tell you. He got here looking like death warmed over only shortly after me. Which will tell you how long Sheard interviewed the bugger.

"Anyhow, Brother Loquacious"—drawing herself back, she looked up at him—"I've a plan. To get you in." She smiled, her jet eyes surveying him. "Here." She canted her head toward the darkened building.

"How did you know he'd come here?"

"Credit me sixth sense that with a man like that, one day, I'd need to know everything I could about him."

"He's alone in there?"

"Which is—you've nailed it—his problem. Socialization. If only Chazz Sweeney could love or trust somebody besides himself, perhaps there might be a remediation of our conditions, yours and mine. Although I have the feeling you're interested in a more immediate and final solution."

The drill was, Bannon explained, that Sweeney would come to the door for her.

"Why?"

"Trust me, he just will."

"Because of your threat at the news conference?"

"Did you see it?" Her smile was full now. "How did I look? More's the point, how did I do?"

When McGarr said nothing, she continued: "It's not just that he'll come to the door—when he does and it opens, his security system won't detect a certain party breaking in the back. That's you. Me, he'll invite me in, and then you'll be the witness to my little chat with the Chazz man."

"How do you know his security system switches off?"

Yet again she flashed her pixieish smile. "It's me stock-in-trade—to know."

"At the back there's a door?"

"Pickable by you."

"You don't know that."

"If not by you, then by nobody."

A smile nearly formed at the corners of McGarr's mouth. "You're shameless."

"And don't you forget it. It'll take you two minutes to get back there, but let's make it five." She released him and glanced at her watch. "In five minutes I'll ring. Say, it takes him another couple to get down and open up. I'll stand in the doorway and refuse his offers for a peek at his etchings for another five. I think he actually likes me. Too much.

"That'll give you a whopping time cushion of ten whole minutes to scope the lock out and let yourself in. The entire house is his, but where he lives—his digs—are on the top floor. Grand view of the harbor. If he bolts, it might be to the boat he's got tied up to the wall. Wouldn't you know it's called the *Boru*."

"You should know what I'm here for, and it's not a wee chat."

"Wouldn't I love to be a witness to history? Yours and his, his and mine, yours and mine."

McGarr turned on his heel, thinking what he had in mind was best done while there were car doors slamming, other ambient urban noise, and the occasional shout. Or curse.

A ship's horn now sounded and echoed around the harbor that was here nearly circular.

The back of the building was hard by the water with a narrow laneway—the width of a horse and cart alone—between the door and the harbor wall.

Standing there digging a smoke from his jacket, McGarr pretended to survey the rather sizable forest of masts and superstructures that made up the Kinsale pleasure-boat fleet, before turning and cupping his hands to light a cigarette.

The lock was complex, case-hardened of the sort that was not easily picked, and he would not try. Stepping back into the shadows of the building, he leaned against the door and drew on the cigarette in a leisurely manner, noting the stile in the harbor wall and the raised decks of the *Boru*, he assumed, on the other side.

Scanning the laneway before grinding out the butt, McGarr drew the Glock from under his belt, took one long stride away from the door, turned, and fired three quick slugs into the lock. Raising a foot, he kicked out at the door. It held. But not for his shoulder. With a pop, it broke open, and he stumbled into a dark room.

Pushing the door to, he listened to the sounds of the building, expecting to hear at least muffled voices from the upper stories. Instead, only a few dull thuds came to him.

But now that he was inside, speed was of the essence. He began moving upstairs, meeting with only one other lock on the door to the first floor, which he opened with a thin supple blade.

The hallway was darkened, with all other doors closed; a second was the same. Catching sight of a glow at the top of the stairs, he climbed toward it, keeping his feet near the wall and the Glock before him.

"McGarr!" he heard when he was two steps from the final landing. "Come in, come in. Two uninvited guests in one night—my, my, I'm such a lucky fella."

Cautiously, McGarr approached the open door from which light was spilling onto the carpet.

"Come in, lad. Don't be bashful. I won't object to your Garda-issue Glock. Haven't I got one of me own, although it's in use at the moment?"

In a mirror hanging on the wall of the room, he could see a desk on which sat a clear plastic bag containing the head of Gillian Reston, eyes splayed, a blue swollen tongue lolling out.

Near it was a photograph of Sweeney with Dan Stewart, their arms looped over each other's shoulders, smiling into the camera.

Taking another step, he caught sight of Sweeney sitting in a wing chair with somebody lying on the carpet before him.

It was Orla Bannon, hands duct-taped behind her; more tape was wrapped around her head and an automatic. The barrel was in her mouth. A length of what looked like fishing line ran from the trigger to Sweeney, who, with jacket off and legs crossed, now reached for a drink on a small table by his side.

"Like my effigy? It was sent me by a caring colleague who will soon enjoy that condition himself, if Jack Sheard has anything to do with it.

"And actually"—Sweeney tried to smile, but it was more a baring of dim, uneven teeth—"I had intended all of this for you. But it stops her bloody gob well enough, I'd say. Which will allow us a tête-à-tête, if I can just have that object in your hand." Sweeney pointed at McGarr's handgun. "Now, if you don't mind."

McGarr did not move. Should he pull the trigger, he asked himself, and risk her life, as he had Noreen's, Fitz's, and Kara Kennedy's? Should he make Orla number four in his litany of collateral damage?

The cord binding Sweeney to the weapon was taut and was being held both by his hand and a wrap, which had been wound around his wrist. A bullet would make Sweeney spasm and perhaps fall over, and Orla would die.

Her eyes were wide with fright and imploring.

"I'll have that," Sweeney repeated.

"Or what?"

"You see it."

McGarr hunched his shoulders. "You plan to kill her anyway. Do it, I'll kill you."

Sweeney began a phlegmy laugh that juddered the taut chain. With his other hand he reached for the goblet, which was filled with an amber liquid. "On one level, which is balls, I must say I love you. Who'da thunk you'da copped—literally—onto my wee device to enrich meself beyond my wildest dreams. And to bring you down in a way that you'd feel daily for the rest of a squalid life."

If McGarr could keep him talking and drinking, he might chance a shot when the chain slackened. Sweeney's meaty features were slick with sweat. There was a large, greasy stain on his red tie.

"And your device was?"

"Ach—don't play dumb, man. I know you're not stupid. Rash, yes. Predictable and therefore controllable, ditto. But all the truly good lads are, don't you know. Nothing new there."

"Delia Manahan—she one of your devices?" An Opus Dei zealot, she could well have been the woman who had spiked Noreen's shotgun, causing her and her father's death two years before.

"Nah, Jaysus. I'll take the 'not stupid' back, since you're a dolt altogether. It was I meself who slipped the smaller shell in the barrel. Hadn't I the access and all the time in the world, with Fitz and Nuala leaving the bloody doors open? The bloody stupid fools."

Glancing down at Orla, who had closed her eyes, McGarr removed his finger from the trigger. "Why?" Her breathing was labored, and her brow was damp with sweat.

"To bring you back to reality, man. To keep you from making further blunders in regard to the holiest and most noble order ever created. God's order, which you had the audacity and bad sense to think you could thwart."

Keeping the chain taut with one hand, Sweeney again reached for the drink with the other. "I don't forget or forgive. You."

He finished the drink, which made his eyes water. A single tear tracked onto the pocked surface of his cheek. "You want the truth? Do you?"

McGarr only regarded him.

"The Trinity security guards, Ray-Boy's hapless father and the other one, something Greene? I had them killed just to get you involved in the case." A smug smile now exposed Sweeney's uneven teeth. "For it was you I wanted as much as the money. Oh, yes. I've got that too, and all of it.

"Kara very-much-effin' Kennedy, my son Dan's darlin' wife? I had her seduce you, just to keep you close."

"Why would she do that?"

"Hah, if I had known you were this stupid, I'd have had a bullet put in you years ago and not bothered with the fraggin'. Why the fuck do you think, man? For the fuckin' money, what else?

"Dan and me told her we'd split the pot. Equal shares. It would be like alimony, only big-time. No more academia for her, no more piss-poor pay check But, you know, Kara wasn't blood, and how could we possibly trust a woman like her, who would bed the likes of you for money?"

He began a low chuckle. "There's a name for women like her. And her." With the tip of his shoe, he kicked out at Bannon's head. "Wake up, you bitch. Wake up!" Raising the chain to keep the lead to the trigger tight, Sweeney moved up in the chair. "Nobody threatens me, especially not in public."

"But Dan, your Dan Stewart—he was blood."

Canting his head, Sweeney looked away, and McGarr's finger moved back onto the trigger. "After a fashion. I can't remember, but I think I was actually paying his mother before he was conceived, and the blood tests were inconclusive. He could have been anybody's bastard, I'd say. She was a right sorry little Scots cunt. We could never have had a future, but Dan, I must say, was pleasant company and useful for a while.

"But enough of this. That one"—Sweeney pointed at Bannon— "she's check. And this one"—plunging his hand into the gap between the cushion and the chair, he came up with another handgun—"is mate, matie." Slowly, haltingly, careful of the tether he had to Orla and the gun he had pointed at McGarr, Sweeney rose to his feet.

"I'm not much of a shot, you'll see." The handgun exploded and the bullet thwacked into the wall only inches from McGarr's head. "But you'd best go out before us." Sweeney placed another shot almost exactly at the same point on the other side of McGarr's head.

"Out!" Sweeney roared. "Get out! I won't have you dying in me house. I'm going to me boat, if your wish is to accompany us." And he began a laugh that ended in a wet hack. Turning his head, Sweeney spat into a mirror on the wall.

With his Glock now raised and pointed at Sweeney's heart, McGarr stepped to the door.

"Go ahead, pull it, you spineless fuck. Pull it, and we'll all die."

McGarr quickly moved down the stairs, trying to gauge where he might position himself for a clean shot at Sweeney. But the doors that he tried were locked, and lights suddenly switched on.

"McGarr? You still with us?"

Outside, McGarr thought, he'd conceal himself behind a car or on the other side of the wall where, when Sweeney climbed over, he could grab his arm and fire with the other hand.

No cars. The narrow laneway was empty; crouched on the other side of the harbor wall, McGarr scanned the several decks of the large yacht, which was unlighted. Water was lapping against its hull.

He heard: "Jaysus—wouldn't you know it, bitch? The motherless fucker's run out on you. Unless he's crouched on the other side of the wall. That's where I'd be, were I brave and true, like Peter McGarr."

Orla appeared first at the top of the high wall, but she did not hesitate when she saw McGarr. There—having to wait for Sweeney—they locked eyes.

With both hands, McGarr raised the Glock.

"You're a cunt! A cowardly cunt, McGarr!" Sweeney roared, as his large head and bulky figure appeared at the top of the wall, silhouetted against the light from the town. "Fucked off on me. And Orla, poor Orla, who'll die alone with her secrets."

It was then, with the Glock aimed at Sweeney's chest, that a chunk of the man's skull burst from his head in a pink mist that sprayed out over the water. A split second later, the unmistakable report of a high-powered rifle echoed around the harbor. A second round caught Sweeney in the neck and nearly severed his head from his body.

Before Sweeney could topple over, McGarr dropped his weapon, lunged for the hand that held the tether, and wrenched Sweeney forward. Throwing himself on top of Sweeney, they skidded down the steep stairs toward Orla and slammed into the side of the yacht.

From his jacket pocket, McGarr pulled out his key ring and severed the line with a pen knife. Only then did he climb off Sweeney, whose body lolled to one side and plunged off the staircase. With a splintering crack, it landed on the rail of a lower deck before spilling into the water.

On the other side of the nearly circular harbor, Ray-Boy Sloane turned to replace the Steyr Aug Bullpup assault rifle in its case. While inconspicuous, the short barrel had produced loud reports, and two cars passing in the street behind him had slowed.

A third stopped. "Are you the police?" a woman asked.

"No, I am." A hand, reaching up, grabbed hold of Ray-Boy's nose ring and ripped it from his face.

As the rifle dropped from Sloane's hands, a fist jacked into his groin, doubling him up into a flurry of punches thrown with such precision that—it would be found later—his nose, pharynx, and one eye socket were broken, and his front teeth removed. The fall from his shooting perch broke both elbows.

As Hugh Ward bent to secure the assault rifle, shiny black wing-tips appeared on the cobblestone footpath before him. Glancing up, Ward caught only a glimpse of something shiny, a hand, three inches of cuff cinched by a gold-and-onyx link, and the arm of a dark pinstriped suit.

The gun roared, and Ray-Boy's body shuddered as a bullet thwacked into his head.

Ward straightened up. "What was that, Jack—endgame?"

"Speak to McGarr." Sheard opened his suit coat and slipped the handgun into its holster. "He'll fill you in." Turning, he walked toward a Volvo that was stopped in the middle of the street.

MORE THAN TWELVE HOURS LATER, McGARR awoke with a start, not knowing where he was. With heavy drapes across tall windows the room was dark, and there was a figure in the bed beside him.

On the telephone, which was positioned on his chest, a red light was blinking.

"I would have answered it, but I suspected it was your daughter, whom I'd like to meet in some other way."

Orla Bannon rolled over to face him, a smooth thigh slipping between his legs. She had unbraided her long black hair, which was arrayed across her breasts. She pushed it away. "Like what you see? All yours, as promised. But maybe you should make that call first."

When he hesitated, she picked up the receiver and dialed in a number. Then, "Nuala, it's Orla. Orla Bannon. Yes, he's right here. Like to speak with him?"

"How do you know my home number?" It was unlisted.

She cocked her head. "As I was saying, I've been interested in you for some time now, but just too shy to make a move."

Which caused McGarr to chuckle. He brought the phone to his ear.